MISSING

a novel by
Jamieson Allom

A young architect's professional journey intersects with his missing father's tragic story.

Published by
Forty South Publishing Pty Ltd,
Hobart, Tasmania
www.fortysouth.com.au

Cover Design: Jamieson Allom

Book design: Imogen Brown

Printer: IngramSpark

For Albert

Pte A. F. McCormack 6RAR
KIA 18th August 1966
Long Tan, Vietnam.

prologue

THANK GOD the rain had stopped. It had started, as if to some sadistic schedule, in the fury of the battle. Sheets of dense rain; misery upon misery.

There were dead and injured out in the darkness. Probably some of his mates, and surely many of the enemy, for they had kept coming, heedless of the hail of Australian fire. In the confusion, Pte Daniel Gardner, 'Danny Boy' or just 'Boy' to his mates, had become separated from the others; he would find the platoon at first light.

First he had to get through the night. Then get through three more weeks of heat, rain, mud, and fear—a gnawing fear that could explode into blind terror, as it had, with little warning, this day. Three weeks, then out of here. Mustn't think about that. Inviting fate.

What was that? He sensed movement in the dark. He knew it was the way of the NVA to retrieve their comrades under cover of darkness. Peering, he could make out a vague form moving around the battlefield, a breeze masking the noises of its movement. The shape was coming closer to where he lay, hugging his rifle to him. *Is there no end to this?*

He raised his weapon. The form moved closer. A fleeting moment of moonlight revealed the characteristically small outline of an enemy soldier. He saw in smudged profile the form of the killer of his countrymen, the cause of his ordeal in this god-forsaken place. Then the smudge was lost in the returning blackness.

He raised his rifle to where the shape had been. *No more. Please, no more.* It must be very close now; he could hear, almost feel, its laboured breathing. He aimed at the sound. The barrel of his SLR must be probing the very breath of the spectre. His hands trembled. His mind careered. *Let this finish it, for God's sake.*

He squeezed the trigger. [1]

DANIEL

a safe island

THE SOLDIER WATCHED the coast pass beneath him. The deep blue of the strait gave way to a white-lipped and lumpy land of green and yellow fields, dark forests, and flashes of snow. A safe island at the bottom of the world, so far from the steamy land where his mate had died. His mate, whose ravaged body would be buried this day.

* * *

He was standing a little apart from the gathering at the graveside at Launceston's Carr Villa cemetery, when a voice asked: 'were you over there with him? Vietnam?'

He looked into the girl's eyes. He nodded. Together, they watched the coffin sink into the earth. Benign earth, restful earth. No tunnels, no mines, no torn bodies, no pounding of fear.

'Are you going to his parents' place?' she asked, as the gathering began to disperse.

'No,' he answered, his voice low. 'I saw them earlier.'

The girl touched his arm. 'Come and have a cup of tea at our place; we're not far from here.'

He tilted the brim of his hat against the afternoon sun as they walked alongside a wide, busy road into King's Meadows, the stocky soldier and the slight girl, he in khaki, she in Mary Quant, strangers but strangely at ease, the funeral having settled its reflective gaze upon them both.

'How did you know him?' he asked, eventually.

It seemed to the girl that the question was an effort for him.

'Until his family moved last year, we lived in the same street. He was one of the local children I used to play with. I sort of grew up with him, although he was a bit older.'

They retreated into their own memories, the silence easier than words.

In a little while she indicated that they should turn left, and they turned off the busy main road into a side street which led to a quiet residential road with green verges and rows of modest red brick houses with well-tended front lawns and gardens. The traffic noise sank to a murmur; a dog barked somewhere, birds chirruped.

'This is our place.' The wrought iron gate in the low brick wall gave a little sigh of welcome as the girl pushed it open.

She led him along a weathered concrete path through the scent of roses and lavender to an entry porch flanked by sturdy brick piers and roofed with a small gable.

The quiet, the warm sunshine, and the girl—this girl he had just met but with whom he felt none of his customary awkwardness—for a moment brought the soldier to a place of peace such as he had not known since he had left behind the sounds of battle.

She opened the front door and turned to him.

'I'm Mary,' she said.

'I'm Daniel.'

And so it was that Daniel Steven Gardner, a good but damaged man, met Mary Lydia Preston, a nurturing and wise young woman, on a sad, sunny day in a safe island a hemisphere away from the madness of a bloody, futile war.

Daniel took off his hat and ran his hand quickly across his hair. Mary saw for the first time that he had a shock of unruly blond hair; she broke into an involuntary smile. He, torn between the impact of her smile and embarrassment at his inability to control the disarray, attempted to tamp the rebellion down into some sort of order.

'Leave it,' she said, not releasing him from her smile, even when she noticed the red line on his forehead.

Inside, the house brought to Daniel images of his parents' home in Ballarat. He took in the floral carpet, the deep arm-chairs, and the plain, tuck-pointed, dark brick fireplace with its embossed metal fire-side boxes and fire screen. There was the ubiquitous china cabinet; there were the framed family photographs set out along the wooden mantelpiece, interrupted only by the familiar streamline mantel clock.

Ordinary things, belonging to ordinary times. How could anything remain ordinary? Remain unchanged? Over there, the nightmare was continuing. He could hear it. Like terrible domestic violence heard through the wall.

'That's mum and dad.' Mary saw that he was looking at a black and white photograph depicting a confettied couple—the dark, slender bride in an elegant suit, the groom in the uniform of the RAAF. 'A war-time wedding.'

Daniel looked at her. Mary was fair-complexioned with dark, compelling eyes, her ebony hair up in the style he thought was a beehive. She was dressed in a sleeveless, deep blue dress of a respectful length, and wore white leather boots.

'They would have been at the funeral today, but they're up at Burnie. Auntie Daphne—Mum's sister—is ill.'

He followed her into the kitchen, conscious of her scent. Conscious too, of the movement of her hips, her slim waist, and the beckon of her exposed neck.

Through a pane in the back door he could see a neat back yard, with fruit trees, a vegetable patch, a chook-house, and a Hills Hoist.

'How do you have your tea?' Mary filled a kettle and lit a gas ring.

The simple domesticity of it all and the shining warmth of this young woman, were suddenly too much for the soldier. Fumbling the back door open, he blundered out onto the bright lawn. Schrapnel of sounds and images struck him without warning, and, despite his trembling defiance, obliterated all else. He was back there.

Mary found him sitting on the slatted garden seat under the apricot tree, an un-lit cigarette in one shaking hand, a *Camel* cigarette pack beside him on the seat. Catching sight of his face, she retreated quietly, as the oblivious kettle whistled its cheerful song.

'I'll bring your tea out,' she called from the safety of the kitchen.

As she watched him through the fly-screen door, she was conscious of her own sheltered existence in this safe place, and wondered what horrors had been encountered by Daniel and her childhood friend.

Although the sun was not hot, the air was warm and the shifting shade of the fruit tree was welcome.

'I'll be mother.' Mary placed a laden tray on a small outdoor table. She gave the china tea-pot a little swirl, placed a silver strainer over Daniel's cup and asked, 'Do you take milk?'

'Thank you, Mary,' he nodded.

'Well, you know where *I* live, Daniel,' she said, 'so, where do *you* come from?'

'I suppose you could call me a country boy.'

'Oh?'

His tea-cup clinked a little dance against its saucer, as he put it down.

'We had a farm near Connorville, that's in Victoria, until we moved to Ballarat.'

'I've only been as far as Melbourne,' said Mary.

Daniel told her that he was the youngest of three brothers. He had, until called up, been living with his ageing parents in Ballarat, the family having moved there when their farm became too much for his father. Like thousands of other young Australian men, Daniel had found himself on the losing end of the infamous 'birthday ballot', their conscription into the country's armed forces being at the whim of impassive, numbered marbles.

At Daniel's faltering reference to the call-up, the grief of the day appeared to revisit Mary. She did not try to hide her tears. He moved, hesitantly, to her. For a long moment they held each other, the girl sobbing quietly for her friend and for all the young men, the soldier fighting to keep his composure.

As the afternoon air began to cool, they moved the seat into the late sunshine and Mary went to make a fresh pot of tea. Watching her go, Daniel struggled with his emotions. Through the morass he was aware of his own vulnerability, and could see that she, too, was exposed.

'Can you stay for tea?'

When Daniel demurred, she said, 'Please do. I have some lamb chops in the fridge.'

That was enough.

'Can I help?' he asked, as she bent to light the grill.

'Perhaps you can get us a drink? Dad has some beer in the laundry. And we have some wine, I think. Yes, here it is.' Mary opened the door of the refrigerator and found a bottle of Porphyry Pearl next to the milk bottles.

'Shall we watch the news?' Mary didn't wait for an answer and went to the television set standing in the corner of the lounge-room. As the set warmed up, a black-and-white picture emerged from the grainy snow, accompanied by the familiar ABC News theme.

Ken Short read from the script on his desk.

'Americans have taken part in peace initiatives across the United States to protest against the continuing war in Vietnam. The Peace Moratorium is believed to be the largest demonstration in US history, with an estimated two million people involved.'

Daniel and Mary shared a glance, but remained silent.

'*The focal point was the capital, Washington DC, where about 250,000 demonstrators gathered to make their voices heard. Senator Edward Kennedy, a vocal anti-war campaigner, called for combat troops to be withdrawn from Vietnam by October next year and all forces to be out by the end of 1972.*'

The sober newsreader shuffled his papers.

'*In local news, the funeral was held in Launceston today of a Tasmanian soldier killed in Vietnam, in an action in Phuoc Tuy province...*'

'I think that's enough news for tonight.' Mary walked across to the television and pushed the dial in, to a crunch of silence. As the world's fears and hopes shrank to a lingering white dot in the screen, she said, 'do you like Herb Alpert and the Tijuana Brass?

'Tell me about your family, Daniel,' she said. She dabbed her lips with her napkin and looked at him across the table.

A new record dropped into place. The early notes of the first track of *West-side Story*, Leonard Bernstein's *Prologue*, brought to Daniel memories of the farm, where his mother loved to play musicals—a means of escape, he came to realise, from the barren silence of her life.

'Well, there's just mum and dad really, in Ballarat,' he said.

'Didn't you say you had brothers?'

'Yeah.' Daniel ran his finger down the side of his place-mat and straightened it. 'DJ and Geoffrey.'

Mary looked at him enquiringly.

'DJ was killed in Korea...'

Mary's eyes filled.

'And Geoffrey,' Daniel shrugged, 'Geoffrey went off somewhere. We've lost touch with him now...'

'What about you mother? Is she in touch with him?'

Daniel was moved by Mary's obvious concern. 'I don't think so.'

'Your dad?'

'He doesn't say much these days. Had the stuffing knocked out of him, I reckon. What with DJ, then having to leave the farm.'

Chops and veg despatched, dishes washed and dried, Mary was serving coffee as her much-loved *Peter Paul and Mary* album dropped into place on the radiogram. The familiar harmony was no more than a muted background to their conversation, until Mary Travers sang the question: *Where have all the young men gone?* The pair fell silent.

'You said you were conscripted, Daniel. That must have disrupted your life,' Mary ventured.

'Mmm.' Daniel realigned his place-mat and looked for something else on the table that needed to be put in order. *Disrupted? Turned inside out, it felt like now. Inside out, upside down, shaken apart. Would the pieces fit back together? Could he find them all?*

Although not lacking in intelligence, Daniel had accepted his conscription to military service without question. To balk, for him, would have been to dishonour those in his family who had fought before him. He accepted the verdict of the unseeing marbles that rolled out a new path for so many young Australians, as fate was clearly intent on putting him to the test that he dreaded so much but dare not shirk. Nor, in his sheltered, youthful innocence, could he question the wisdom of his country's leaders. Not yet a man, he would go to war.

Their mood was lifted by the Beatles, and the conversation re-started, now turning to music and fashion. It appeared to him that Mary was interested in both. Perhaps all girls of her age were. His own notion of what was important and what wasn't had been shattered in the last year or two. Was that why his usual shyness, his reserve, was absent?

'Is it important in your job?' he asked. 'To keep up with fashion?' Mary had explained that she worked in a record shop, Wills and Co, in a little curved street called The Quadrant.

'Yes, they expect me to look smart. But I won't be there much longer.'

'Why not?'

'I like the job all right, but I've decided I want to teach. I've signed up at the Teachers College for next year.'

'Seems to me that would be exactly right for you.' Daniel couldn't say why, but he knew it was true. Perhaps it was her readiness to listen. Perhaps it was the compassion and understanding in those dark eyes. Or her intelligence and humour.

'Thank you, Daniel.' She touched his hand.

Just a small gesture, but he had to look away.

'Stay tonight, Daniel,' Mary said, in a quiet, matter-of-fact manner, as she put the dishes away. 'We have a spare room. And I can send you off in the morning with scrambled eggs.' At this, Daniel grinned, and Mary glimpsed the boy behind the embattled soldier. *Was it the eggs or the idea of staying over?*

When he awoke at first light, he was momentarily puzzled by his unfamiliar surroundings: a dark timber bed-head, a round bedside table covered with a white, fringed cloth, and above him a drooping, frosted glass light fitting, the centrepiece of a ceiling bordered with a geometric-patterned plaster cornice—a pattern that he found himself following, tracking it as if it might lead him somewhere important.

When he moved, he felt a weight against his shoulder. It was an arm. The girl's arm. Mary's. She was clothed in her dressing-gown and slippers, lying above the covers beside him. He eased around, slowly so as not to wake her. Her face was serene in sleep, her mouth slightly open, her hair in disarray.

His movement caused her to stir. Her eyes opened and after a moment of comprehension, she greeted him drowsily. 'Hello.'

'Hello.' Daniel responded with an enquiring smile.

She returned his smile shyly, and moved away from him. 'I heard you last night. Daniel, you were shouting. It was awful. I didn't want to leave you alone.'

* * *

A silver-haired lady tending her front garden looked across the fence as Daniel left Mary's house, squinting at the low morning sun and adjusting his slouch hat. Their eyes met. He nodded to her. He felt her eyes following him as he walked away. Away from a place of unexpected refuge, away from the warmth of a shared breakfast, the warmth of human contact. How he had wanted to stay with Mary Preston this morning. She must seen how he wanted to immerse himself in her, never to surface again.

He walked along the quiet street in the chill morning air, past a busy brickworks, arriving eventually at a broad intersection. He crossed, as Mary had suggested, to Talbot Road, one of six converging roads, where he located the trolleybus stop.

As the electric bus surged up the steep hill, passing safe brick houses interrupted only by a modern ice-cream factory, Daniel was feeling that he had left something very important behind, that he was going in the wrong direction. The feeling grew, pulled at him. *Get off. Go back.*

The road ran along the top of a ridge which fell away on both sides. To his left, he could look out across crowded inner suburbs to a wooded skyline; to his right, the view swept across green hills to a distant mountain range. He was glad that Mary had suggested that he take the high route into town; he was warming to her small city. It was, he guessed, about the size of his own adopted town. And apparently the boom gold-rush years had helped shape this place too.

Retrieving his pack from the hotel, Daniel pulled out some dollar notes, the strange new money, and paid the wizened attendant. The old fellow gave him a *thanks cobber* and a nod of acknowledgement. As if he knew.

As the TAA bus bounced along Hobart Road towards the airport, a young man got up from his seat and approached Daniel. He leaned over awkwardly, glanced at Daniel's service badge and said, 'G'day. Do you mind me asking: were you called up?'

Daniel found himself looking at a lanky, clean-cut boy, fair-skinned and freckled, with light, anxious eyes. Had he himself once been that young, that innocent? Un-touched?

He nodded.

'Me too,' said the boy, 'I'm off to report in now. You got a minute?'

That morning, at the Preston house, Mary discovered a little sketch left by Daniel. She could see that he had used the ball-point pen and note-book from the phone table in the hall. There she was, busy in the kitchen, instantly recognisable by her hair. Mary was moved by the tenderness she could see in the simple drawing.

'That's lovely; who drew it?' her mother later asked.

'A new friend. I have a feeling you and dad will get to meet him.'

As he climbed the steps to board the shiny *Vickers Viscount* prop-jet, Daniel paused to look back at the modest terminal building. People were waving. He felt sure he would be back, back to this island where his mate now lay, and where he had, for a short time, felt safe, felt almost at home.

home is

THE PLANE DRONED towards the sun. Daniel looked out across meadows of snowy cloud and saw, in their slow swirls, the shifting patterns of his life. Memories murmured through the sound of the propellers, echoes of battle churned with innocuous noises of the time before, when home was the farm and, for a time, the farm was a home.

Back then, home was a noisy household, crowded with his everywhere mother, his never-stopping father, and his towering, always-talking brothers. A mother whose love he never doubted, two big brothers destined to be lost to him before he could properly know them, and an unknowable father.

As a child, Daniel could sense the power inside his father's gruff, dour exterior, this man whose leathery hands could make, mend, fashion and improvise with an assurance that he regarded with a kind of awe. Perhaps it was love.

As an adult, he came to learn more about the man Duncan Gardner. But the knowledge was always second-hand, as if read in some impersonal account, some stilted family memoir.

* * *

Duncan's merciless classmates saw it, even if his parents hadn't. The embossed initials on his Gladstone bag, although he had scuffed them as much as he dare, told them to their delight that Duncan Alexander Gardner was a D.A.G. The boy called Dag was compelled to prove his worth, to show the smirkers that he amounted to much more than a mildly amusing piece of sheep excrement. For Duncan, this meant building the family farm into something that would be acknowledged and respected by his erstwhile schoolmates and pastoral peers.

He took as his bride a robust country girl, a bonzer sheila, Pauline Shephard, a girl who would surely help him to achieve his goal. A farm girl herself, Pauline was at home milking cows, tending to crops or crutching sheep, her long hair pulled back from her freckled face into a severe bun.

When their first son, Duncan junior, was born, Duncan's world began to right itself. He could see the fruits of his labour coming into alignment with the fruits of his loins. He could foresee the consolidation of a proud line; the younger Duncan, DJ, a university degree in agriculture under his belt, would expand the property and diversify its produce; the Gardner name would resound around the area, around the state, even.

Then Geoffrey arrived. Another son. Unexpected and a little inconvenient, but never mind, he would in time be an extra pair of hands about the place

Duncan's decision to enlist in 1942 had been no surprise to anyone. When duty called, Gardners responded.

The ungainly limp he brought home from the Malayan Peninsular in 'forty-five—the result of a clumsy accident involving a slippery ditch and a wheeled gun—impeded his practical capabilities, but did not diminish his compulsion to prove himself. His reluctance to talk about his injury was never questioned.

On his return, Duncan found the farm in good shape. Pauline had widened a little, DJ had filled upwards and outwards into a strapping teenager, and Geoffrey, well, Geoffrey was Geoffrey. Could that comment he overheard at the sale-yard possibly be true? True of a Gardner? *You mark my words, that young Geoffrey is a nancy-boy.*

With the help of his sons and the steadfast Pauline, Duncan threw himself with such tireless passion into his mission of building up the farm that Pauline feared for his well-being. 'Glory be, Duncan, you'll bust something if you don't ease up.'

When Daniel was born, one of countless new arrivals in the post-war baby-boom years, his mother was delighted, but Duncan saw little to celebrate in an accidental child who was another mouth to feed and a distraction to Pauline.

The real shock came in the early fifties. With little warning, at least none that had registered with Duncan, his two adult sons departed the farm, and Duncan's hopes followed them through the farm gate. For what did he have left? Just a dreamy drainpipe of a kid in Daniel, whose adulthood was too far distant to build any new hopes on, and an idiotic injury that made him less of a farmer, less of a man.

Part of Geoffrey had yearned to stay with the family and to help shape his little brother's enquiring mind. To open him to a world beyond the farm fences and the hemming hills. But Geoffrey's own need was greater.

With every passing year he became more conscious of his separateness. He could not stay. He owed it to himself to find his place in the world. He could not say it to his parents, but here, his spirit would die.

Daniel, six years old, was left bewildered and unsettled by the sudden absence of his big brothers. He regressed to tantrums and bed-wetting, his mother protecting him from the scorn of his father.

For DJ, the idea of adventure had been to join the army. He died a cold, violent and premature death in Korea in 'fifty-three, the final year of that soon-to-be-forgotten war. With the news of his passing, the family reeled. And withered.

Duncan was shaken to the core. It was now certain: the prodigal son would never return to work the farm. And Geoffrey had never really been a prospect, had he?

Duncan made the agonising decision to do the unthinkable: to surrender, to leave the farm, leave the memories, walk out on the dreams.

The *For Sale* sign at the farm gate and the brittle silence had been as another bereavement to Daniel the boy; at every opportunity he took flight to the calm certainty of his hideaway in the bush that fringed the lower part of the property. There, to the companionable murmur of a little creek and the whispering of the gum-leaves, he quieted his mind by occupying his able hands building and modifying, with whatever was to hand, his secret 'fort'. Finding patterns in the delicate interplay of branches and twigs around him. Bending branches to weave them into patterns of his own. Packing the woven walls with wool scraps to keep out the wind. Spreading grass and hay to make a welcoming floor. Then ensconcing himself within this private refuge and losing himself in his reading and drawing, safe from the bleak uncertainties that roamed outside.

His father survived the depleted family's new environment in suburban Ballarat by attacking every task he could find with a haunted, hobbling energy: painting, fixing fences, repairing clotheslines, replacing gutters, planting vegetables, stripping engines—often calling upon his drafted, dutiful helper. *Stop that scribbling, Daniel; come here and learn how to do something useful.*

* * *

The engines sounded a different message as the plane began its descent into Essendon airport. The snowfields rose to surround the bumping plane, rushing madly past the windows, before becoming just another memory, just an ordinary grey ceiling above an ordinary world.

Where was he going now? Where did he belong? His platoon, his blood-brothers, had dispersed, carried their kits, their memories, their re-shaped selves and severed pieces, back to their homes. But where was his home?

Daniel felt an urge to stay in the anonymity of Melbourne for a while, before pressing on to Ballarat. To lose himself, find himself, piece himself together, before he had to face people, face questions.

And perhaps he would write a note to Mary Preston; the memory of her was an island of light in the murk.

But he should go home to Ballarat. It was expected of him. His father, wounded in service, and his brother, killed while serving, would expect it of him. *His fucking country would expect it of him.*

a wedding

SATURDAY, 20TH OCTOBER, 1973 was a breezy, sunny spring day in Sydney, as Queen Elizabeth officially opened the Sydney Opera House. Far to the south, in provincial Launceston, where the weather was also benign, another ceremony was taking place.

'I do.' Daniel said, looking into Mary's shining eyes. *Til death us do part, my darling. Nothing else will.*

'I do.' Mary said, looking up into his face. Then, unscripted and to the smiles of the gathered, the bride reached up and smoothed the groom's recalcitrant hair.

The black-robed, white-haired minister leaned forward with a crumpled smile, and squinted over his glasses at the couple, who found themselves, at that propitious moment, held in a slab of pale sunlight. 'I now pronounce you man and wife.'

The wedding had been a long time coming. They had exchanged shy letters for a time, gradually revealing more of themselves, until Daniel gained the courage to make the trip back to Tasmania. Their courtship had been stretched-out, intermittent. Daniel had felt obliged to spend time at the Gardner house in Ballarat. He had worked with a local house builder, completing a carpentry apprenticeship in the process, and finding that the work—nutting things out, putting things together—filled his mind, leaving fewer openings for the raiding parties of unwelcome memories. But still they came. Mary, in the meantime, had achieved her ambition to become a teacher, finding fulfilment in helping to shape young minds.

The bridal party left the little church, emerging to mild sunshine, the scent of wattle and cut grass, and the small echoes of ordinary suburban life. Mary's parents and Alex's mother tossed confetti and laughed happily, friends and relatives of Mary and her parents greatly outnumbering Daniel's meagre contribution.

His father, grizzled and cantankerous these days, having pushed his three sons—the dead, the departed and Daniel—into the farthest corner of his heart where pain and disappointment could not reach, saw no point in making the trip, or perhaps was afraid of making it.

And Daniel had no best man. The irony did not escape him that the mate he would have asked to fill that role now lay in Carr Villa Cemetery, just a mile or so away, but had his mate not died Daniel may never have met Mary. He found the thought excruciating, and could never voice it, not even to his beautiful bride.

A camera flashed. The groom flinched.

The father of the bride rose. 'Thank you.' He looked across his glasses at the gathering. 'Well, public speaking's not my thing, but I know I'm among friends here ...'

Colin Preston was a retired grocer. His less than robust health had made easy the decision to retire when he had been made a good offer for his business by a younger, more adventurous man who saw that the future lay with the proliferating supermarkets.

A stout man with a ruddy face and thinning hair, awkward in his unaccustomed suit, the father of the bride unfolded a small piece of paper and peered at it. Daniel knew that Mary was a little nervous for her father, but she need not have been, for what he said was right, he was indeed among friends.

The reception hall, St Ailbe's, housed memories for many of the guests; Daniel and Mary had recently danced there too, Mary shining with happiness, Daniel feeling awkward and inept but fortified by love. Today, the room was bright and be-flowered; white-clothed trestle tables were arranged parallel with three walls: the bridal party at the head table, the newly-weds front and centre, smiling faces on all sides.

'Four years ago,' the father of the bride continued, 'when Audrey and I came home from the coast to find that our Mary had a man in the house overnight,' he looked up at his audience, whose attention he had quickly gained, ' fair to say we were shocked. But when we learned the circumstances, we were proud of our girl.' His voice wobbled, 'seems we did something right.' He looked at his wife, then at his radiant daughter, and his eyes filled. 'Blimey, what a sook I am.'

He paused a moment, blinked, and continued. 'Since then, we have come to know young Daniel here, and we couldn't be happier with the choice our Mary has made. If only he'd comb his hair, the bloke'd be perfect,' Colin made a little snort at his own humour. 'Just kidding, son. I'm envious.' He patted his own balding pate.

As Mary's father continued with his homespun tribute, Daniel looked at his mother; did she feel comfortable among so many strangers? He need not have been concerned; Pauline was happily engaged in a smiling exchange with her neighbour, Mary's Aunt Daphne. His mother, nearing sixty now, seemed to bloom when out of Duncan's heavy shadow.

Mary was listening, but not really listening, to her father, when she heard: '… and he's a straight shooter…'

She saw Daniel's coy-under-praise expression momentarily flee somewhere distant and bleak, until he managed to assemble a faint, crooked grin. And she saw that Pauline, too, had shot her son a glance.

Her dear father. A simple man, a good man. Would never knowingly hurt a soul.

'I give you Mary and Daniel, the bride and groom!' Colin stuffed his crumpled notes into his pocket and raised his glass.

Chairs scraped noisily as the guests rose in ragged unison to toast the newlyweds. *The bride and groom! Mary and Daniel!*

A red Chrysler Valiant convertible, driven by a cousin of Mary's and trailing the obligatory array of cans, carried the waving couple noisily off into their new life. A new life that, for Daniel, was a sunlit jungle, an unknown territory of beauty and menacing calm.

renters

'OH, NOT NEAR the gasworks!' This was Audrey Preston's reaction to the location of the married couple's first home, a rented house in Inveresk. It was a modest Victorian cottage boasting a pretty, if overgrown, garden and an iron lacework veranda, in a less-than-salubrious area, just the toss of a lump of dirty coal from the Launceston Gasworks. The looming gasometers dominated the area and the faint odour of gas was ever-present.

'They're closing it down, mum. There'll be no more town gas. And anyway, the rent's affordable and we're practically over the road from the City Park.'

Yes, Audrey had to concede to herself, that was a benefit. The city's principal formal park was a delight, a beautiful place to escape to.

'But how will you get to school?'

'Easy, Mum. I'll walk into town and get a bus up Wellington Street.' Mary regretted the demise of the city's trolleybuses, and wickedly savoured her memories of frustrated drivers exiting their immobilised vehicles to attempt to re-connect the wildly waving antennae to the life-giving wires above.

'She'll be alright, Aud,' said Colin, smiling across the sports pages at his daughter. *Newcombe Wins Open.*

* * *

Word of mouth in the small city worked to Daniel's advantage. He soon gained himself a reputation among the town's builders as an honest and reliable 'Mr. Fixit', whose remarkable know-how spanned across several trades, and who was always willing to take on new challenges. It was Daniel Gardner who single-handedly constructed a new timber pedestrian bridge across the Wattle Gully rivulet, who built, to the artist's drawings, a new concrete, steel and timber sculpture in the Royal Park, and who built numerous one-off gazebos, conservatories, and verandas in the backyards of Launceston.

The second time a builder called him *Mr Fixit*, he took the hint and adopted that as his business name, having it sign-written gratis by a happy home-owner on the sides of his Holden HG utility.

But Mr Fixit, the maker and mender, knew not how to repair the fractures in his own psyche, the dark fissures which could open and suck the light from his day. His sudden departures from building sites, his bouts of anger or bleak apathy, were thankfully rare enough to have little effect on his livelihood.

The couple's landlord, a Mr Madden, known to the local children as Mad Man Madden for his surly nature, realised that he had the ideal tenants when Daniel began to effect minor repairs to the old place without seeking any compensation. Mad Man was chastened somewhat by the discovery, late in his narrow life, that not all renters were irresponsible no-hopers.

Daniel's stuttering but sure income, together with Mary's teaching salary, allowed them to plan for the day when they could buy their own home. Watching their savings grow as they built their marriage, stone by uncertain stone, gave them both quiet satisfaction.

For Daniel, this sense of purpose helped to hold him together. But the nightmares still came; anger and fear still launched surprise attacks.

* * *

Daniel had been reading in *The Examiner* about the aftermath of the disastrous collapse of part of Hobart's Tasman Bridge, when he heard a cry.

'Daniel! I'm bleeding!'

At the sight of his wife standing awkwardly in a bloodied dress, Daniel was shocked. His mind spun.

Shots. Where had they come from? He dropped to his stomach in the undergrowth. Silence. He peered through the long grass. Someone was still standing. God, it was Smithy. Just standing there. With this puzzled, emptying look on his face. His front a terrible wash of red. And his scared shitless mates, us, just watching.

'Daniel,' Mary said, more quietly.

Unprepared, and uncertain what should be done, Daniel wrapped Mary in a blanket and bundled her gently into the passenger's side of the ute. Few words were spoken as he drove up Charles Street towards the

Launceston General Hospital, but Daniel, when he could, shakily found Mary's hand.

The foetus, just a miniscule imagining of a person, released its tiny hold on life in the hospital's casualty department.

This was the first of three early-term miscarriages suffered by Mary, before she was to carry a child for its full term.

names

'AND IF IT'S A BOY?' Mary and Daniel had decided on the names for a girl, should the baby be of that gender. She would be Catherine Audrey after Mary's deceased maternal grandmother and her own mother. Daniel's mother would have to wait.

'Well, I'm sure my father would like it to be a Gardner family name, but I don't mind.'

They had been careful not to discuss names until Mary was nearing her ninth month and the birth seemed assured.

'Let's start there, then. What names, Danny-boy?' Mary was making a late-morning cup of tea. It was Saturday, and she and Daniel had just returned from shopping in town. Baby clothes and two dozen nappies.

'Well, there's *Duncan* of course.' Daniel offered, as he reached for the teapot.

'For your father or your brother?'

'My father, I suppose.'

'Who didn't even come to our wedding...'

Daniel glanced at his wife. Mary had been hurt by Duncan's absence. *What sort of a grandfather would he be if he wouldn't even attend his own son's wedding?*

'Sorry, Daniel.' She touched his arm.

'Then there's *Charles*, I think, back there somewhere...'

'What about *Geoffrey*?'

'My brother's name? I think he's the first Geoffrey. A one-off.' Daniel let the memory of his dear, one-off brother take hold for a moment. What had become of him? Had he gone to London, as his mother had heard? Had he found his place?

'Then there's *Alexander*, Dad's middle name and his father's Christian name.'

'Alexander! I love that name, Daniel.'

Daniel smiled at his heavily pregnant wife as he swirled the tea-pot. 'Well, that was easy, wasn't it?'

How could he tell her that he hoped for all their sakes that their baby would be a girl, for what did he know about being a father, about guiding a boy into manhood, whatever that was?

From outside, little spurts of metallic whirring began as old Mr Zanker, two doors down, began to mow his small, already immaculate lawn. The scent of fresh-cut grass wafted in on a mild spring breeze—a clean, new smell, new life growing.

Then: unwelcome, mud-smelling thoughts of lives expunged. Of lives bled out. And for what? Daniel swept the tea-pot onto the floor and fled.

* * *

Alexander Duncan Gardner was born at Launceston's Queen Victoria Hospital in the spring of 1980. Mary's joy was tempered by the delivering doctor's advice that, sadly, this child would be her last. *How she would love him.*

In her congratulatory card, Grandma Pauline wrote for Daniel: *When I told your father the baby's names, he didn't say much. Nothing unusual there, but I saw a tear in his eye.*

Soon after the scrawny red infant had shed his abundant, dark birth hair, it became evident that he would be a blond like his father, and as his paternal grandfather Duncan had once been.

What other traits would the boy have in common with his grandfather? Would he be good with his hands? Would he be stubborn? Uncommunicative? Would he be single-minded? Obsessive, even?

heaven and hell

'I WONDER IF heaven's like this.' Mary lazed on a huge towel in the shady glow of a beach umbrella, a discarded Frederick Forsyth paperback at her side. She looked through her over-sized sunglasses at Daniel, who was sitting up, reading *The Examiner* and keeping a watchful eye on the small figure fossicking in the sand lower down the beach.

The sun made a glowing halo in the five-year-old's blond hair, and Daniel's heart swelled with the pain of a love whose intensity he could not have imagined before the birth of his son. He got to his feet and stood for a moment, savouring the liberating warmth of the air, the sound and smell of the ocean, the floating cries of sea-birds. Life. The light between the visits of the darkness.

'I hope so,' he said.

He stood and walked across the sand towards the boy. 'What're you doing Alex? What's this?'

Alex was engrossed in the construction of Sand City, a complex of canals, tunnels, bridges and castles, with twig fences, pebble walls and feather flags.

'A town, dad. Watch this.' He raced to the water's edge with his bucket, squatted to fill it with seawater, then ran back, his little legs bouncing.

'Look.' Alex carefully poured the water into his canal system. 'I need more.' Ignoring his father, he ran back to the water's edge and repeated the exercise.

Daniel could see his own influence in his son's fascination with building things. A fascination that he had seen grow as the pair worked together in their shed. He could see too, Mary's influence in the child's patience, thoughtfulness and enquiring mind.

'Wow, that's great, Alex!' Sand City's waterways were up and running, although their young creator was having difficulty maintaining the water level. Next time, with Daniel's guidance, the boy would build a little closer to the ocean, where the water table was closer to the surface.

'Hey, let's see if we can find a cowrie for mum.'

Father and son set off along the tide-line of Green's Beach, their eyes scouring the sand, seeking, among the sparsely scattered shells and bits and pieces of nature's flotsam, the beautiful little egg-shaped shell treasured by Mary.

'Look for shells of similar shape and size, Alex. The sea sorts them out for you.'

'Okay daddy.'

The faith this little boy had in him made his heart ache.

'Look at this, Alex.' Daniel bent to pick up a shell, much bigger than the cowrie they sought, and decorated with a pattern of wavy lines. 'Mum'll know what it's called.'

Alex went back to his determined search. He'd find a cowrie for mummy.

Daniel spotted them first, but said nothing. He placed himself where Alex would have to detour around him and walk right over the patch of smooth sand where the little treasures lay.

'Daddy!' Alex's squeal must surely have carried back to Mary. The child bent and, with reverential care, picked up a small cowrie.

'Well done,' said Daniel. 'Where did you find it?'

'Just here.' Alex pointed at a scattering of small shells on the sand. His eyes widened and his little body shook with excitement. 'Daddy! Another one!'

'Goodness, two cowries! So tiny, how did you ever find them? And they're beautiful Alex. These are ribbed cowries, quite rare. Thank you. I shall put them in my collection.' Mary hugged her beaming son.

Watching them, Daniel could not decide whose pleasure was the greater—that of his sun–flushed, beaming wife or that of his tousle-headed, hopping son. Or indeed his own pleasure at watching these two, whom he loved more than life itself.

But why did it hurt so much, scare him so much, this loving?

* * *

Daniel had survived his tour of duty, suffering—at least in the eyes of the army—only a single, superficial injury. Little more than a graze: a Russian-made 7.62mm bullet travelling at 2,300 feet per second steaked across the thin flesh of his forehead, the glancing impact with his skull felling Daniel but barely deflecting the missile as it continued its lethal journey. Daniel's real, insidious injury was hidden, hidden even from himself.

On his return from Vietnam, Daniel brought with him a dark stranger, an anger whose ferocity frightened him; he feared it could spin out of control and damage those he loved. For some time his anger embraced all those who had made him like this. The politicians. The army brass. His trainers. Those of his fellow Australians who had reviled the young diggers returning home. The dismissive veterans of earlier, 'real' wars. And the enemy, for their senseless bravery, for making him a villainous invader, for showing him his own dark side.

He could not believe, if indeed his mind had allowed him to contemplate it, that in battle he had become a beast, killing fellow humans with whom he had no quarrel. And a great fear, unspoken and only dimly recognised, was that the beast was still in him, lurking in the shadows, and that it would re-surface and devastate those closest to him. Something in him, something battered and deformed, told him that to open himself up fully to the love he felt for Mary and their child would expose him to his circling predators, and his family to the consequences.

Sometimes he sensed the rage returning, and would separate himself from those around him. But too often the monster gave no warning. On those occasions when he was taken unawares, an upset table, a splintered door—or worse, the fear in Mary's eyes—would bear terrible testament to the visitation.

It's happening again. They're getting into my head. The pictures. The obscenities. What the hell was it all for? No-one gives a shit. I don't give a shit. Get away. I'll kill you again! Oh Christ.

He began to take off on his motorbike—bought with his final army pay and kept over the years—to disappear for days into remote parts of the Tasmanian bush, blindly seeking to put distance between himself and his torment.

The solitude and quiet were a balm, although the wild was not without hazard. A fine creeper in the rain forest was a trip-wire; that mass of foliage a sniper, that fallen branch caught in a tree, a human limb; a kangaroo carcass, wretched human remains. Thus, Pte Danny 'Boy' Gardner was sometimes seized and thrown mercilessly back into the mud and blood of Phuoc Tuy.

He learned to avoid the rain forests and favour open forest and bushland, where the more familiar smells and sounds of the Australian bush brought comfort, not threat. He liked to make camp in a sheltered location with an open outlook. He would not be ambushed again. He favoured the coast, too, with its cleansing salt air and fewer places for his assailants to hide.

Daniel's rational mind could understand what had made him like this. He had heard that others were suffering similar torments. But there was something more, something deeper, buried within him in a place he dared not approach. Something which at times twisted his insides, implying an unbearable truth.

It would happen without warning. It would happen when his eyes caught an un-expected flash of light in the dimness. A camera flash. A sheet of lightning. A sudden sweep of car headlights. He came to fear the flash, and what it might mean.

He could not venture near the door that kept his devils contained. Even removed in distance and time from the horrors of the battle-fields, he could not take the risk of remembering. And he feared most of all the meaning of the flash.

flashback

DANIEL RAISED HIS RIFLE to where the shape had been. It must be very close now; he could hear, almost feel, its breathing. He aimed at the sound. The barrel of his SLR must be probing the very breath of the spectre.

Was it fear or anger? Or devastating fatigue? Or some lethal curdling of these? You had to blame something, someone, didn't you? Hate someone for being sentenced to this hell. For your lost and mangled mates. For what you had become.

His hands trembled. His mind careered. *Let this finish it, for God's sake.* He squeezed the trigger.

A flash.

Daniel was not conscious of any sound. Only the muzzle-flash. For as he felt the gun jerk against his shoulder, he saw in the flash a face. And in the very same instant, the face was obliterated.

He had fired on the enemy before, seen figures fall, as if in some surreal charade. But this was different.

With the vomit, Daniel felt a hunk of his humanity wrenched from his insides.

The face in the muzzle-flash. A bare-headed, mud-smeared and startlingly near face that seemed to be peering straight at him. Peering with eyes that, even after they were brutally extinguished, would continue to stare.

He pulled a shell-shattered branch across himself and closed his eyes. He was back in his hideaway at the bottom of the farm, listening to the burble of the little creek.

The morning after the battle, in the deathly grey dawn, Daniel found that he could not look back at the battlefield. Something had happened during the night, some horror he could not revisit. He made his way through the steaming quiet towards the first fragment of familiar voice that he heard.

Days later, in the relative safety of the base camp, a stalking truth found him. A truth, a realization, a possibility, what did it matter what you called it?

The talk at the base was of others who might not return home—companions not yet accounted for. Lofty was one of them. Private Brian 'Lofty' McGuiness, the smallest bloke in the platoon. Was it the air of vulnerability about the sweet little Tassie bloke with the bat's ears and perplexed eyes that brought him to Daniel's mind? He could see his face now.

And as he saw it, Lofty's face and the face in the gun-flash became one.

The recall was fleeting. Remembered and rejected in the one instant. Just an inexplicable, ugly tic, then gone. Bludgeoned deep into the lost reaches of his mind.

a scented shed

'CAN YOU HOLD THIS, MATE?' his father asked.

Alex looked up at his dad. Helping dad in the shed was one of his favourite things. Just as good as going to the beach. Or to the bush. Or drawing with dad. Or having a ride on the back of the motorbike. Yeah, the bike; that was probably the very best thing.

Alex reached up and took hold of the end of a board that his father was adjusting into a vice. 'What sort of wood is this, dad?'

'It's myrtle. Can you smell it?'

Alex leaned close to the pink wood and sniffed it, caressing its straight grain.

'Yeah.'

Really?'

'No, I don't think so.'

'Here, smell this.' His father handed him a small block of pale yellow wood.

'Hey, yeah, I can smell that. Nice. That's, um, no don't tell me, hewing pine.'

'Huon pine, yes. I'll show you a Huon pine tree one day.'

The shed, the outbuilding that had made the decision to buy the compact East Launceston house an easy one, had been a garage. It was clad with galvanized iron and was set well back on the block, so its side door could be entered from the backyard. These days, the utility, the HG, was parked on the gravel driveway, denied the privilege of shelter by the incursion of an assemblage of construction equipment and a cache of building materials, both new and salvaged. A parade of tools, each in its regimented place on the wall above a long wooden workbench, waited for their call to action. To one side of the bench, low on the wall, hung a collection of colourful, boy-size tools.

The only acknowledgement of the shed's prior use was the presence of a lurking, tarp-covered form next to the cement-mixer. The BSA.

'What're you doing with this, dad?' Alex was examining the piece of myrtle.

'You remember old Mrs White? At Mowbray?'

Alex nodded. 'You built a porch for her. She was nice.'

'She remembers you, too. Well, I'm replacing a missing shelf for her. Helping out a bit.' A missing shelf. God, what a little thing.

The village stank of mud and effluent. The woman held a crying infant in her arms. He could see her now. She stood before her broken hut staring at the soldiers. Staring at these strangers from a land of wealth and weaponry, as they passed through her country, cut through her life. Her eyes held Daniel's.

'Helping out is a good thing to do, Alex.'

Alex looked at his dad and nodded.

'Hey, maybe you could make something for Mrs White,' Daniel looked towards the off-cut bin, a treasure chest of small wood pieces of all shapes and hues, 'something for her to put on the shelf. To remember us by.'

together

'WILL WE BE TAKING THIS, DAD?' Eight-year-old Alex had brought a small auger from the shed.

'No, thanks Al, The hut we're going to is already finished.'

'Is it one that you built, dad?'

'Yes. We can just fix it up a bit. Maybe build a new fireplace. Would you like to do that?'

'Yeah, great, dad.'

Always Daniel stayed long enough at his chosen site to make some form of shelter, using only those materials which the location offered. Looking for what was there, working with it, piecing it together, the way it was meant to be. Piecing himself together, at least for a time.

On those occasions when he took Alex with him, Daniel most often went to a shelter he had made previously. That way, they had immediate, if rudimentary, shelter. Together, man and boy would repair, refine and modify the structure.

The simplicity and beauty of these shelters was evident even to Alex's young eye, and the images of them, the feel and weight of their parts, stayed with him over the years. He could see in their careful framing the veins of a tender leaf, the intricate branches of a tree, or the fine bones of a bird's skeleton. That they kept out the rain and even the bitter wind was unsurprising to Alex, who knew for certain that nothing was beyond the capability of his father.

This day Daniel and Alex were setting out for the lake country. The air chilled as the BSA rumbled up the long, snaking rise from the orderly yellow farmlands to the patchily forested highlands. The young boy, a slight form in his out-sized helmet, clung to his leathered hero and exhilarated in the rushing wind and the closeness of the two of them with the machine.

The hut was an hour's walk from Arthur's Lake. Daniel's spirits lifted as soon as he and Alex had concealed the bike, hoisted their packs and entered the bush. Daniel loved the eucalypt forests, where he savoured the familiar, reassuring scent of the Australian bush, the calls of the wattle-birds, currawongs and parrots, the dusk-thumping of wallabies, and the sheer timelessness, where in the purple shadows he imagined the spirits of the aborigines, still moving about their land—perhaps, like him, looking for peace.

He and Alex walked on, their footfalls hushed on a carpet of bark, between lichen-mottled rocks, ferns and ghostly gums. Occasionally, through the trees, they could see the glint of sun on water and the movement of musk ducks.

As they walked, Daniel stooped to pick up a fallen bird's nest. He picked gently at the dense mass of twigs and fibres. He caught Alex's eye, and together they silently marvelled at the small miracle. How, somewhere in the tiny brain of a bird lay the knowledge of how to weave such a robust refuge from such insubstantial bits and pieces.

'Will it take our weight, dad?' They had arrived at their destination and were considering how best to mend the roof, whose bark layers had been disturbed—by a storm, perhaps, or by those pesky possums.

'What do you think?'

The boy looked again at the roof. He could see from beneath how the many fine branches were interlaced, and how they formed a kind of domed shape over which bark strips had been laid, over-lapped and secured.

'They're only thin.'

Daniel smiled. 'The thing is, all those thin branches are working together, Alex. Sharing the load. And the domed shape that they make is a strong shape. Remember the egg? And the sea-shells?'

Yes, Alex did remember. The egg that he could not break when his father had challenged him to do so, when exerting pressure only at its domed ends. And the thin but strong shells on Green's Beach.

'Let's do it together, Alex. I'll be down here, you climb up there, and we'll work together. Careful now.'

small arms

'OFF AGAIN?' A smiling Mary watched as her husband and her son went about preparing to head off into the bush. This was so good for them both. She could see how Daniel was calmer, more settled, on these occasions. Not like the times when he just disappeared on his own, took off as though the Devil was chasing him. And Alex loved these trips so much; there was no doubting that. Just look at him now.

'When will the explorers be back?' she asked.

'Sunday afternoon. Before dark,' replied Daniel, as he closed the bike's panniers. He turned to his wife and embraced her.

'I love you, Daniel,' she said.

'Me too.'

'Hey you,' she said to Alex, who had climbed onto the pillion seat, 'haven't you forgotten something?'

Alex scrambled down and came to her.

'Sorry, mum,' he said, and kissed her vigorously.

* * *

Alex, his face screwed up in concentration, was drawing the motorbike near their camp south of Musselroe Bay, on the island's far northeast coast. Not as isolated as Daniel would have liked, but with its wide beach and sheltered sites for camping, more amenable to a relaxed father–son excursion.

They had put together their shelter quickly, the weather being benign and the likelihood of their re-using the hut being remote. They gathered grasses and fallen branches and built a simple humpy covered with crudely woven thatch, threaded branches tying the covering in place. Their sleeping bags lay on the sandy soil; a circle of rocks formed a fire-place.

Alex had tired of drawing the plovers and diving petrels and had turned his attention to the motorcycle.

'What's BSA mean, Dad?'

Daniel thought for a moment. 'I think it stands for Birmingham Small Arms.'

'Small arms?'

'Guns. Not great big ones like canons. Ones that people can carry.'

'Is that why they're called arms?'

'The word 'arms' has more than one meaning, Al. One meaning is arms like your arms ...'

'My small arms?'

'Smartypants. The other meaning is weapons, like guns. Armaments.'

'What's that got to do with motorbikes?'

'Good question. Seems like the BSA people were good at making mechanical things. Maybe they started out making weapons, then began to make other stuff, like motorbikes.'

'That's better isn't it dad?'

'Yes, Alex, that's a lot better.'

Alex was thoughtfully jigging his precious graphite stick, shading his drawing the way he had seen his father do it, when he asked: 'Did you carry small arms, Dad?

SLR, semi-automatic, 7.62mm calibre, 300 yards battle range, weight with full magazine about 11 pounds, could be relied upon to kill an enemy outright ...

'Dad?'

a wild beach

'LISTEN TO THE WAVES, DAD.'

Daniel smiled at his growing son. Nine years old already. Perhaps he could manage this fatherhood thing after all. Perhaps his little family could survive.

The pair left the quiet shelter of the trees and walked in bright sunlight across a sandy, flat area through low scrub, heading for the ocean, north of where the dark waters of the Pieman River spilled into the Southern Ocean, on the island's west coast. Their every sense told them that the beach was close: the ragged line of dunes before them, the gulls riding the wind—their cries darting away behind them, the rhythmic roar of the breakers, and the salty smell of the ocean.

They emerged from the warm refuge of the dunes each with a little loping run down the final steep slope onto a vast tumultuous beach, where the force of wind and noise assailed them. The beach, whose scalloped undulations reflected the ferocity of the pounding surf, stretched on to the south until it disappeared into a salty mist, and to the north to a rocky headland. In between were several haphazard scatterings of rocks.

Daniel used a piece of driftwood to draw a long, deep line in the sand, from the foot of the dune out to where the sand was wet from the reaching tide.

'What's that for, dad?'

'That, Alex, is to make sure we don't get lost. So we'll know where we came onto the beach, and the direction to our camp.'

'That's a good idea.'

'The wind and tide will eventually wash away the line of course, but we'll be back long before that happens. Sometimes I make a row of big rocks, if I need a line to last a long time.'

The pair walked northward, unsteady in the boisterous wind, just above the incoming tide, jumping aside occasionally to evade the foam-edged arcs sizzling indignantly up the sand at the intruders. Alex kept one eye open for the treasured cowrie shells that his mother so loved, the other on the insistent sea.

They drew closer to the headland, where the shore formed a small cove and the wind was less raucous. Daniel pointed his stick at a dune, whose eroded face revealed dense layers of shells.

'See those shells there, Al? These are aboriginal middens along here.'

Alex looked closely. He knew from school what middens were.

'Can you imagine, Al, how long it must have taken for those millions of shells to accumulate? To gather? How many people feasted on those shellfish, how many lives have been lived right here over the centuries?'

Before Daniel could stop him, Alex gently took a flat, pearlescent oyster shell from the face of one of the middens and brushed sand from it.

'It's for time and the elements to do that, Al, not us.' said Daniel, putting a large hand on the boy's small shoulder. 'There's not much left to remind us of the people who once lived here, so we shouldn't disturb what there is.'

It was several hours later when they returned to the line. Alex had found a rare paper nautilus shell for his mother (who would later explain to him that it was actually an egg-sac), and Daniel had collected various pieces of useful driftwood, half carrying, half towing them with a rope sling he had devised.

They followed the line back across the dunes and were passing a stand of blooming tea-tree on their way back to the campsite, when Alex reached up and picked one tiny white flower from the wafting crowd. As they walked, he examined the flower: a slender, star-topped stamen in the heart of a bejeweled coronet, with five cupped petals arrayed precisely around it.

'Look at this, dad.'

His father stared in silence at the perfection of one of nature's miniature masterpieces.

Face in the mud, again. Chaos. And before his eyes, right there, a tiny white flower. It had no place in this brutal domain, but there it was. A defiant survivor. Intact. A trace of beauty in the midst of ugliness. Of hope where there seemed only to be despair. Just another cruel joke.

'I might try to draw it, dad.'

* * *

Their meal cans bashed and buried in the last light of the long day, the pair sat by the flickering light of an encircled fire. Setting aside his labored sketches of the tea-tree flower, Alex was struggling to trap in pencil the form of a shore-bird he had seen, while his father had opened his leather portfolio and launched a feverish charcoal assault on his own private page.

As the darkness deepened and his son's eyelids began to droop, Daniel said, 'Time for bed, Alex.'

What's that you have there, Alexander?

I've designed a bird, God.

Show me Alexander. Oh, my goodness, you're quite the designer, aren't you?

Thank you, God.

I like the wonderful contrast between its black back and head and the white underside you've given it. And the sharp orange beak and matching legs are perfect. Where shall we put it, Alexander?

On the beach, please God. At the water's edge.

Very well. It can feed on bi-valves—shellfish—in the wet sand. And we'll call it a pied oyster-catcher. Is that all right with you?

'Alex?'

'Huh?'

'Is that all right with you?'

Alex emerged from his dream to find his father bending over him. 'We'll pack up and leave in an hour. Is that all right with you?'

perspective

NEAR THE SHORE of Lake Echo Daniel had built a low hut, its curved rear wall nestling into a natural recess in a rock-strewn bank. The wall was built of local boulders packed together with clay and mud; several fallen eucalypt limbs spanned its width to form the curved spine of a roof made up of densely intertwined branches and bark shingles. The weaving had a disciplined intricacy to rival the beauty of nature, the bark roofing the colour and pattern of some giant reptile's discarded skin.

The shelter was magical to Alex. He marveled that his father had made it—that it was not some creation of nature, some natural part of the bush.

'What can we do to it, dad?'

'Let's see. Why don't we make a door, Al?'

'How?'

'Well, we need something that will close off the doorway, keep out the wind. How do you think we can do that?'

Alex and his father were sitting in a companionable silence as the sky darkened above them and the bush began to speak of the presence of night creatures. Behind them, a new wood-framed, woven reed door, the pair's handiwork of the day, stood ready to be moved into place.

'Look at the stars, dad.'

'They're brighter out here in the bush, aren't they Al? '

'Yeah. And there are more of them.'

'Remember what a star is, Al?'

'Yes, they're suns. Like our sun, only further away.'

'Imagine how far away those suns must be, so that they are only pin-pricks of light to us, and only visible in the dark.'

'Yeah, wow.' Alex stared in wonderment.

'The further away they are, the smaller things become. Things that are closer to you seem bigger. '

'Like prospective, dad?'

'Perspective. Yes, exactly, Alex.'

Daniel knew that sometimes things got so close and so big that you could no longer see them, no longer recognise them for what they truly were. They had got right inside you.

dreams

SAFELY HOME, in his bedroom, a tired Alex was sitting up in bed. He opened his sketch pad and reviewed his drawings of the day. The most precious drawing was the last, drawn by the light of their small gas lamp, an ambitious attempt to capture the deeply shadowed, intense face of his father, who was absorbed in his own drawing.

'Oh, I love that, darling.' His mother had come to say goodnight, and was looking over his shoulder. 'You'd better show me the rest in the morning. School tomorrow.' She kissed him and said, 'turn the light out in a minute.'

The day before, Alex had drawn a star-fish, the shell—the *carapace*—of a decorator crab, a fern frond, and two birds: a big, soaring Pacific Gull and a noisy Cockatoo. *Those Cockatoos...* The pad slipped from his grasp.

And God?
Yes Alexander?
Can I ask you a question?
Of course, Alexander.
It's about another bird.
You like birds, don't you Alexander?
Yes, I do.
What is your question?
It's about the white cockatoo.
Ah. The sulphur-crested cockatoo?
Yes God.
I was pleased with that one, Alexander. I thought the concentric golden arcs of its crest related well to the dramatic curve of its beak. Do you agree?
Yes, I do, God. And I love how when it spreads its wings you see the golden edges against the sky.
Thank you Alexander. I thought that was a nice touch.
But, God, with jew respect, ...
God smiled. That's due, Alexander.
But ... alright, with due respect, God, I think the bird has a design floor.

Alex heard a collective gasp of horror from a gaggle of God's minions, whose presence he had been unaware of until that very moment. The little crowd of Casper-like figures rustled and fussed in agitation, looking with trepidation at God.

I think you mean a flaw, Alexander.

How spooky was that? It dawned on Alex that God knew he had the wrong spelling for the word due, now the word flaw, when Alex hadn't even put pen to paper. And, spookier still, Alex knew exactly how God had corrected him. This gave Alex pause: God knows things. But he decided to soldier on anyway.

Well, God, You have given a lot of birds such beautiful calls, how come the sulphur-crested cockatoo ended up with such a horrible screech?

Oh dear, had he gone too far? He fidgeted anxiously, tugging at one of his own feathers, waiting for God's reaction.

'Alex, time to wake up.' His mother was gently tugging at his sleeve.

At the breakfast table, Alex told his mother, 'I dreamt I was talking to God about cockatoos.'

'Which ones, darling? White or black?'

'The white ones. You know.'

Daniel laughed. Yesterday they had found themselves surrounded by a chaotic flock of the raucous creatures. Like loud-mouthed, often annoying, friends, you still loved them even as they misbehaved.

'I asked him why they screeched like they do. I can't remember if he answered me.'

Daniel was smiling as he went about preparing their breakfast.

'Do *you* know, Dad?'

What wonderful, impossible questions his son asked. Daniel couldn't recall asking his own father such questions, but then he couldn't seem to find in his memory any time at all when he and his father had shared this kind of simple closeness. The thought saddened him, and the sadness rolled into a dark well of pain and surged up inside him, catching him unawares.

'Dad?'

* * *

'What's that hole in the wall, mum?' Alex was looking at a jagged, fist-size hole in the sheet plaster of the kitchen wall.

Last night he had heard a groan and a loud thump. Or had he been dreaming?

'Just an accident, darling. Dad will fix it when he comes back.'

# of sky

DANIEL FOUND, to his relief and gratitude, that the devils of the rainforest kept their distance while his son was by his side.

Quietly and safely the pair had trod the cushioned ground, past and under ferns of all sizes, taking in the fairy world of fungi, liverwort, mosses and lichen, and savouring the cool quiet beneath sassafras, celery-top, leatherwood and myrtle, and, by the river, the unprepossessing but amazing Huon Pine—the stuff of countless stories, the prize that drew the legendary piners to remote and inhospitable parts.

'There's one, Alex. That's a Huon Pine.'

'That one? That straggly one hanging over the water?'

Alex was clearly underwhelmed by the appearance of the ancient tree whose dense and aromatic wood was so highly prized. He had pictured something taller, prouder, more heroic.

In the far north-west of the island, near the Arthur River, the pair climbed to a high rocky outcrop above dense forest, and made camp beneath a sheltering overhang.

'What are you drawing, Alex?' The long summer evening was still light as Daniel was preparing a simple meal. No open fires at this time of year; even here, the risk of bushfire was too great.

'I'm trying to draw the view.' Seated on a rock, Alex nodded out towards the hilly, forested country, the view commanded by their elevated site.

'Can I see?' Daniel moved to Alex's side. 'That's good Al. The perspective is good; I like the way you have the rocks so big here in the foreground.'

'What about the hills, Dad? They don't look right, do they?'

'Can I show you something?'

'Sure.'

Daniel rubbed Alex's charcoal stick briefly on the end of his thumb, then lightly made a loose, snake-like smudge across Alex's drawing. Alex was captivated. With that one deft stroke, his father had drawn the most distant mountain range. And he could see that it was *far away*.

'You see how the hills get lighter and fuzzier, the further away they are?'

Daniel said, directing his son's gaze to the distant layered hills, serene in the hazy evening light. 'Watch.' He used his blackened thumb to slightly darken the next layer of hills that Alex had drawn, then more vigorously worked on the nearer hills.

Alex's drawing had suddenly become real. As Daniel completed his little master class by loosely rendering the rocks in the foreground, the picture became something else: no longer a sheet of paper, but a three-dimensional dream world. Alex felt as if he could fall into the picture and fly to that faraway, thumb-smudge range, and beyond, to the fading, endless sky.

'Where do we go when we die, dad?' Night had lowered its gentle curtain around their little camp, leaving only the heavens revealed to them. Alex was thinking of his grandmother, Grandma Prescott, who they told him had *passed away* that year, 1990. Mum said she had gone to heaven.

'Some people believe that their spirit, their soul, will go to a place in the sky, a peaceful place they call heaven.'

'Do you believe that, dad?'

'I think we go back to nature, where our spirit will be in everything.' Daniel said, as he packed away the scuffed portfolio that contained his sketch-books, the scratchings of an assaulted soul.

'What do you mean?'

'Remember that dead Tasmanian devil we saw this morning?'

'Yeah?'

'Well, it's already being consumed. That means …'

'I know what *consumed* means.'

'Sorry. Anyway, it's already being consumed by the living things around it, the creatures and the plants. So it becomes part of many other things, new lives. Every little part of it, every atom, lives on. Just as your memories of Grandma live on. That's beautiful, don't you think?'

But Alex didn't think that the motley remains of the devil had been at all beautiful. He was silent for a moment.

'So, if we go into the things all around us, how can we go to heaven too?'

'I'm not sure anyone can really answer that, Alex.' Daniel looked heavenwards. 'Maybe it's the same thing.'

Alex looked to the glittering night sky. This was confusing and mysterious stuff.

Daniel had boiled the billy on his camp-stove and was brewing tea when a tousled Alex joined him. The morning was mild, the familiar scent of the forest comforting, and the rhythmic sound of the distant surf deeply calming.

But, for Daniel, calm was a fickle friend.

missing

'SO, MRS GARDNER, it's your husband who's missing?'

The policeman carefully placed his hat on the table, reached inside his jacket, creased from sitting in his hot car, and looked across at Mary.

'That's right, Sergeant. He went bush, as he often does, and hasn't come back.'

'When did you expect him back?'

'A week ago.'

'Ok, let's get the details.' He opened his notebook and clicked a biro into action. She noticed a blue ink-spot in the pocket of his pale blue shirt, and vaguely wondered if there was a wife somewhere to scold him for it. To welcome him home. To hold her man close.

'His full name?'

'Daniel Steven Gardner. That's Steven with a v.'

'Occupation?'

'You can put down carpenter. He does other work as well, metalwork, machinery repairs, other things.' She heard herself using the present tense, and pushed back the dull pain that threatened to engulf her. 'He has a shed out the back.'

The policeman nodded. 'Age?'

'Forty-five.'

'Height?'

'About five nine. Whatever that is.'

'Weight? '

'I think about seventy kilos. A bit more maybe.'

'Fair hair?' She saw that the Sergeant was looking through the wide opening to the small, formal dining room, where her straw-headed son sat drawing, jabbing at the page in a manner painfully like the familiar actions of his father, seemingly oblivious to the solemn exchange taking place in the next room.

'Yes, but getting a bit darker. Not as blond as young Alex there.' At the sound of his name, Alex looked up, glanced at his mother, then immediately retreated into his sketch-book, punishing the paper with renewed vigour.

'Any distinguishing features?'

'Um, he had a scar on his forehead. Horizontal, near the side, just here. But you wouldn't really notice it.'

But it would help to identify a body. She saw the unspoken thought in the policeman's eyes. She wanted to protest, to quash that thought, but no words would come.

'Do you know what caused the scar?'

Mary crossed her legs and smoothed her skirt. 'No. He always said it was nothing.'

The big man sipped at his tea and adjusted his frame on the kitchen chair. 'When did you last see your husband, Mrs Gardner?'

'When he left here early on Wednesday, the thirteenth.'

'That's this month? November?'

'Yes.' She saw him write *13/11/91*.

'I expected him back by the twentieth. He said he'd be a week. Ten days at the most.'

The Sergeant continued to write diligently in his little book.

'And what was he wearing when he left?'

'Khaki trousers. Brown boots. An old brown leather jacket.'

'How was he travelling?'

'On his motorbike. Here are the registration papers.' Sliding the creased form across the table felt to Mary like some sort of surrender to an unassailable truth. Her eyes brimmed.

'Thank you.' He copied down the particulars, mouthing the words as he wrote *1967 BSA Spitfire*, with a faint nod of recognition. 'Where was he going?'

'I'm not certain, but probably to the west coast, near the Pieman.'

'Probably?'

'Yes, I'm sorry, but it's quite possible he went somewhere else altogether.'

'Why do you say that?'

'Daniel would go where the spirit moved him.'

The policeman looked awkward; Mary saw him glance at Alex, who was drawing feverishly now. 'I hope you don't mind me asking, Mrs Gardner, but was your marriage all right?'

'I understand, Sergeant,' Mary said quietly, 'Daniel hasn't gone off to another woman. He loves Alex and me. He just needs his solitude.'

The man nodded. 'Do you have a photograph of your husband, Mrs Gardner?'

'Yes, several.' Mary spread the photographs on the table: a family snap in front of their neat weatherboard home, Daniel in uniform, Daniel with

Alex on the old BSA.

'He was in the army, I see.'

'Yes, Vietnam.'

'Regular or nasho?'

'He was conscripted. National Service.'

'Ah.'

The big policeman clicked his pen shut. 'Thank you, Mrs Gardner.' He eased his chair back and stood, causing the kitchen to shrink. 'All police stations around the state will be notified. Our Savage River officer will check the roadsides out that way; as I recall there are some bendy roads through thick bush, and if someone went off the road ...' his broad face took on a doleful expression. 'We'll make enquiries in Corinna too, and mount a search in that area if we get any leads. But because we can't be sure where he was heading, there's only so much we can do.'

As the policeman's car crunched down the driveway, an emptiness moved into the house. A creak as the house adjusted itself. A distant murmur of traffic. The tapping of charcoal on paper.

Mary moved to her son and hugged his shoulders. Then went quietly to her bedroom and closed the door.

* * *

In the *Examiner* and *Advocate* newspapers on 2nd December 1991, below a photograph of Daniel, appeared a small notice:

MISSING
Anyone knowing the whereabouts
of Daniel Steven Gardner, aged 45,
of East Launceston, is asked to
contact their local police station.
Mr Gardner was last seen on
Wednesday 13th November, 1991.
He was riding a BSA motorcycle
Reg. no W1573, and may have been
travelling towards the west coast.

ALEX

missing dad

IN LATER YEARS Alex could conjure up only disjointed images of the visit by the police to his parents' East Launceston home.

What he did recall was how the form of a dark blue policeman had filled the doorway of the modest house, how the big man's voice had rumbled in the kitchen, next to the dining room where he sat, losing himself in a thicket of charcoal lines.

His mother had made a pot of tea and brought out warm scones with butter and raspberry jam. She sat opposite the policeman at their kitchen table, with its silken Huon pine top and finely muscled blackwood legs. Alex could still see his father hefting that table from the back of the ute; he could see him working its stained and pitted top back to a soft glow, the shed filled with the fragrance of the wood; he could hear his father explaining how the lost stories hinted at by its dents and gouges should be allowed to whisper on. Alex could see too the restored bentwood chairs, upon which his mother always looked elegant, but which the big policeman made to look quite inadequate.

How could some memories be so clear and others so elusive? His feelings at the time were difficult to retrieve, trapped perhaps in that charcoal morass. *Why isn't dad here? This is all a mistake. It has to be. Dad will sort it out when he gets back, tell that policeman what's happened. This is stupid. Stupid. Stupid.*

moving

OIL SPOTS on the concrete floor, a bunched tarpaulin: the only signs that the bike had ever been there. Apart from a faint smell of grease, that is, laying under the odour of paint and turpentine, of plaster dust, of grass clippings on the lawnmower, and the sweetness of wood shavings.

Mary stood still. The scent of Daniel's stuff. Of *him*. She had not ventured into the shed since the day the policeman visited.

'Where do you reckon he is, mum?' Alex had seen his mother enter the side door of the shed, and followed her.

'Come here darling.' Mary sat on a scarred wooden workhorse and drew her son in close. 'We just don't know, Alex, but I'm very worried that something might have happened to him.'

Alex frowned at the spattered and stained floor.

'There's something I need to tell you, darling,' she held her son tight, 'we may have to move to a new place.'

'Why, mum?'

'Well, with your dad not here, there's not enough money coming in to pay for the house.'

'Is that the mortgage?'

'Yes.'

''I'll help. I can earn some money. Mowing lawns and stuff.'

'Thanks darling, but it still wouldn't be enough. Anyway, you need to do your schoolwork.'

Alex's eyes wandered. 'Will we still have a shed?'

Mary had been unable, months after Daniel's failure to return, to claim on his modest life insurance. The man from the insurance company had been appropriately sympathetic when he visited and gave her the unwelcome news: until her husband's death could be established, there could be no payout. And now that Daniel's contribution to the household budget had ceased, the mortgage payments on their East Launceston house would be too much for her.

Her father had offered to raise a loan on her parents' home, but Mary would not hear of it. She sold the house, paid off the mortgage and used the residual amount to start a new savings account. To start all over again. Without Daniel.

Oh, Daniel. Was our love not enough?

* * *

The rent was cheap. Understandably so. Their new home was a flat above a hairdressing salon in the inner suburb of Invermay. Upstairs: a lounge and two bedrooms, one large, one tiny. Downstairs: bathroom, kitchen-dining. Outside: laundry, toilet, and a narrow back yard. And a shed. Not a big shed, but Daniel's work bench somehow fitted in.

In the shed, Alex contemplated the stack of boxes containing his father's tools. Tools which he could use when he was bigger, his mother had promised. Until then his own small tools would have to do.

It was in the shed that he made a promise to himself: when he was big he would find his father, and they would use the big tools together. He would somehow get their house back, too; that would make his mother happy.

cutting

'YOU'VE DISAPPOINTED ME, ALEX.'

Alex and his mother were sitting in the hospital's emergency department, waiting. Alex's left hand was wrapped in a blood-stained tea-towel. It hurt, and the blood had scared him. But his mother's words cut deeper, hurt him more.

'I'm sorry, mum.'

The electric jig-saw had seemed such a simple tool. His father had used it with such ease, making such wonderful shapes.

Alex had waited until his mother had gone to visit a friend before lifting the embargoed article from its box and trailing an extension cord from the laundry to the shed. He found a piece of flat board and secured it into the vice, still bolted to his father's workbench.

Now to cut out a shape. What could he make for mum? Maybe he would just get the feel of the tool before he decided. He pushed the switch and the thing came to life in his hand. He put its jigging blade to the edge of the board. This was harder than it looked. He steadied the board with his free hand. There, now it's cutting...

But, without warning, the thin blade snapped, and the jagged, jumping edge hammered wildly into the surface of the board and, before he could react, into his hand. Blood everywhere. His shriek brought one of the hairdressers from the back door of the salon.

'When you're older, I said, Alex.'

'I know mum. I'm sorry.'

'Did you say thank you to Lois from the salon?'

'I can't remember. I think so.'

'Well, make sure you do, young man.'

'I wish I *was* a young man. Not just a useless kid. Then I could do things for you.' *And make dad proud.*

He felt her squeeze and ventured a sideways look. 'Then I could use dad's tools properly.'

a scar

SOMETIMES, when the weather was hot and still, the back door of the salon would be left open. Sometimes Lois, or one of the other young women, would stand in the doorway, cigarette in hand, letting the cooling draft waft her skirt. From the shed, he could see her standing there now, her red hair pulled up into a loose coil.

'How's your hand Alex?' she called.

'Good thanks, Lois. The stitches are out now, but the doctor said I'll have a scar.' Surely a scar was a sign of a man.

'Can I see?'

He walked along the yard and offered his hand. She reached out a bare arm and took his hand in her own. Then ran a finger along the ragged line. He liked the feeling; he liked her smell, her nearness. His tummy seemed to be doing something funny.

* * *

'I don't need pocket money any more, mum.'

'And why is that, young man?'

'Because I have a job.'

'Really? What it is?'

'Lois will pay me ten dollars to clean the floor of the salon twice a week. They have an electric polisher. She showed me what to do. She said I should ask you.'

'Electric? I didn't think that you and electricity were friends.'

'Ha ha.'

'Of course you can do it, darling. And thank you, that'll help our budget.'

'And, mum...'

'Yes?'

'I have an idea for another job.'

'Goodness. What's that?'

'The butcher over the road says he'll let me try my hand at signwriting on his shop window. If it's ok, he might pay me to do it regularly.'

'What a great idea. You'll need some special paint and brushes, won't you?'

'Yeah. I can buy them when I've earned my cleaning money.'

'I think you've earned a hug already. Come here.'

* * *

'How's high school going, Alex?' Lois asked, over the whine of the polisher.

Alex kicked the button and the machine settled.

'Yeah, good thanks, Lois. I'm enjoying it so far.'

'What's your favourite subject?'

That was what everyone seemed to ask. Even so, he always had to think about it, all over again. 'Well, I definitely like art best, but that doesn't feel like schoolwork. I really like science, too. And English is good. And...'

Lois laughed that warm laugh of hers.

* * *

'Hey mum, guess what.' Alex dropped his school bag on the kitchen floor.

'What darling?'

'There's a gazebo that dad built in the school grounds. It's really excellent. A bit quirky. All the kids love it.'

'I remember him doing something there, but I never saw it. How did you find out that your dad built it?'

'The headmaster told me. Mr Jenkins. He said my dad was a fine builder and a good man. That's what he said, mum.'

* * *

This Week's Specials:
Pork sausages Beef burgers Top Side Kangaroo patties

on the move

WHEN THE AGENT said that the place just needed a bit of TLC, Mary knew what that meant. It meant extensive renovation. But the small brick house perched on a barren lawn was within her budget, that's what mattered most.

The house was in her old neighbourhood, Kings Meadows. Close to her parents' place, and close to the care home they had set their ageing sights on.

Mary was comforted by the fact that Alex, sixteen now, was busting out of his skin to help renovate the place. To put his father's tools and his own growing capabilities and interests to good use. She understood that her son needed to show that he was now the man of the house, that he could look after his mother, repay her.

She watched him cut back his father's workbench so that it would fit at the end of the house's small garage, then set up places for the tools.

* * *

Alex achieved his driver's license in the same year that he and his mother left the Mowbray flat to move to Kings Meadows. His license enabled Alex to start the search that was a recurring dream during his adolescent years. Years of seeing his school friends knocking about with their dads. Kicking a footy with them. Wrestling with them. Holding onto them.

His boyhood dream of finding his own dad had not died, but *I will find him* had become: *I will find out what became of him.*

From his own memories and from interrogation of his mother, he drew up a list of places his father had visited, or might have visited, and marked them on a topographical map of the island. This annotated map replaced one he had drawn in a school exercise book, much earlier.

Alex resolved to search those wild areas—country which ranged from rain forest, though near-impenetrable bush, to open forest, to the lake country, to the coast of the Southern Ocean with its tea-tree flats and dunes, and broad, wild beaches with lichen-covered rocky outcrops. High on his list were secluded areas near the west coast, remembering that his father was attracted to the wild, untamed seas that frequently pounded that edge of the island.

He would visit all these places, until he found an answer.

* * *

Alex stared at the hut. It had become part of the bush, its making and its memories now as one with the spirit of this place. He approached the overgrown mound slowly. The lake glittered a distant greeting through a stand of tall gums. No-one had been here for a long time, that much was evident. There was no sign of the motorbike, no evidence of occupation at all. This was not the place.

He put down his back-pack. There was the fireplace he had made with his dad long ago, a simple ring of rocks, now overgrown with grasses. The memories rushed back, the feelings not part of his plan. He picked up one of the rocks. How he had struggled to lift them as a boy. A little lizard—a skink—watched him.

No, this was not the place he was looking for—the final place. But his search had begun.

* * *

The near-futility of searching so many remote places did not weigh too heavily on Alex, as on these trips he felt he was communing both with the land and with his father. His father, so dear to him, yet, as he looked back, such a mystery.

It was only with effort that he was able to recall clues to that mystery; even then he was uncertain of his memory, or perhaps unwilling to accept the signs. The night noises. The accidents. The raised voices. The silences. The sudden exits. The absences.

He was aware that his mother knew more of his father's inner world, and where it might have taken him. She, while deeply saddened, had never, in his patchy memory at least, seemed mystified, even surprised, by Daniel's disappearance.

But for Alex, it would be some time before he gained his mother's insight. His was a simple and compelling mission, to find the answer to the question which would not leave him: what had become of his dad?

awakenings

ALEX GARDNER grew up a *Lonnie* boy. He loved, in that familiar, unconscious way, that the city was surrounded by rich and varied countryside—rolling hills, grazing country, pretty villages, and distant, snow-capped peaks. The bush was never far away, and the coast was easy to reach.

He continued to visit Green's Beach with his mother, then as he and his friends eventually acquired their own cheap and often noisy transport (Alex's first car was an old, faded Fiat 125 Mirafiori whose only real asset was its stirring exhaust note), the seaside town of Bridport, with its sheltered beaches, its pub and its summertime girls, became—between his trips to the bush—a favourite haunt.

It was at Bridport, on the Bass Strait coast, an hour's sinuous drive from Launceston, where, in his teens, Alex first became conscious of how his love of building things was evolving into an interest in architecture. A school friend, Handie—Warren Hand to his parents—had taken him to see the secluded shack of a family friend on the undulating, warm-sand road from Bridport to nearby Lades Beach…

Ah, Lades Beach, later the scene of several fumbling sexual adventures. Limited, though; Alex was mindful of the exhortations of his far more experienced friend Albie: *never do it on the beach, mate. Sand, mate.* This said with a rueful grimace. So more penetrative excursions had to wait for more benign conditions. If the steamed and squashed interior of a little third-hand Corolla was indeed more benign. The car's owner, Glorious Gloria, a holiday camping student from down south, had obviously been a few places too, while that was his inaugural outing. He well remembered, with an embarrassment only slightly dulled by time, how Gloria had ended his frantic probings by taking him in hand and guiding him into her lush territory.

'How'd you make out, Al?'

Alex would never reveal such personal information, of course. But this was Handie, who shared his ethics, so he knew it would go no further. Even so, he had kept his response to a self-satisfied *that's for me to know* smile. The virginal Handie had been desperate for all the steamy details, and when he saw that none were forthcoming, his shoulders sagged. 'You wanker.'

'Speak for yourself!' was Alex's rejoinder, upon which the friends fell about laughing.

But back to that shack: amid the banksias, tea-tree, she-oaks and white gums, nestled a simple but elegant shack, a weekender, whose owner was Will Howarth, a retired architect.

The building sat snug on a concrete slab, a simple rectangle in plan, with a pitched iron roof. The long side of the rectangle faced north and was shaded by a deep eaves overhang, which, Will explained, would keep out the hot summer sun but still allow the lower winter sun to enter the house and warm the tiled floor. Inside, the large living area was open in plan, with a central, free-standing fireplace. The rear of the building was dug into the gently rising sandy site, so that from inside, the vegetated ground outside was level with the long, waist-high window sill, and looking out in that green direction had felt to Alex as if he were crouching to observe from their level the private domain of the creatures of the bush.

The image took Alex's thoughts to his lost father. He would have liked this simple, unpretentious shack amid the trees; liked the way it spoke to the bush, saluted the sun, belonged to its place.

Looking back, the design was not revolutionary and not particularly fashionable, but for Alex it had struck a spark. He could see that a little thought and some simple design measures could elevate a building above the ordinary, give it a sense of belonging, make it uplifting to inhabit.

It was this Bridport spark that lit in him a fire whose kindling was the woven wood of the bush structures built by his father, years ago. It was a fire destined to burn for many years.

life drawing

SEX. It hadn't really been on Alex's mind, at least no more than usual for a youth standing at the door of manhood, until he heard his name called in Salamanca Place.

'Alex?'

In the Launceston College's winter break of 1997, his first of two college years, Alex was accepted for an unpaid work experience position. The two-week stint was at ABC Architects in Hobart, the island's capital, little more than two hours drive south of his home town. He had enjoyed his occasional visits to the envied southern city, the seat of the state's government and, to many northerners, the over-rated beneficiary of national pork-barreling, but this visit was more than just weekend hi-jinks.

It was lunch-time, and Alex had trailed other ABC employees down the stairway from their offices and out into the welcome winter sunshine of the city's favourite waterfront eating strip. In his short time with ABC, he had developed a routine of sorts: he would buy a bulging sandwich from *Lord Sandwich* and look for a seat in one of the nearby parks, either St David's Park, girl-watching, or in Battery Square, where he could look out over the broad, glittering River Derwent, where little white triangles moved to the music of the breeze.

This day, though, he was contemplating expanding his limited culinary experience by trying a bowl of laksa in the aromatically enticing *Vietnamese Kitchen*, when he heard the voice.

'Alex?'

She was smiling at him, a little uncertainly, from a table outside the next restaurant. The two girls with her were watching with open interest.

Was it? Yes, it was. Gloria. Glorious Gloria. The question in her voice was understandable, he supposed; his amorous efforts back then at Bridport could not have made him very memorable.

'Gloria!'

'It *is* you, Alex! Are you living here in Hobart?'

The sun-burnt student had in a few years become a young woman. Her dark hair was somehow different, shorter and more sophisticated, and, despite her bulky winter sweater, he could discern that she had filled out.

'Only for two weeks. I'm doing some work experience at ABC Architects.' He tilted his head back in the direction of their offices, upstairs in one of the long line of sandstone former warehouses.

'Oh wow, I've heard of them. Aren't they doing that big project in Collins Street?'

'That's right.' Alex enjoyed a moment of reflected pride.

'Are you studying architecture?' Her smile was warm. So very warm.

Alex was beginning to feel a little awkward, standing there, particularly as her intoxicating smile and the memories it triggered began to have their unwanted effect on his anatomy.

'Sit down.' Gloria commanded, dragging an empty chair from the next table.

As her friends shuffled around, she said: 'Alex, these are my friends Clare and Rosie. Girls, this is Alex. You look so good, Alex!' She ruffled his hair as though they were great mates.

He reddened. *Why must I blush so?*

'Ooh.' Gloria stroked his pink cheek.

'Are you girls students?' Alex asked, as much to deflect attention from himself as out of any interest. Although he *was* interested. Sitting there in the sunshine with three pretty girls, in a strange city, he felt that at this moment, he stood—or rather sat—at the threshold of his adult life, that the world and all its mysteries and charms might be his for the taking.

'Yes,' replied the Rosie girl, a petite, elfin blonde wearing over-sized red spectacles. She scrunched her paper napkin. 'We're law students. Second year.'

Through her lenses he could see startlingly blue eyes.

'On vacation, now, thank God,' put in Clare, a rather serious-looking, slim brunette with square shoulders under a carefully coiled scarf.

'Wow, a table-full of lawyers. What do you call that? Y'know, like a murder of crows, or a parliament of owls?' The deflection had worked; his face felt cool again.

'I reckon that would have to be a *cell* of lawyers, wouldn't it?' this from Gloria, who had her hand on Alex's arm, as if afraid he would leave her life again. Or, more likely, it was a proprietorial gesture: *he is mine.*

'Or a *motion*?' said Clare. 'After all we're learning that lawyers give a lot of people the motions!'

'*Ex gratia excretia!*' giggled Rosie.

'*Et cetera, ad infinitum …*' said Clare in mock solemnity.

As the easy laughter subsided, Gloria leaned into Alex and said, *sotto voce*, 'Come and visit me, my flat's just up the road in Battery Point. It'd be excellent to catch up. Here's my number.'

'I'd like to draw her, Handie. A life drawing, I mean. I've never tried one, and she'd be the perfect model, I reckon.' Back upstairs, Alex was making a surreptitious call to his friend before the others returned. Alex imagined that under Gloria's winter clothes was a Rubenesque figure. Rubens, he knew from his father's art books—actually his Uncle Geoffrey's art books which were left with Daniel—had favoured female models of generous proportions. Cuddly.

'You want to *draw* her?' Warren Hand sputtered back through the phone. 'You're sure you don't want to *bonk* her?'

'Well, yeah, actually. That most of all.

* * *

'Call me William, Alex. Mr Carey in front of clients, but otherwise William.'

Alex figured that William Carey must be about the age his dad would have been now. Others in the ABC office seemed quite matey with William, yet in a respectful way. Perhaps one day he too could have that confidence. Grown, Alex wondered what sort of adult relationship he would have had with his father.

'You sketch very well indeed, Alex.' One of the associates had set Alex the task of making a free, illustrative sketch from a technical elevation, intending to test his ability to interpret the drawing, but also a convenient way of keeping him occupied and out of her hair. William was looking at the sketch now.

'Thank you … William. I've always enjoyed drawing.' *From my father,* he wanted to say to the man leaning over his shoulder and making a disquieting but not unwelcome visit into his personal space.

'Foster that skill, Alex. The way things are heading with our profession, you'll find that you'll be spending a lot of time at the computer screen, handling a mouse rather than a pencil. I may be a dinosaur, but I still believe that the ability to draw is fundamental to what architects do.'

It was during this time at ABC that Hobart's Mount Wellington, just *the mountain* to the locals, loomed into Alex's consciousness, thereafter always to occupy some part of that widening terrain. He was struck by how the mountain was sometimes aloof and at other times, when the light was right, leaned forward to peer down onto the city. He envisioned its rocky mantel fanning out behind it all the way to the far, white sands and wild seas of the island's south-west coast.

Its presence became, for him, a constant reminder, a symbol, of the wild places that lay beyond the craggy line where the mountain met the heavens. Wild places that had left their imprint on him, and on his father

* * *

As Alex walked up the sweeping curve of Hampden Road from the waterfront, the mountain came into view. There it was, like a giant stage backdrop, filling the sky above the curved crest of the road, crowded between an elegant neo-gothic house and a row of modest colonial cottages. The mountain had that week received its first heavy fall of winter snow; its cloaked summit, which that morning had shone white, was now a dark outline behind which a red sun was sinking. Sinking over the wild country.

Gloria's flat turned out to be a renovated Georgian house in Waterloo Crescent, which she shared with three other uni students. Two of them had left for the break, the other, a nerdy economics student, was apparently rarely seen outside his malodorous room.

'Sugar?' They were sitting at a spartan wooden table in the kitchen. It was growing dark outside and, through the window over the sink, Alex could make out the awakening lights of houses on the Sandy Bay hillsides. Gloria had extracted two large mugs from a purple-painted overhead cupboard and was making coffee. She had only instant.

'Yeah, just a little, thanks.'

'So, tell me about what you're doing at ABC Architects.' She sat opposite him and stretched unselfconsciously. When her foot touched his leg under the table, neither pulled back, and as Alex spoke of his rather tame exploits at the Salamanca Place office, she began to softly run her toes up and down his shin, inside his trouser leg, in the manner that a pet owner might idly fondle their pet whilst engaged in some other activity.

'That's interesting, Alex,' she said, when he explained what little he knew of the Collins Centre, 'I've studied a little planning law, and I'm thinking that it might even be an area of the law that I eventually go into...' Her tone was changing, a distracted look had replaced her attentive expression, and her toes became more adventurous.

When Gloria said 'Come,' and took his hand, Alex allowed himself to be led to a room which turned out to be a bedroom, crowded and somewhat untidy, but, to him, as magical and mysterious as some exotic, fictional bordello. She did something to a CD player and romantic strings floated on the air.

'Undress me, Alex.' It was a whispered command which caused Alex's heart to drum an uneven beat. She came close to him and raised her arms, like a child. Alex took hold of the hem of her sweater and slowly raised it over her head, negotiating first the swell of her breasts, then the contours of her smiling face. Nose and ears, hair, then free. Beneath the pullover Gloria wore only a bra, a brief red thing that fought to contain her milky white bosom.

Her eyes never left his. Was there amusement there?

She undid a hidden clasp in the waist of her skirt; her downward glance was Alex's sign to take over. Obediently, he eased the skirt from her hips, and she stepped out of it as he lowered it. *This is not the time to stop and fold it.* Alex tossed the skirt onto a chair and regarded the girl standing before him. Surely she must hear his wild heart.

Feigning confidence, he reached around her, and in a loose but intimate embrace unclipped her bra. To his relief, he accomplished this Seduction 1.01 move without incident. The red material became a vibrant slash on the dark skirt.

Oh God, she was beautiful. He had guessed right about the Rubens thing.

Now, wordlessly, she commanded him to remove the last barrier to her nakedness. Alex knelt at her feet on the retro shag pile mat. He could see a dark area through the thin fabric. As he worked the little garment off her amazing hips, a luxuriant tangle of dark hair appeared.

The knickers missed the chair.

* * *

'We've enjoyed having you here, Alex. From what I've seen, you'll be well suited to architecture.'

'Thanks, William, I've enjoyed being here.'

He had indeed enjoyed it. He had witnessed, fly-on-wall, the daily comings and goings of an architectural practice, watched with admiration one old hand performing on his drawing-board and labouring over codes and technical specifications, the younger brigade conjuring up complex images on computer screens, and the partners frowning over contract documents. He had explored the office library, puzzled over architectural drawings and specifications, eaves-dropped on client meetings, listened to the in-house banter and gossip, and always admired the dedication of the whole ABC team.

'Keep us in mind if you need any vacation work during your studies. We sometimes have need for some help about the place.'

'I will. Thanks.' They shook hands.

'Oh, and Alex, have you got a CV? I expect it'll be pretty brief now, but keep it up to date. Make sure you include your time here. It all helps to show that you're committed to what you're doing.'

As he made his way out of the long ABC drawing-office, past waves, nods and smiles from faces behind computers or over drawing-boards, the thought came to him that there were things he had experienced here in Hobart, more specifically in Battery Point, that would never appear on his resumé. Things that were, however, burned forever into his own, personal, *curriculum vitae*.

TLC

'CUP OF TEA, ALEX?'

'Yes, thanks mum. I'll just trim this beam first.'

Their new house was beginning to smile, its fog of gloom lifting under the care—the TLC—of its new occupants. Drab drapes were cast out. Threadbare carpets pulled up. Walls patched and painted, light tones replacing sombre. Hardwood floors were sanded and finished, to bounce golden light into every awakening corner. And the bleak lawn, even more threadbare than the pre-war carpet, was beginning to enjoy the attention of its happy new owner. A young apricot tree in the back yard spoke of promise and hope, and several quick-growing natives in the front garden signaled an impatience to get on with life.

His mother set two mugs down on an outdoor table, part of a setting which was a present from her to the house, acquired when Alex had announced his plan to build a sheltering pergola outside the back door. They sat beneath its emerging structure now.

'It's starting to look good, darling.'

'Thanks. I went back to have a closer look at that school gazebo, to see what dad did there.'

His mother smiled and looked up.

'Dad put it together beautifully, better than I can hope to do. And he does unexpected things…'

Unexpected things. There was a moment of blurred shade as a cloud passed across the sun. Across Mary's smile.

'He's mixed in some bits of old timber, recycled stuff, even raw branches in places. And every bit looks as if it was meant to be just there and nowhere else.'

His mother nodded her understanding. She looked at him. 'Your father would be proud of you, Alex.'

'I still miss him, mum, even now.'

'So do I, darling. So do I.'

'Mum, can I ask you something?

'Mmm?'

'You never really seemed surprised that dad had gone missing. Sad, of course, but not surprised …'

The new framework held the unspoken question in its bars of shadow.

'I didn't know your father when he was young…' her voice was small, Alex had to lean forward to hear, '…before he went to Vietnam…'

His mother's eyes were clouded, and looking for a safe place to rest.

At last she said, 'are you looking forward to starting uni next year?'

the getting

ALEX'S DECISION to study architecture seemed wonderfully vindicated the moment he, eighteen years old, walked into the first-year design studio at Newnham, the northern campus of the state's university. Models large and small, cryptic sketches, and bits of building stuff all resonated with him strongly. In what seemed like a primary school classroom for lucky grownups, it was the little skeletal, wooden models that really did it. They reached deep inside him, in to where the memories of other skeletons, other wooden frameworks, were still alive.

His first academic leap would, if successful, land him a degree in environmental design, to be followed, here or elsewhere, by a post-graduate degree in architecture. He knew that some of his fellow students would take their first degree and move on, either quickly or over the years, into fields other than architecture. But for Alex, his objective was as clear as the sky had been over Lade's Beach the day he resolved that he would follow this course—he would become an architect.

Starting out, Alex had a vague plan of taking an overseas gap year after UTas, then doing his second degree at RMIT University in Melbourne. Assuming that he got that far. That way, he figured, his life experience should be massively expanded. He would be able to look at his ideas, his passions, from a wider perspective. Would they prove to be childish preoccupations, sentimental reflections? Or was there, in the integrity and beauty that he saw in his father's creations, a guidepost, a motif, for his future work?

His first solo assignment, set by his lecturer in first-year design, was to design a transportable outdoor puppet theatre for a local amateur puppet-theatre company. The studio was filled with laughter and feeble jokes, throwing up such names as *Punch and Judy, Miss Piggy*, and *Kermit*.

After all the practical and not-so-practical matters were identified, what life could Alex as a designer give to his creation, just as the puppeteers gave life to their inanimate marionettes? Just as his father had imbued life and beauty into his modest bush shelters? How could he lift a mobile theatre from the utilitarian to the magical? How does an architect elevate a structure from mere building to *architecture*? And was that very question elitist and pointless?

His solution, which he would later think was a little too serious, was to design a versatile timber enclosure rather like a small, intriguingly distorted caravan, which met all of the company's functional needs. Its exterior grade plywood panels were deeply colour-stained; their edges were black-painted to minimise water ingress; their stainless steel fastenings were visually exaggerated and carefully set out. And the primary structure was of sculpted, clear-lacquered wood, with articulated connections that brought to mind the bony buildings of Gaudi or the craftsmanship of Geppetto, the maker of Pinnochio. Or, for Alex, the beautiful skeletons put together by his father.

Eager to learn from constructive criticism, and to enjoy a debate on matters esoteric, Alex was a little disappointed that his tutor's only real criticism related to his choice of applied finish.

'Very good, Alex. But I think you'll find that a clear finish is not very durable on any timber that's exposed to the weather.'

Deflating though that comment may have been, it was an early reminder that in his chosen profession he would be concerned not only with big questions, but with practical minutiae—the fittings, fastenings and finishes of buildings.

Where shall we build it, dad? Are we allowed to do it here? What about this spot? Can we use these stones? Will these branches be strong enough? How will we hold the bark down, dad? Why don't you ever use nails? Can you show me how to weave the walls? Why do you make that pattern? Is this mud sticky enough?

Alex's time at uni seemed to race by. Making new friends, taking on new challenges, slowly learning to like beer, and navigating his way through the sometimes unclear expectations of his lecturers.

More than once along the way, Alex offered private thanks to Gloria for initiating him into the precarious world of boy-meets-girl. It was quickly confirmed for him what he had already suspected, that Gloria was a rarity. That her liberal and unabashed behavior was not often to be encountered in a young woman, at least not by him, not among the many and varied girls whose presence on campus was a sensory smorgasbord.

* * *

Late in his first year, Alex worked as a labourer for Barney Benson, a cottage builder who had been a friend of his father's. Barney was in his late sixties now and his son Justin had taken over the business.

Alex had been carrying pre-cut radiata pine studs from the truck to a levelled area beside the emerging skeleton of a house amid a rising crop of dream homes. Justin Benson, his thick calves bulging beneath dusty khaki shorts and his curly hair dancing in the breeze, was nailing together a section of wall framing, before it was to be raised into position.

Thunk. Thunk. Thunk. Thunk. His nail gun spat its abrupt sounds as the timbers were quickly joined.

'Hey, Alex.' It was the older man, Barney, calling from the top of a ladder. Alex looked up to see that the grey-haired, leather-faced builder was speaking from the side of his mouth, several nails held between his lips, a battered nail pouch on his belt. 'Pass us up that rafter, would you, son?'

Alex slid the three-metre length of timber up over a top wall plate to where Barney could take hold of it and pull it into position. He watched with admiration as the three-inch nails (Barney still spoke in inches) were plucked from his mouth, deftly held in the awkward skew-nailing position, and – *Bang, bang, bang, bang, bang* - driven home with rhythmic precision, hammer flashing in the sun.

Bang, bang, bang, bang, bang.
Bang, bang, bang, bang, bang.

'The old man's not bad, is he?' Justin said with a grin. 'Hope I'm half as good at his age.'

Alex could only smile and nod, as he went back to his labouring, and Justin aimed his nail-gun.

Thunk. Thunk. Thunk. Thunk.

'Got a splinter, Al? You should be wearing gloves.'

He and Barney were taking a break, the older man pouring tea from a Thermos, Alex unscrewing his water bottle.

'That's what dad used to say.'

'And he'd have been right.' Barney looked across the steam at Alex. 'He was a good bloke, your dad.'

Alex let the *was* go unchallenged. He was happy with *good bloke*.

'Very clever, he was, could turn his hand to anything.'

'Yeah, I remember that alright. We built some stuff together.'

'Oh yeah, course you did. I remember Danny talking about how you two would go bush and build huts and whatnot. I reckon those times were real important to him—y'know, father and son?' Barney looked to where Justin was working.

Thunk. Thunk. Thunk.

'Reminds me. Your dad didn't like nail guns. Not sure why. He had this thing about *integrity*; maybe that was part of it. But I thought it might have been something else...'

Face pressed into the stinking mud. Fumbling with your weapon. The whip-crack sounds of bullets cutting the air above your head, each chased closely by the thud of the gunfire. Crackthud. Crackthud. The gunfire increasing to a murderous maelstrom. Don't raise your head. Pete did, the poor bastard. Thud. Thud. Thud...

* * *

Alex's vacation work during his UTas years also included several periods as a casual employee down south at ABC. These were fruitful periods for him; with each visit he felt his understanding of the profession growing and his career choice affirmed.

He would sometimes graciously be asked for his opinion regarding a design, before being allocated a menial task relating to it. That was fine by Alex. He knew that it wouldn't be quick or easy. He witnessed his colleagues struggle with a maze of planning requirements and a plethora of codes and building regulations. He heard them talk of potential mistakes that could lead to litigation, he waded stoically through the querulous quagmire of the firm's quality assurance manual, and he read both the pro-forma client agreements and the suite of building contracts commonly utilised by the practice. Occasionally admitted to a project management meeting, he watched the amiable banter and collaborative decision-making of the consultant team headed by one of the ABC partners or associates and attended by a gaggle of specialist consultants.

His confidence was growing and the rightness of his decision to pursue architecture as a career was shining through.

I reckon I'm on the right track, dad.

meaning

BETWEEN SEMESTERS, if Alex was not working to augment his practical experience and his modest savings, or helping his mother on the Kings Meadows house, he ventured into the bush in order to cancel out another area on a patchwork quilt of aerial photos that he had set up in his bedroom.

Had his quest become an obsession? He did wonder sometimes. He preferred to think of it as *resolve*. His earlier more emotional response had given way to a calm resolve that the truth be one day found. A resolve that he could not allow to weaken, for it had become part of his essence, part of who he was.

This time, he was speculating. He had explored, by car, mountain bike and foot, a forested area on the east coast—an area that both he and his mother felt would have appealed to Daniel.

He was on foot when his own fate was held briefly in the hands of the impassive gods of the wild places—an abrupt reminder of the hazards faced by his father.

It was a towering White Gum, *Eucalyptus viminalis*, which erosion had left hanging at a precarious angle over a sheltered cove, held only by a few slender but tenacious roots. Further along the shore, monstrous silver-grey bones of other gums spoke of this tree's certain fate.

He was walking high on the beach, pushed there by the tide; his path would take him directly beneath the tree. Underfoot was claggy, sand mixed with clay from the eroding bank. As he approached the tree, Alex began to ponder on how one would calculate the odds of being under it when it fell. The tree was clearly going to fall soon, probably another wet season would do it; maybe it would happen even sooner.

This typically *Alex* rumination was rudely interrupted. A sudden, dreadful, rending sound startled him. Time stopped and his mind raced, as the giant lurched above him. To jump clear? No, even if he could get traction in the muck, there was no time to escape the reach of those murderous boughs. To dive down? Perhaps he would be lucky and find himself safe under an arched branch, but more likely not.

For eternal milliseconds, he watched a tortured hand bear down on him. He saw in its giant clutch the patterns of his father's shelters. He relived his long search as if in some bizarre slow-motion replay. Was this to be how he would be reconciled with his father?

Then, in a clarity born of the imperative of survival, Alex saw, as if on one of his architectural drawings, what a small form the human body took when viewed from above—from that perspective, what a small target.

In that moment of compressed time, he tracked the tenuous voids of blue sky between the huge fingers; he took one quick, calculated step sideways, and stood, ready for his little allotment of heaven.

The fallen branches shuddered and the still-living leaves gave a resigned sigh. Standing unscathed amid the chaos, Alex felt only exultation. It was as if the bush itself understood his mission and was keeping him from harm. His search would continue.

Still elated, but now feeling shaken, Alex walked to the end of the cove, where a smooth, rust-coloured sandstone point speared into the great body of shining water. The Tasman Sea. Around the point he could see a miniature landscape of curved and layered cliffs, canyons and craters, another world shaped by the ceaseless, irresistible cycles of nature.

On the flat stone platform, he paused to reflect on what had happened. He could see how the wilderness could wreck so easily the plans of feeble intruders. Had such misadventure befallen his father? Did what was left of his broken body lie beneath some massive limb, or at the foot of some crumbling cliff, going back to the natural world around him?

Alex stared at the water; it was clear and shallow, he could see the sandy bottom. The surface was alive with a pattern of concave dimples, and below, an endless, bright golden thread laced the water, dancing on the sand, breaking and rejoining with every surging breath of the ocean.

The world was full of such intricate beauty, such mystery. Who was he to think he might find meaning in it all? To find answers?

The smooth stone spear-head he stood on directed Alex's gaze out and beyond. Had he not known how very cold the water would be at this time of year, the call of the sea would have had him shed his clothes and renew himself in its vastness, its fluid calm. He could understand how his father was so drawn to the ocean.

Is there something that calls us back to the sea? Some remnant of primordial memory that draws us back to where it all began?

a gap

SURVIVAL. Alex was aware that there were many places in the world where buildings were still little more than a response to the basic human need to find shelter, to survive. His research told him that these buildings, unsurprisingly, took their form from local skills and the materials that the place offered. Just as his father's bush shelters had done.

Financed by his hard-won savings and the sale of his precious car, he planned a crowded gap year between his first and second degrees. A year in which he would seek out those elemental buildings and see what he could learn from them. See whether the kinship with his father's bush structures was real or imagined. See whether simplicity and frugality still made any sense in an increasingly complex and wanton world. And see whether his ideas, those of a sheltered person from a sheltered island, had any place out there in the open.

There were of course the irresistible jewels that called to him; how could he travel without succumbing to the twinkling allure of some of those? But his purpose was more serious; his planned itinerary had played a not-insignificant part in his being accepted into Melbourne's RMIT University for his second degree—architecture.

Alex eased into the trials and challenges of international travel by first visiting the UK, then other countries where English was widely spoken. Having gained experience and confidence, he could be more adventurous.

By the time he took flight for India, Alex had tubed London, cycled Amsterdam, strolled Paris, and, despite himself, marvelled at the new talk of the profession, Frank Ghery's gleaming Guggenheim art museum in the revitalised Spanish port city of Bilbao.

The seething dissonance of the sounds and smells of India was a sensory curry, so startlingly different from anything he had hitherto experienced that he had to remind himself why it had looked good on the menu.

Because it *was* different, that's why. And he needed to test his ideas in a world wider than the small, safe place of his birth.

Following a route suggested by an Indian friend and fellow student, he travelled by train—an adventure in itself—to the centre of the teeming continent. There, in the Indian villages he found the traditional round mud houses with their thatched grass roofs and round windows, he saw the simple beds made from the wood of the coconut trees, the mattress a webbing of coconut fibre rope.

In Mumbai, could he brave the urban slums? Would he be safe? Would his voyeuristic visit offend? A new acquaintance, a backpacker who was exploring his own country, assured him that all would be well, and accompanied him on the mission.

Alex marvelled at the resilience of the slum-dwellers. *How can they be so happy with so little?* The dense maze of narrow lanes were lined with pitiful structures, cheek by jowl, erected from bamboo poles, plastic and cardboard, with reed mats for walls. The floor was sometimes bare earth. *And those smells.* The air was filled with the smells of spices, cooking and incense and, with a shift in the breeze, something else. The common latrines.

In Sri Lanka, his pleasure at seeing first-hand the traditional, but disappearing, mud houses with their cow-dung floors and walls was heightened by the welcoming friendship of the villagers.

In Burma—Myanmar—he saw the elevated houses of wood and bamboo, thatched roofs and bamboo walls. What a shame that the traditional skills were fading.

Alex would have liked to see the round, wooden, felt-lined, demountable *yurts* of Mongolia, but visiting that country was just not a practical proposition given his limitations of time and funds.

In Cambodia, he learned that the typical rural Khmer house had been slowly evolving, but, helped by a friendly Khmer *sthabatyakar*—an architect—managed to find and visit several buildings which were of the traditional construction. These were elevated wooden structures whose walls were lined with panels of palm matting and whose 'bonnet-style' roofs were of thatched rice straw. The construction utilised basic carpentry techniques; Alex made a series of small sketches of the simple but elegant connections, and was moved when he saw in them the work of his father, the simple elegance of his father's bush shelters.

* * *

'Hello mum. It's me.' Alex was calling from a phone in a bar run by an ex-pat Australian in Vung Tau. 'I'm in Vietnam now.'

'Hello darling.' Mary's voice told Alex of her pleasure at hearing from him. 'I thought you must be there by now. Is it all going well?'

'Yes, it really is. Tiring, especially in the heat, but always interesting.'

'I'll feel better when you're back home, Al.'

'I know.'

'At least you're getting closer,' she laughed.

'True.' He gathered himself. 'Mum, I've been to visit the Long Tan and Hat Dich battlefields.'

His mother was silent.

'I wanted to experience the kind of country where dad spent time. I found it impossible to imagine what it was like, though.'

'That was a long time ago,' Mary said quietly, 'a different world.'

'I visited the Long Tan memorial cross. Ran into an Australian veteran there. A farmer from Toowoomba. We had a good talk.'

'That's good.'

'Yeah.'

'I love you, Alex.'

'I love you too, mum.'

* * *

Alex was in southern Thailand, two weeks before his intended return to Australia, when a message found him—a message to call his mother.

'Daniel, we think your father's motor-bike has been sighted.'

'Say again, mum, the line's not too good.'

Hunched over the counter in the reception alcove of a back-packer hostel, Alex pressed the bulky black telephone receiver to his ear.

'We've heard that someone sighted your dad's bike abandoned in the bush.'

It had been nearly a decade since Daniel went missing. Apparently a gold prospector, who had been unaware of the earlier search for the missing man, happened to remark to his fellow drinkers at the little settlement of Corinna in Tasmania's remote north-west, that he had seen an abandoned motor-bike in the bush north of the Pieman River several years earlier. The bar attendant had passed this snippet on to the local policeman, who in turn had contacted Mary.

'Of course, we can't be sure it was Daniel's bike.'

The cacophony of noise from the steamy street outside pressed in on Alex. The cool, quiet bush was a world away.

'I'll come home, mum.'

silence

'GUSTAW?' Alex addressed the seated figure in the clearing, a weathered figure barely distinguishable from the bush itself—the bush that Alex had made his way to after his arrival back in Tasmania.

'Mary-friggin-mother-of-Jesus, who told you that? One o' them drongoes back at Savage River, I s'pose.' The prospector's voice was gravelly.

'Corinna actually,' Alex grinned apologetically.

'The name's Gus. Don't go callin' me nothin' else, cobber.'

Gustaw/Gus Kuchinke, Alex had learned back at Corinna, was a son of one of the many post-war eastern European immigrants who had come to Tasmania in the fifties and sixties to labour on the ambitious Poatina hydro-electric power station—the latest in a long line of Hydro-electric schemes whose concrete salutes to the future were graced with names purloined from a lost past. Names like *Waddamana*, *Wayatinah*, *Tarraleah*, *Liapootah*…

Hunched forward over a steaming billy, Gus's angular form was wrapped in a frayed great-coat, whose original colour had long ago yielded to the elements. An imprint of the beaten leather hat on the log beside him showed around his bony head, where his thinning, grey hair had been compressed.

'Wanna cuppa?'

'Thanks, that'd be good, Gus. I'm Alex. Alex Gardner.'

Gus's proffered hand was deep-tanned and calloused. Alex's must have revealed his soft life.

'You'd be his son then? The bloke that went missin' them years ago?'

'That's right Gus. I heard that you'd spotted his motorbike somewhere out here. Or at least a bike that might have been his.'

'There y'go,' Gus passed Alex a steaming tin mug of dark tea. 'Ain't got no sugar.'

'That's fine, thanks. '

'So y'wanna know about the bike, then?'

'Yeah. What can you tell me, Gus?'

'Can't remember exactly when I saw it, but I reckon it was about the time I found me that nugget in ninety-four. The only friggin one I ever found that was worth anything much.'

Alex sat back and tried to ease himself into the older man's rhythm.

'You look for gold, then?'

'Sure do. Lotta old workin's around here. You can still come across 'em in the bush. Old crushers and sluices and stuff.'

'You find much gold?'

'Just enough to keep me goin'. That'll do me.'

Alex knew from previous excursions to the area, which was coming to be known as the Tarkine, that alluvial gold was to be found in these parts, but that finds were hard-won and meagre. He had learned that the area had seen gold-prospecting and mining for nearly a century and a half, and that the forests and creeks around Corinna were dotted with artefacts from those earlier activities.

'You pan for it?' he asked.

'Yeah. That or make up a sluice box. Same difference. Dunno if you know it, but in the old days the miners built water races for friggin miles, just to bring enough water to their workin's. Y'can still see the marks where them races were.'

'I think I might have seen some,' Alex's memory was jogged and he recalled the mysterious, narrow channels he had seen running around the contours of several hills, 'I didn't know what they were at the time though.'

'Used to be a lot of stuff went on round 'ere that people don't know about,' retorted Gus, 'Forestry 'n' that. You wouldn't know it now though; everythin' grows back so friggin quick. 'Ceptin' the Huon pines o' course. Them'll take a little while yet.' A faint smile. 'Some people reckon these parts is all *priss-teen*. They don't have a friggin clue.'

In the companionable quiet, they sipped at the hot tea.

'You're lucky y'caught me. I'm just off to follow a couple of creeks up that mount'n over there. I'm always lookin' for where the creek gold comes from. Ain't figured it out yet, but I will.'

'Can you recall where you saw the bike, Gus?' Alex struggled to contain his impatience to get some answers.

'Yeah, sure, cobber. It stayed in my mind 'cause I couldn't figure how it had friggin got there. The nearest trail that I knew of was 'alf a friggin mile away.'

Alex smiled inwardly and felt a strange mixture of pride and sorrow as he remembered what his father had been capable of.

'*When's* a bit hard, but *where* is easy.' The old-timer's face crinkled into a jagged, leathery grin. 'Was just south o' the big'un, the big tree.'

Oh Christ, that narrows it down. 'Do you remember which big tree?'

'Yeah, cobber, like I said, the big-un. Y'got a map? I'll show you.'

Alex's excitement rose; he turned and fished into his pack. Sliding out his map, he folded it several times so that just the area around the Pieman and Savage rivers was displayed.

Gus stoked the little fire with a stick before tossing it on the flames, then leaned across to take the pencil Alex offered. As he did so, Alex noticed a metal tag hanging around his neck.

'You a veteran, Gus?' It was small-talk on Alex's part, but even as the words came out, he knew it was anything but small-talk. Gus didn't answer quickly.

'Yeah cobber. Viet-friggin-Nam. Sent us ignorant young punks over there for some friggin stupid war, to kill blokes who never did us no harm.' He touched the place where the tag hung. 'Wear this for me mates. Least I can do.' He fell silent, his eyes shining in the light of the fire.

It was a silence that Alex had heard before. The silence was his father's silence. Hearing it from Gus Kuchinke, like his father an absconder from the world of questions, opened in Alex a little window of insight. And in through that window, the silence shouted.

Without warning, Alex was slammed by a sudden, crushing guilt. Why had he not listened to its message before? Never delved deeper? The man from Toowoomba, the man he had talked to in Vietnam, had been trying to tell him this stuff, he realized now. And his mother, too, had tried, but couldn't.

'What about your dad?' Gus's question knifed into his knotted reverie.

'Yeah. Vietnam.'

Another silence.

'Lotta blokes did it tough when we came back. Still doin' it tough, some. No-one to look after you, those days. Was even spat on, some blokes. Now it's all this post-trauma whatsit.'

'Post-Traumatic Stress Disorder.'

'Too friggin late.' Gus looked at the ground. 'Me best mate's a total alkie now. Can't even have a proper talk with him no more.' The weathered bushman seemed to crumple; the forlorn look which shadowed his face grabbed at Alex's heart. 'Another bloke I know from over there did himself in last year. Wasn't the first, neither.' He looked at Alex. 'It never leaves you, y'know.'

Silent tears made their way down Alex's cheeks as the older man watched, nodding in the silence.

'There y'go, son.' Gus had marked with a little circle his reckoning of the location of the big tree, and was holding the map out to Alex.

Son. The quiet bush, the crackling of the fire, the smell of eucalypt and wood-smoke. And now, *Son*. Alex gulped down the great mass which had invaded his throat and threatened to have him bawl like a child. Like an eleven-year-old child who wanted his dad back.

He took the map from Gus and tucked it into his back-pack.

the bike

DAWN. Alex had followed the white gravel road north from Corinna, crossed the Savage river, and turned off into the bush. He urged his mother's car as far as he dared along a rough, four-wheel-drive trail, then set out on foot. *I'm coming, dad.*

The vegetation changed as he made his way through the bush; he clambered up rocky slopes through forests of Celery Top and Blackwood, emerging to cross a small plateau of eucalypt forest, before descending steeply into a deep valley. That it was indeed a valley was not evident from the ridge, since the trees within it rose to a great height. They inspired awe in Alex, as he scrambled down to the valley floor.

Stopping to rest and take a drink, Alex looked up. The giant gums, even the smallest wider at its base than his own height, soared towards the sky. Shafts of sunlight penetrated their distant canopies, a few rays reaching the hushed forest floor. The stillness closed around him, the giants appraising the puny intruder.

Alex slipped off his back-pack, took a compass bearing and examined the topographical map. How to find the tree? They all seemed to be 'big-uns'.

As he approached the place where he reckoned the big tree should be, he had an eerie sense of some powerful presence. Then, there it was! Un-mistakable. A huge tree which reached a good twenty metres above its neighbours. No expert, Alex took it to be a stringy bark, *Eucalyptus Regnans*. Certainly it was a *big-un*. Its massive trunk must have been all of six metres across, perhaps more.

Finding a patch of sunlight, Alex set down his pack and sat on a mossy fallen limb. The silence was profound. At first Alex could hear only his own heart-beat. Then he could detect the occasional minute sound in the undergrowth, and the faintest of breezes in the tree canopies, far above. Then, ringing through the silence, a sweet, pure bird-call, echoed by another, farther away. This, he thought, must have been the kind of peace that his father sought.

Alex decided on a strategy for his search for the bike. He would venture out from the giant tree, moving in a straight line for about seventy-five paces, then returning along a different, but parallel, line. This he would repeat until his in-and-out lines formed a segment of a circle fanning out from the tree, towards the south.

He was returning to the tree for the fourth time when something in the coarse, damp tapestry of the bush caught his eye, resonating with some hidden memory. Was there colour or form there that was not of nature? Alex's heart seemed to pause, his whole being held in a space between hope and disbelief. And as the reality came into focus, he felt his boyhood grief well up inside him. It was surely the form of a motor-bike.

Wedged beneath a moss-covered fallen tree, its once-black struts were reduced to bleached bones, its chromework was dulled, pitted and scarred with countless pustules of invasive rust, and the formerly red paintwork had faded to the palest autumn russet. Ferns and delicate creepers threaded its spokes, and the scant remnants of its cracked and wildly distorted tyres were evidence of sorties by marauding devils. But Alex could see enough. There were the remains of the familiar pillion seat, *his* seat all those years ago, now just a tattered, shredded carcass, its stuffing dispersed and lost. And there, barely discernible, was the proud BSA badge, the familiar teardrop and star.

What does the picture mean, Dad?
What picture, Alex?
On the petrol tank. The letters inside that egg shape with the star behind it. That's the bike's badge, Al; its logo. You think it's an egg? Looks like a tear-drop to me. A sort of flying tear-drop.
Maybe it's chasing the star, Dad.

And there, waiting to put the matter beyond any doubt, was a number plate. The little plate, affixed to the front mud-guard, was totally obscured, and as Alex scraped away the years of accumulated dirt and growth it felt as though he was peeling back the scars that had grown over his youthful wound. He could make out the number: W1573. His father's number.

He stood quietly, not resisting the rush of memories. And with the memories came the thought that his dad would have approved of the way that the bike was being taken back to the earth.

* * *

'Mum, I've found dad's bike.'

There was a moment's silence.

'Where are you, Alex?'

'I'm at Corinna. I'll stay here tonight and come back home tomorrow.'

'Are you alright?'

'Yes, mum. I met the prospector, Gus. Followed his instructions to the bike. In the middle of nowhere, it was. I need to come back and think about what to do next.'

'Alex?'

'Yes?'

'You'll need to notify the police.'

'Yeah, thanks. I think the nearest police station is at Savage River. I've photographed the bike and recorded the location. I'll drop in there and talk to them.'

* * *

'Sorry, mate,' said the country copper, 'but we don't have the resources to go looking for a person who's been missing that long. Specially out there. But it'll go into the file, and we'll make a point of keeping an eye open anytime we've got someone in the area. Sorry.'

Alex had been un-surprised by the policeman's response, and back in Launceston set about planning his own search.

a puzzle

LIFE WAS CROWDED. Christmas was upon him, he needed to properly record his overseas experience, prepare for moving to Melbourne, and catch up with his friends. On top of which, he had planned to replenish his depleted savings by working for three weeks with Barney Benson. But, for Alex, this mission trumped all other plans.

He was sitting in their Kings Meadows kitchen listing in a little note-book the things he would need to take. The back door was open, just the fly-screen closed; the morning outside was warm and twittering.

After a few minutes he disappeared out the back door. His collection of aerial photographs of the wilder parts of the state, obtained over several years at no small expense from the state government's mapping office, had been pinned to a large sheet of Caneite to form a disjointed patchwork in many shades of green interspersed with an occasional black-and-white patch.

Alex came to realize that its presence on his bedroom wall unsettled his mother, and he had some time ago taken the board down and put it out of sight in the shed.

Now he withdrew the precious board and laid it on his father's chipped and grooved work-bench. He scanned the patchwork and his finger quickly went to the area near Corinna, where the little black ball-head pins held in place three adjoining sheets.

Tracking up the board, to the north-west, he gave a little sigh of satisfaction. This was the area where he had located the BSA. Squinting closely, he saw that the shadow of one of the forest trees was cast over the others. That surely had to be the *big-un*. Fortuitously, the tree was near the centre of one of the photographs. The wide area that the photo covered would surely contain his father's last destination.

Alex un-pinned the photo, exposing in its place an irregular white rectangle, the void left by the missing piece of a jigsaw puzzle. He turned off the light and took the vital piece into the house.

Back at the kitchen table, he checked the scale of the photograph from the fine print along its edge. He then proceeded to draw with a felt-tipped pen a series of elongated rings which radiated out from the big tree, the marker for the abandoned bike.

'What are you doing, darling?' Mary asked. She had been writing school report cards.

'Just trying to work out a systematic way of covering the area.'

'You do know, don't you, darling, that I've come to terms with the fact that your father is lost to us?'

'Yes, I know that, mum, but this feels like something I have to do. It's all I *can* do.' He remembered what Gus had said: *Least I can do.* 'Can you manage without your car for a few days?'

He saw his mother move behind him, felt her hug his shoulders.

'Mum, Gus, the prospector, was a Vietnam vet.'

His mother was silent, but he felt her stiffen.

'I guess he was about dad's age—the age dad would be now. Would have been now.' Alex turned his head a little. 'He lives alone in the bush, mum. Told me about some of his mates. What the war did to them.'

He barely heard his mother whisper, 'I'm glad you met him, Alex. I could never explain.'

* * *

Back in the forest, Alex set up camp next to the BSA and each day explored one or more of the areas he had ringed. It was a strange feeling, coming back from his search to be confronted by his father's ghostly bike. Sometimes, as he approached, he imagined that he could hear movement in the bush, catch the smell of a camp fire, even hear the staccato sound of charcoal striking paper.

Several times he became excited by the nature of some location, when he sensed that the spot would have been attractive to his father. A high, natural platform on a craggy outcrop with a long view towards the ocean; a quiet mossy clearing next to a burbling creek; a secluded patch of forest embraced by a rise in the ground. But none gave up any secrets, none bore any sign for Alex of his father having been there.

In the end, when the last of the loops had been completed, he had to accept that he had failed. He had followed creeks, traversed forests, climbed to higher terrain, even gone to within sight of the coast, but all to no avail. Not a single clue had he encountered. The frustration, the disappointment, the sense of failure, kept him there, by the bike, for a long while before he started back. *Where are you, dad?*

It seemed that he had no option but to retreat to his other life, and to hope that some further information or inspiration might come his way.

across the strait

THE PEOPLE WORE BLACK. The faces and voices revealed many origins. The footpaths teemed and jostled. But the strangest thing was: in this city across the strait, he could find no horizon. Not the near hills and distant mountain range of his home town or the majestic presence of Hobart's mountain, just a Leggo outline of building after building, building *upon* building. Where do I look, he would ask himself, to see what weather is on the way, to see what the day will bring?

He knew that there was a vast bay nearby, he saw the famous river that snaked brown through the city, and he knew that that there were indeed some city hills - Clifton Hill, Box Hill, Eastern Hill, and others yet to be discovered. But these were mere rises in the plain really, not proper hills where you had to get up off your bike seat and work hard. Although they did, for a lucky few, open up an extended view, offer a more distant outlook, a bigger sky.

No such extended view in Prahan, to which lively and convenient area Alex moved after briefly sharing a tiny flat in nearby, well-to-do South Yarra.

Alex's first real home in the city was a slightly run-down share house only three blocks removed from the hubbub of Chapel Street. Handy to the shops, cafés and pubs. A choice of railway stations within walking distance. Tram routes right there. A large bedroom of his own. Affordable. And the others in the house seemed like interesting people.

There was Aaron, a long-haired escapee from the seventies, who was trying to break into the city's live music scene; there was clean-cut Peter, studying economics at Melbourne Uni; and there was Lucy, a well-rounded, high-spirited girl who was setting up an edgy little fashion design shop which cohabited with a tattoo parlour in nearby Windsor.

Alex's fruitless search of the area around the BSA was a disappointment that he carried with him to Melbourne and was never far from his thoughts. It was on his mind now, as he stood swaying in the tram, the grey, drizzled images of wet streets and rain-streaked buildings scrolling past the foggy windows. He clutched his precious drawing tube close and absently checked that its plastic ends were screwed tight.

Had he missed something in the bush? Had he walked right past some sign of his father? That was quite possible, given the nature of the place and the passage of time. Or, had he not extended his search far enough?

He determined that he would re-visit the bike in the bush at least once a year, to widen his search even further and to see if he was favoured with some new insight. That resolve gave him some peace, and allowed him to focus on his studies at the boisterous city campus of RMIT University, his destination now.

* * *

It was at RMIT that Alex encountered Karl Fischer, also an architecture student, also from a provincial city. He and Karl first met when arbitrarily paired on an assignment. The warm-up assignment, given by their lecturer in architectural theory, was to choose a significant Australian building that both were familiar with, and to write a one-thousand-word analysis of it in the form of a discussion between two academics, one taking the viewpoint of a harsh critic, the other of an unabashed devotee.

The pair had discovered that they worked well together. They enjoyed the interaction, had fun even, briefly adopting and exaggerating the sometimes obscure and pompous language of academia.

Alex, from Tassie, and Karl, from just outside Geelong, found that their own apparently different perspectives—in their banter, green vs slick—were not all that far apart after all. And both were certain that architecture was where they belonged.

Alex learned that Karl's father had been a design engineer at Ford's Altona plant until the scaling-down of production had seen him made redundant.

'What does he do now, Karl?' Alex was watching Karl's screen as his fellow student tried to come to grips with AutoCad's 3D capabilities in the first year studio. He, Alex, had an advantage there, having played with the software at ABC. Even produced some useful images.

'Just this and that. He hasn't found a permanent job, and his age works against him. Mum's working, though. She's had an admin job at Deakin Uni for yonks now. Reckons she's part of the furniture.' Karl clicked and scrolled. 'Bugger', he said to the screen.

'You have any brothers or sisters?'

'Two sisters. They can't do enough for their big brother.' Karl feigned a smug look, but Alex could see past it. He felt a pang of envy.

'What about you, Alex?'

'Just me and mum.' Perhaps his father's story would be told later.

In their break, paper coffee cups balanced precariously as they sat in voluminous bean-bags, Alex asked Karl about his ambitions. Why architecture?

'I've always like nutting things out, seeing how things work. From my dad, I suppose.' Karl took a careful sip of his coffee. 'And I've admired a few very nice houses belonging to friends and associates of my parents. Maybe I just want to join the rich and famous.'

'But everyone keeps telling us that architects don't get rich. At least not by practising architecture.'

'Yeah, well, I suppose if you live comfortably doing something you enjoy...'

Alex wondered how much the fate of Karl's father— apparently on the professional scrap-heap despite his credentials—had to do with his new friend's ambitions.

He could see that Karl's sneakers and his clothes were inexpensive, but so very carefully chosen. *He cares about his image. Or, is he making a statement about what can be achieved on a modest budget? Thumbing his nose at the costly labels. Probably a good attitude for an architect.*

A friendship grew, and their association began to extend beyond the permeable yet confining bounds of the campus. Going to the football together became a frequent and enjoyable occurrence, while during the week the pair often met at one or other of the innumerable lunch-time eateries in the city's many bustling lanes.

It didn't take Alex long to work out that he wasn't really a big-city person, that this wasn't the place where he really belonged. Sure, he enjoyed the activity and excitement, the footy, the galleries, the night-life and, oh yes, the girls. There was no shortage of young women on the campus, and he and Alex would often urge each other to make the first move. A move which, if executed successfully, could become a second move. Even, occasionally, a thrilling third.

But Alex missed the bush, the mountains, the lakes, the empty beaches. Simplicity. His real interest lay with simple architecture: green architecture, modest sustainable building, eco-friendly development. Fashionable catch-words that he knew well and often mistrusted as they became, for many, mere platitude, but relating to real and important issues. Important to him.

Alex knew that to practice that sort of architecture, any sort of architecture, he first needed to gain all-round, hands-on experience, and to expose himself to a diversity of ideas. That's why he was here, in the city.

factory work

THEIR FINAL YEAR. The venue was Hardware Lane, the two students having wandered down from the university campus to admire the colourful cavalcade of shiny new motor-cycles in nearby Elizabeth Street, all standing in snorting equine readiness along the footpath or flaunted in sensual resplendence in the shop windows.

The lane was crowded; the friends passed half a dozen buzzing eateries before seizing a momentarily empty table in a pizzeria which spilled out into the lane. The talk soon moved from *Ducati* and *Kawasaki* to *Denton*, *Katsalidis*, and other champions of the Melbourne architectural circuit.

Fender Katsalidis's Eureka Tower, long under construction in Melbourne's Southbank precinct, had just overtaken the Rialto as the city's tallest building and was still inching skyward, soon to become the hemisphere's tallest residential building. It was, for Alex, the antithesis of the modest housing he had sought out on his travels, yet he could not help but admire it. Karl had no reservations; in the confident yet controlled assertiveness of the building its architects had achieved what he himself could, as yet, only aspire to.

When their shared homage to the city's emerging new landmark had petered out Karl asked, 'how's your final project going?'

'Pretty well, I think.'

Alex knew that the increasingly complex global economy depended on flourishing trade between nations; he was aware that all of the technology and all of the sophisticated materials from around the globe were available to architects in developed countries like his own. The right few lines written into the building's specifications, and glass would float from the USA, windows from Germany, tiles from Italy, and containers of cladding from China.

So, did the remedy for those in more wretched places, those whose housing needs were more elemental than the well-to-do apartment dwellers of Southbank or Docklands, lie with tapping into that world of possibilities, with better utilisation of technology, greater sophistication, mass production, perhaps? Or might it lie with a return to local traditions, from factory-made back to hand-made? From fly-in, pan-continental panaceas to the use of local skills and materials? Or indeed, might the answer lie in some unlikely melding of the two extremes? It was this conundrum which Alex was tackling in his final year major study.

'As you know, I'm hoping that I can make a solid case for a local approach, but I'm putting the pros and cons for both.' Alex glanced at Karl to see if his friend was still listening. 'I'm preparing some alternative housing solutions, using both the low-key, low-tech, local approach and the global, state-of-the-art, hi-tech approach.'

'Low-cost housing seems a long way away from what BNG are into, mate.'

Karl *had* been listening. And he was right of course, Alex acknowledged with a smile. The large city practice of BNG wouldn't have been his first choice, but he knew that his part-time work there would benefit him and look good on his thin CV. He wanted to understand the role of technology in both design and construction, and perhaps a bigger firm would offer him more in that quest. And he expected that his experience there would directly aid his preparation for the much-anticipated registration examination.

Karl, meantime, had found himself an occasional, casual position with a small firm in Hawthorn. Just two principals and a staff of six. Lavish extensions and renovations to already luxurious homes a specialty. Karl was getting a little closer to the rich and famous.

* * *

Alex was twenty-five and sporting a hard-won B Arch, Hons, from RMIT when, in early 2005, he moved from part-time to full-time work at 'The Factory', as BNG was known to its scornful (envious?) detractors.

Warwick Barnes and Neville Newlands had started the firm as Barnes, Newlands in the fifties and led it to towering prominence through the swashbuckling sixties. Both Barnes and Newlands had gone to another dimension, that great drawing-board in the sky. Peter Greene, who had earned partnership in 'seventy-five, had recently retired to his rural retreat on the Mornington Peninsular, although his Melbourne etablishment network still occasionally threw up new clients for his old firm.

When Alex came on board, BNG boasted four directors, ten associates, about twenty-five other architects, another twenty or so technicians and a collection of administrative staff.

A fancied few scribbled their 4B ideas on yellow butcher's paper—a tradition of the practice, ran them up the office flagpole, and had them quashed, praised or appropriated, by this, that, or all directors. Alex could only fantasize about wielding a creative pencil; he caught sight of a client only occasionally, never witnessed a client presentation, rarely met a director, and never a builder. He quickly came to see the value of his very different experience at ABC in Hobart.

Of late, Alex had been spending his working days preparing, on his computer, meticulous detail drawings of the service cores and toilet blocks of the latest high-rise office building on the firm's books, *The Turret*. He remembered, from an earlier life, scouting with his father for a suitable location in the bush and digging a shallow latrine. Prevailing wind and ground absorbency, so important then, would matter not at all for the sanitary show-pieces in the sky he was working on now.

Others on the project team were preparing the scores of small-scale, general arrangement drawings—plans, elevations and sections—and the specification writer was drafting detailed clauses in readiness for the compilation of the building specifications. All of this was taking place under the watchful eye of the project director.

Before long, Alex found that this isolated detail work, detached from the complex whole that was being planned, was becoming mind-numbing. He needed to understand it all, see how everything fitted together, how it stood up, kept the rain out, occupied its place in the urban terrain.

He found his thoughts drifting dangerously off-line; drifting to the wild west coast of Tassie, to the hazy heat of India, to the sheltered coves of Bridport, to the memorable mounds and valleys of new acquaintance, arts student Sandra and, oh dear, the rising intruder below his desk.

He longed for involvement in the real business of design. That, he knew, would seize his attention and hold it fast.

Until that time came, until he could leap into the unknown and hazardous waters of design and re-connect with the inspiration of his father, Alex would learn what he could from his place on the assembly-line, immerse himself in the swirling energy of the big city and, when he could, re-charge his spirit in the wild country of his home island.

* * *

By the end of the year, Alex had accrued enough leave to fly home to Tassie for a couple of weeks. His holiday itinerary centred around time at home with his mother, with a few outings together, maybe Green's Beach included. Then a couple of nights reminiscing with Handie at the Hand family's shack at Bridport, and an excursion to the Tarkine.

'How is your grandmother, Alex? You did get to see her, didn't you?' Mary looked at him across her teacup.

Alex had suggested he and his mother have lunch at the tea-rooms in the exotic gardens of Launceston's Cataract Gorge. They were sitting at a veranda table now, enjoying a pot of English breakfast tea after their meal.

'Yes, I went up to Ballarat last month. Caught the train. I've come to look forward to my visits, actually. And I know Grandma Pauline does.'

Alex smiled at the memory of how the old lady's face crinkled with delight as she opened the door and her arms to him, how she had fussed around her kitchen with impressive vigour, making them a pot of tea. That had been English Breakfast, too. Leaves, not bags.

'I'm so glad you're keeping in touch with her, Alex.'

Mary picked up her white china cup, its elegance only slightly diminished by its challenging handle. Together, they watched a peacock strut regally across the oasis of quiet lawn before them.

'Does Melbourne feel like home yet?' she asked.

'It's exciting. There's always lots on offer, and Karl and I get around quite a bit. But, you know, I always miss the quiet of the bush.' He absently rearranged the table accoutrements in front of him. 'You know I'll be going out there, don't you?'

His mother's touch told him that she knew.

* * *

In the bush now, well beyond the bike, Alex was walking slowly uphill from a trickling creek, myrtle and sassafras gradually giving way to tall eucalypts; the ground was uneven and strewn with lichen-spattered rocks and rotting branches. The only sounds were his own footfalls, the whisper of a breeze above him, and the warble of an invisible honey-eater.

On each successive visit he had ventured further out from the overgrown bike, the area to be searched growing larger each time. He carefully marked on his aerial photograph the areas he had covered, and the image was taking on the appearance of a sixties op-art flower, a flower whose petals continued, one by one, to grow outwards from its hidden heart. A flower which took his mind back to a stand of tea-tree in full bloom, to a young boy and his dad, to a campfire, and a childish drawing of a perfect flower, a tiny symbol of hope.

He reached what would become the extremity of one of the petals now, a rocky ridge from where he could see the coast, only a kilometre or two away. The ridge was a promising site, he thought; he could see his father camped on that sheltered ledge, frowning as his charcoal beat against the paper. But again there was no sign that Daniel might have been there.

If he had found nothing when the flower was fully drawn, when all of its empty petals lay open to him, what then?

* * *

As the friends sat in the thin, throbbing lane with its enticing aromas of brewed coffee, fresh-baked delights, and a tingling mix of herbs and spices, watching the sharp-shod, dark-dressed city-goers pass each way in stuttering streams, they inevitably returned to their different designs for the future. Karl ran his lean fingers across his designer stubble, peered at Alex through his squat, red-framed spectacles and asked, 'How are things at The Factory, Alex?'

Karl, also by now a graduate architect—graduated, but but not yet registered to practice architecture—had a permanent position with the Hawthorn firm, Meredith Dunlap. George Meredith had recently retired, leaving Gareth Dunlap the sole principal. Alex could see that Karl was enjoying mixing, even if as an underling, with the wealthy residents of Melbourne's inner eastern suburbs.

'I'm still working on The Turret,' Alex said, straightening the menu on the table.

Karl raised a trimmed eyebrow above the red frames.

'It'll be Australia's tallest office tower,' Alex heard and did not like the defensive tone in his own voice.

'Any trouble getting the development approval?'

'Don't know; all that front end stuff happens upstairs. We worker bees only know what we read in the paper'.

Alex was playing along, deliberately overstating the situation, but not by much. There had been plenty of media coverage of the ambitious project, but he couldn't recall any reference to planning approval issues, nor was it talked about in the lower echelons of the firm.

Alex knew that his salary was larger than Karl's, but Karl liked to boast, with some justification, that he was exposed to broader experience, being involved in projects through every phase, from initial briefing and fee budgeting through design and documentation to the overseeing of building works. And, if the tales Karl told were to be believed, house clients were in some ways more demanding than the commercial clients favoured by the directors of BNG.

'Nothing at all happens upstairs at MD, Mate,' Karl said, looking thoughtfully at his near-empty cup. 'I'm in on it all.'

But *all* for the MD practice, thought Alex, was limited to posh houses and little else. BNG, on the other hand, took on a broad banquet of work, much of it impressively large. Admittedly, he himself tasted only a tiny morsel of that generous spread.

'I think Designark have got it about right,' Alex said, referring to an architectural practice located in Geelong. 'A mid-size firm that does small to medium-size projects, and does them really well. And where, so we hear, they have a happy team where everyone gets involved.' He was thinking too, of ABC Architects in Hobart.

'I'm with you there, mate,' Karl said, a little to Alex's surprise. 'I did some work experience there a long time ago. That's exactly the kind of firm I'd like to one day be part of.' He glanced at his watch. 'You having another coffee?'

* * *

'Have you seen Google Earth, Karl?' Alex asked, his eyes scanning a line of tables along the unadorned edge of Causeway Lane.

'Yeah, Gareth is right into it.'

'I've been thinking it might help me with my search.'

'You've seen it in action yourself, then?'

'Only looking over Sonia's shoulder,' responded Alex. Sonia Wong was one of the associates working on the Turret project. Alex was full of admiration for her, and was coming to regard her as a friend. 'It looked pretty amazing.'

Sonia had been studying the inner city of Melbourne on Google Earth when Alex had seen the much-heralded new program on her computer screen. He had yet to play with it himself, but had been impressed by its possibilities, and had seen how it might help him.

'Here's a place,' said Karl, and the pair settled themselves at a round, shiny table for two, close to where the lane met Little Collins Street.

'Mate, it was made for you,' Karl said, 'all those expensive aerial photos of yours could soon be relics of the past.'

'You think so?' Alex asked, as he picked up a menu.

'I do.'

Alex resolved then and there to familiarize himself with the amazing new tool.

He found, to his delight, that he could fly the world as if on a magic carpet, zooming down to more closely examine areas of interest. In his first intoxicated hour he re-traced his way around the places visited in his gap year, zoomed into the site where The Turret was soon to rise, found his mother's house in Launceston, and surfed excitedly up Tasmania's west coast. Karl had been right; when he next returned to his search, he might no longer need his aerial photographs.

the girl

'ECO-FREAKS?' Karl was looking at him strangely.

Alex's view, born early in his studies, that there were many different types of architects, was a view that took more definite form as he progressed along his professional path. The narrow lane that ran alongside the former post office in the Bourke Street Mall, was, as usual, buzzing during the lunch hour, and Alex had to speak up as he aired his view to Karl, in the spring of 2006.

'Yeah. Well, to name a few other types: there's the the Egoists, the Nerds, the Artists ... Humanists, um, the Business Types, their cousins the Marketers, and that rare breed, the All-Rounders. Have I missed any?'

'Yes, you missed out the intellectuals and academics.' Karl breathed on his glasses, and cleaned them with a small cloth which he then carefully folded and slipped back into the beast pocket of his recycled Harris tweed jacket.

'True. I suppose I was showing my bias towards those who practice rather than teach.'

'Wait on, mate. It's possible to do both. There are plenty of examples.' Karl had now set about cleaning the face of his precious new mobile phone, a compact device which Apple had recently released to much fanfare. 'And anyway, I think you're generalising too much. Don't most architects have a bit of most of those characteristics in them?'

Alex was thinking about this when his attention was directed by Karl's covert eye movement to a dark-haired girl hurrying along the lane, steering an over-size black leather handbag before her. Her long hair framed an attractive oval face; her simple black dress, worn under a fine-striped black-and-white top, fell to mid-thigh; her stockings were dark and densely patterned, and her black shoes stood on slender high heels.

Not wishing to stare, or at least knowing it was impolite to do so, Alex returned his gaze to his less discreet friend. But the temptation was too great. He again turned his head to follow Karl's changing eye-line, and, to his embarrassment, found himself looking into the girl's face.

Vincenza was running late. She had known that coming downtown to pick up the tickets was chancy, that she could not be late back to work. Work was at Pages, a little bookshop just off the top end of Swanston Street. (Rumour had it that Adrian Page, an obsessive bibliophile, had changed his name to wed himself more intimately to the object of his affections - his beloved shop.)

She cut through the block as she gathered pace, clutching her bulky handbag containing the precious tickets. Her shoes were not made for hurrying; she sashayed precariously. And perhaps Postal Lane at this time of day was not really a short-cut.

A shock of blond hair caught her eye. One could walk the city's crowded streets for weeks without seeing a familiar face, but when Vin spied that blond head at a lane-side table, she knew it had registered with her before. It was not an unfashionable head of hair, but its owner clearly was indifferent to its composure. Studied indifference she could recognise; this was real. She liked that.

Blond Boy was sitting with his back to her, opposite a shorter, dark-complexioned, more preened young man who appeared to favour Retro-Cool attire: above the table-top, she could see he had on a fifties-style, patterned grass-green open-neck shirt and a tweed jacket, label possibly her namesake, Vinnies. Blondie was less adventurous—less of a slave to fashion?—a wrinkled black linen jacket with a steel-grey shirt.

As she neared their little table, Vin saw Retro look at her and murmur something to his friend. Blond Boy suddenly turned his head and looked directly at her. His rising blush and the beginnings of a shy smile surprised and charmed her. She could not help but smile in return.

As the girl disappeared into the lunch-time throng, the two young men fell briefly into worshipful silence. A look passed between them; Karl's eyebrows were raised, Alex's expression was one of faraway dreams. He was re-living the moment of her smile.

* * *

Alex thought it was architect Robin Boyd, wasn't it, who had expounded in his heyday in the sixties that, as he addressed any new design challenge, he looked for the emergence of an aesthetic, a pattern or order, inherent in the complex and often contradictory requirements of the client's brief and the nature of the site. With that approach, presumably no external values or pre-conceptions were papered over the building; rather, its physical form married with the brief and its location to give a beautiful, tangible solution to an abstract problem.

When Alex voiced this vicarious concept over lunch in the shelter of the busy Centre Place on a blustery late spring day, Karl was unconvinced.

Tossing his wind-swept scarf over his shoulder, Karl challenged: 'So, what if you can't find a *pattern* as you call it? What if there is none? Wouldn't you then just apply all your own preferences, prejudices, and ideas to the task at hand? And what's wrong with that? So long as you put your client's interests first and don't go on your own private ego trip...'

Karl stopped talking. His eyes had left Alex.

'Hang on,' he spoke quietly, his lips barely moving, 'here comes that girl.'

The young men were suddenly hushed, attentive to their menus, only their sliding eyes betraying where their real interest lay.

Was that a faint smile on the girl's face as she passed by?

* * *

And where does ART come into it all? Alex was asking himself. *What, for that matter, is art? (Duh. I bet no one's asked that question before.) For me, it implies something free of discipline as we usually think of that. Or should I say free of rules, of constraints? Perhaps it's a yielding to un-logic. A preparedness to go where whim or imagination takes you, without the need to explain. Taking your mind into the dream world, where all things are possible. Except having this little conversation with your client.*

'You're right there, mate', responded Karl, when this little thought bubble of Alex's broke the surface, as they lunched at a crowded café in the popular Block Place thoroughfare. 'The last bit, I mean. Our house clients would walk away quick-smart if we started talking like that. They don't need that sort of wank; they're after practical advice, good service, the best and most impressive materials and finishes, latest technology, and a bit of a wow factor—even better than what they see on *The Block*.'

Alex laughed. 'Yeah, right. We're Masters of the Wow Factor. Our important role in life.'

'Admittedly one or two clients are interested in the way architects think, and like to have a story to tell to their dinner guests. But, in the main ....'
Karl never finished his sentence—he must have seen that Alex's attention

had suddenly departed from his profound exposition to another place. He realised that Alex was deaf to him. It had to be the girl.

Before Karl could turn his head, Alex was on his feet. He stood with his back to the girl's approach and leaned over the table as if inspecting something of great importance, in doing so effectively blocking her passage.

The girl waited patiently, with a bemused expression, for him to move aside.

'Oh, sorry', said Alex, feigning surprise and flashing his winning smile. He stepped aside and bowed an exaggerated Raleigh-like gesture. The smile he received in return was so spontaneous and so warm that he was quite floored. His bravado evaporated and, to his horror—and to Karl's growing amusement—he felt the burning humiliation of a blush.

But the Tassie boy had broken the ice.

Vincenza

IT HAPPENED EASILY, in the end. It was a warm morning in late January. Alex was walking through Hardware Lane, she doing the same, but in the opposite direction. When Alex spotted her, eye-catching in a simple but elegant white dress with black trim—a throw-back to the sixties, perhaps?—he was thankful that he had no time to think, no time to *pike out*. It had seemed natural that they should stop and say hello.

They both, tentatively at first, paused, smiling their recognition. Then, as felicitous fate had placed a vacant table at the very place their lives intersected, Alex gestured to the table as if he had conjured it up himself, and said: 'coffee?'

She gave a warm *yes, why not?* smile and they sat.

'We meet at last.' Alex couldn't keep the smile from his face. *This girl is lovely.*

She lowered her dark eyes from his open admiration.

'I'm Alex. Alex Gardner.' Alex offered his hand across the little stainless-steel table.

'I'm Vin. Vin Genovese.'

'That would be Vincenza?'

'That would be Alexander?'

They both laughed and nodded.

Her hand was warm, her grip nicely firm. Her nails were painted black; he hadn't noticed that before. Perhaps they hadn't been black before.

'Where do you work, Vin?'

'At Pages. It's a little bookshop not far from here.'

Now that I know that much, you won't get away from me again.

'What about you, Alex?'

'Have you heard of BNG?'

'They make garage doors, don't they?'

Is she being mischievous? 'Sorry.' Alex chuckled. 'I should have said I work for a firm of architects called BNG. In the city.'

'Oh. Maybe I do know of them. Are they the ones doing that new really tall office tower?'

'That's them. I'm actually working on that project. It's called The Turret.' *But please don't ask me exactly what my role is. Drawing toilets. For now, just be impressed.*

'Wow, that's impressive. What's your role, Alex?'

As Alex was assembling his answer, their coffees arrived.

'One cappuccino?'

Alex raised a finger. 'Thanks.'

'One skinny flat white?'

Vin smiled her thanks.

'Did you study architecture here in Melbourne?' she asked.

'Yes, I did my second tier at RMIT.'

'Oh, that's right, architecture is a two-tier course, isn't it?'

'Yes.' Alex scooped up some of his coffee's froth and took the spoon to his mouth. *Whoa, Alex, is this proper etiquette? Oh what the heck. If she's offended, then she's too proper for me.* In that moment of hesitation, the girl's own teaspoon darted out like some tiny silver bird of prey and seized some of Alex's froth.

'Do you mind? I love the froth.'

He laughed. 'Of course not.' Vin's child-like action felt deliciously intimate to Alex. Or had she been rescuing him?

'I went to RMIT for a while, too.' She sipped at her coffee. 'A Graduate Diploma in Information Management. Librarianship, if you like. But I've done creative writing courses, and that's where my interest really lies.'

'You're a word nerd, then?' He immediately regretted the ridiculous expression.

'Never call me that, Alexander.' She frowned at him with mock severity. 'But I will own up to loving words.'

'Sorry', he said. 'I quite like words myself. The influence of my mother. She's a teacher. *Media* and *criteria* are plural nouns, Alex, she would say. Use them correctly.'

'Wow, you get points from me on that score. I'd almost given up on those two.'

They laughed together. Little crinkles appeared around her dark eyes when she laughed, and a tiny dimple visited one cheek.

Vin looked at her over-sized watch. 'Sorry Alex, I must get back to work.'

Pages, thought Alex, inscribing the name into his memory.

'I don't think we finished our conversation.' said Alex. Her smile encouraged him. 'Lunch?'

'Thursday?' said Vin.

'Same place?' said Alex. 'One-thirty?'

'Deal.' said Vin, picking up her bag.

Alex arrived early and contrived to secure the same table, *their* table. It felt like a romantic thing to do. It was another warm day, but the shifting clouds suggested that a change might be coming. Alex had dressed with careful nonchalance, a white linen shirt and faded grey jeans. He was keyed-up but determined not to show it.

And there she was. Was this lovely girl making her way along the busy lane really coming to meet him? He stood to greet her.

'Hello Vincenza.'

'Hello Alexander.'

They shook hands, a little awkwardly, and sat, each discreetly appraising the other. Her dark hair was swept back into a high pony-tail *(did you still call them that?)* exposing her graceful, slender neck. She wore a simple but flattering dress—a shift, he thought it was called—of a spice–coloured fabric, and carried the huge bag that had caught his eye when he first saw her, now with a little red ornament hanging from its handle. Her nails were no longer black, but deep red. The same red as her lipstick. And as the little dangly thing.

'I like your colours,' Alex ventured.

'Thank you,' said Vin, smiling. 'In my job, it's expected of me to look neat and tidy.'

Now there was an understatement.

In an easy conversation over a warm chicken salad, Alex learned that Vin was, like him, an only child. Her Italian parents had come to Australia just before she was born. She had lived at the family home in Footscray during her years of study, but now shared a small flat in Carlton. With a girlfriend, he happily noted.

'You a Blues supporter? Carlton?'

'Yes, I am actually, but never tell my dad. He assumes that I support the Bulldogs. He's fanatical about them.' Her grin told Alex that she loved her father.

Alex chuckled. He was enjoying the sound of her voice. *And those eyes.*

He learned that Vin had acquired a Bachelor of Arts at Melbourne Uni, majoring in English literature, before taking on her part-time post-graduate studies at RMIT, conveniently close to her new job at Pages. He was impressed.

Alex in turn told Vin of his studies at UTas in Launceston and his stints at ABC in Hobart. And of course he told her of his mother, Mary. He knew that Vin must have noticed that he made no reference to his father. How many times had he struggled to answer when asked the unthinking question: *What does your father do, Alex?*

They both understood that more intimate revelations would come when it felt right.

The next time they lunched together it was at a different place, in Menzies Lane, but table six at *Tony's Tucker* in Hardware Lane would remain a special spot for them, even when, in years to come, the management, the name, and the tucker were all to change.

Their first dinner was in China Town. They had met for a drink at a wine bar in the Melbourne Central complex when Vin had finished work, then walked down Swanston Street to Little Bourke. Alex wanted to hold her hand, but settled for ushering her safely through the evening throng, touching the small of her back in a gentlemanly fashion. He switched to the outside of the footpath in that old-fashioned manner that his mother had taught him. *You'll love her mum.* Then, when there came a moment that they were in danger of being separated, he grabbed her hand. And it stayed grabbed; Vin gave his hand a little squeeze of approval.

Upstairs in the *Golden Dragon*, in a semi-private alcove, they enjoyed a leisurely meal and savoured the gradual opening of their lives to one another.

Vin spoke of her work, her ambitions, her parents, and her grandmother.

'Nonna is dad's mother. She's wonderful. She moved out here ten years ago when we were all expecting a new baby in the house. But mum miscarried. I would have had a little brother.' Vin's smile was wistful.

'That's sad.'

'I think dad was the most upset of us all. He would have loved to have a son. To kick a football with, to muck about with in the shed.'

The shed. That brought a smile back to Alex's face. 'Same with my dad. He used to enjoy it when we made something in our shed.'

'Used to?'

Alex straightened his place-mat. 'He's not there any more.' He could see the question in Vin's eyes. A question he felt able to answer.

'He went missing in the bush years ago. I've been looking for signs of him ever since.'

Vin looked stricken. She reached across and put her hand over his. The gesture moved him.

But the Tarkine flower was wilting. Alex's much-worked-over flower-patterned aerial photo was creased, crumpled and faded, and the hope it had promised was fading with it.

Messages from fortune cookies:
Time heals all wounds, but first you must bandage them with love. (Alex).
Fulfil your duties, but never neglect your heart. (Vin).

koala country

'HEY KARL, have you seen the ad for the Otways design competition?'

'No, mate. What's it all about?' Karl set down his espresso and folded his paper. Alex could see on the back page: *Pies lose Swan for big game.*

'The Shire Council is inviting designs for a new visitor centre in the Otway Ranges. Open to all architects registered in Australia.'

'That lets us out then,' Karl observed, his eyes wandering to a giggly gaggle of girls seated across the way.

Both young men had diligently accumulated and documented the requisite amount of practical, post-graduation experience to allow them to apply for professional registration. Only then could they legally call themselves architects and, if they chose, 'hang out a shingle' and start their own practice.

'I'm thinking I might have a go at it anyway,' said Alex. This was an opportunity to do some real design work. 'If I come up with a design I'm happy with I'll talk to the guys at BNG to see if they want to take it on.'

Karl returned his gaze to Alex. 'Good thinking. Good experience, whatever comes of it. Go for it, mate.'

'Should you and I do it together?'

'No, thanks anyway,' Karl gave Alex a knowing smile, 'No offence, happy to help a bit if I can, but I wouldn't want to end up working for The Factory.'

Alex found that getting hold of the design brief was relatively simple. To the question: *are you registered in Australia?* His response was: *Registration expected to be in place at time of submitting entry.* Optimising the truth a little, (the registration examination was to take place next month, with a positive outcome far from assured) but it earned him access to the full design brief prepared by the Council: the project objectives, detailed maps and site surveys, lengthy schedules of functional requirements, studies of expected visitor numbers and demographics, and internet links to various studies relating to the area.

As Karl had said, this would be good experience.

* * *

They clambered into Karl's car, a collectible but costly-to-maintain Alfa Romeo, their layers of cold-weather clothing making the compact car seem even smaller. The mountain bikes had been clamped on the back. Karl's high-end machine showed very few signs of wear and tear, Alex couldn't help observing. He was coming to understand that his friend was attracted to sophisticated design in its many manifestations, whether or not it had a useful place in his life.

'Let's go via Colac,' Karl suggested, 'then if we have time we can go down to the coast and come back through Geelong.'

'Sounds good to me.'

As they eased away from Alex's house, where Karl had collected him, the chill air and the grey light triggered in Alex a nostalgic recollection of heading off to the bush in the pre-dawn with his father. This whole adventure felt like a grown-up version of his childhood excursions. Off to the bush to make something from what they found there. He recognized now, as they drove, that this exercise was more than an intellectual, professional one; it was a response to a need in himself. To reconnect? To validate? He couldn't find the words, just the feelings.

After a stop for coffee at Colac, and muffins to go, they headed south-east into the ranges, wending their way on damp roads through shadowy forests in the direction of the coast. Now the talk was of the fast-approaching registration examinations, of frequently-asked-questions and tricky topics likely to arise: contract pitfalls, the dangers of estimating building costs, risk management, liability in tort… then, as the weight of that subject became too much to sustain on this free-wheeling morning, they moved on to more compelling stuff. Bikes. Footy. Girls.

'So you're getting on well with the Italian girl?'

'I am.' Alex's smile must have revealed his pleasure at the fact that he was indeed *getting on well* with Vin.

'You know Al, I was greatly impressed by the way you accosted Vin that day. Forced her to notice you.' Karl eased the car carefully around a frosty bend, working the gears and clearly enjoying the car's ribald exhaust note. 'I confess to being a little envious now.'

'You, the great Lothario, envious?' It seemed to Alex that Karl never lacked a partner for social occasions. And never the same partner.

'Yeah, strange. Isn't it?' Karl played along. 'But I reckon you've found a treasure there, mate.'

They arrived at the site at mid-morning. It was easy for the two to see why the shire council had stipulated this location: it was close to a major tourist route, it was already largely cleared, of adequate size and reasonably level. The setting was pleasant: tall gums, light understorey, outlook to wooded hills.

'Let's have a poke around,' suggested Alex, gathering up his satchel and digital camera. Karl locked the car and followed Alex into the bush. A big koala ensconced in the fork of a low branch eyed them, but carried on with its meal of gum-leaves. A pair of resplendent king parrots looked on from another tree, while a posse of noisy gang-gang cockatoos flew overhead.

A half-hour later, when the blueberry muffins were calling to them from the car, Alex called a halt.

'Here.' He said, standing motionless in a clearing.

The place they had come to might not be as clear as the Council's site, and it might not be as close to the road, but a narrow view between the hills culminated in a distant, shining triangle—the waters of Bass Strait.

'From here, you can orientate yourself, right? Back there, you don't know where you are.'

'I'm with you, mate,' said Karl, 'risky though, ignoring the Council's choice.'

'The location is everything.' Alex was wandering the site, snapping and writing happily. The distant laugh of a kookaburra carried across the valley from somewhere on the opposite hill. Was his choice of site being ridiculed or applauded?

He pulled a Google Earth printout from his satchel and marked the site, then found a rock to sit on with his sketchbook.

What would you have made of this place, Dad? How do you think I should approach this?

a family

'ALEX, YOU HAVE A CALL on line five.' It was the practised, melodic voice of Angela at reception.

'Thanks Angie. Hello?'

'Seldom.'

'Sorry?'

'Seldom. The answer to nine across.'

Alex smiled. 'Hello Vin.'

'*Some heartlessly led round on occasions*, six letters: S, something, L, something, something, M. *Seldom.*'

'Alex, it's that young lady again, line three.' Was there a teasing note in Angela's voice?

'Thank you Angie.' Alex glanced around the drawing office. Personal calls were tolerated at BNG, but only within reason.

'Vin?'

'Hello darling.'

Darling filled Alex with warmth and brought a smile to his face. He glanced around again, this time catching the eye of Sonia, who gave him a knowing wink.

'Have you heard the news about Beaconsfield?'

'No.' Alex was alert, his smile fading.

'There's been a collapse in the gold mine. Three men are missing. Do you have any family there?"

He didn't, but the news from so close to home affected him. Not for the first time, Alex wished he still had a God to pray to. The God he had privately entreated as a boy, when another man went missing.

* * *

Just a short walk from the train station, the couple turned into a quiet, narrow street. Walking with Vin, holding hands with Vin, being a couple with Vin, were experiences still new to Alex, and they filled him with a fusion of feelings all warm and buoyant. Walking on air, as the love songs would have it.

'This is our street,' said Vin, tugging Alex by the hand across to the shady side, 'and here we are.'

The Genovese home, several houses from the corner, sat on a narrow lot in a street of narrow lots. At the kerb, a white, dual cab utility bore the name *Genovese Concrete and Render.* The low, concrete front fence to the house was finished with a pebbled render; the small front garden, if it could be called that, consisted of green-painted concrete crowded with earthenware and concrete pots, each boasting a thriving plant. A small portico supported, purportedly, by two concrete Doric columns sheltered the front door.

He knew it might be derided by some of his fellow designers, but Alex loved the house; everything about it said *home.*

The humming of bees filled the fragrant air as they approached the wood-framed, obscure glass front door. Vin rang the door chimes to warn her parents, then led Alex inside. At the far end of a dim hall graced with a group of framed family photographs, a couple of prints of Italian scenes, and religious icons on a little shelf, stood Vin's mother, arms outstretched in welcome.

The likeness to Vin was undeniable; Mrs Genovese—*call me Maria*—had her daughter's dark eyes and wide, brilliant smile. Her luxuriant hair held just a hint of grey.

'I'm so pleased to meet you, Alex,' she said, taking his hand warmly. 'You'll be staying for lunch, won't you?'

'Of course he will, won't you Alex?' said Vin. 'Mum's lasagna is wonderful, *stupendo.*' That was settled. 'Where's dad?'

'Sergio is out the back.' Mrs Genovese shrugged with a resigned smile which said: *where else?*

'I'll take Alex out.' Vin led Alex out through a large, outdoor, roofed area into a sunny green oasis bordered by a thriving vegetable garden, olive trees, tomato plants and a chaotic array of herbs in containers of all sorts. There, tending what looked to Alex to be a grape vine, was a stocky, wide-shouldered man. His bare arms were sinewed and brown—*you'd better treat his daughter well*—his face weathered, his hair thick and greying.

Alex smiled at the incongruity of the sleeveless football guernsey that Vin's father was wearing over his bib-and-brace overalls. The Footscray Football Club, the Bulldogs.

'Liberatore,' said Alex, recognising the number 39 on the guernsey.

The man's face creased into a smile. 'Ah, you know my Libba? You are a Doggies fan?' He wiped his hand on his overalls and offered it to Alex.

'Dad, this is Alex,' put in Vin.

'No, Mr Genovese, I'm afraid not.' He took her father's hand and accepted his crushing grip. 'I was a fan of your Libba, though.'

'Ah. Come Alex, you must try my grappa.'

'That's my nonna.' Vin saw that Alex was looking at a photograph on the Genovese mantelpiece. Two lovely, smiling faces, crammed into the small photo in obvious mutual affection; one was his Vin, the other a bright-eyed elderly woman. The resemblance and the love touched Alex. This was a real family. Complete.

'She lived here for years, as I told you. But she missed her home town and her friends. She moved back to Italy last year.' Vin's face softened as she spoke of her grandmother.

Hearing this, Mrs Genovese said with a mischievous smile in the direction of the couple: 'a new bambino might have kept her here.' This time it was Vincenza who blushed.

thinking too much

'WHAT DO YOU THINK of the Eureka Tower, now that it's finished?' Alex asked.

'I really like it,' said Karl, 'Sophisticated. Polished. Lots of energy. Their brand all over it. Nonda's become something of a brand himself, hasn't he?'

'Yes. Interesting how developers are keen to attach the name of a well-known architect to their projects.'

Karl examined a triangle of pizza, finding it acceptable. 'Good for the profession, I would have thought.'

Still on architecture, the field that occupied so many of the friend's exchanges, he asked, 'How's the Otways design going, Alex?'

'Not too bad. I've decided to use some of the little sketches I made on site. Remember?'

'Really?' That eyebrow again.

'It'll save me the time and effort of putting together a lot of computer images.'

'Yeah, I can see that, but ...'

'But what?'

'But mightn't it suggest to the competition assessors that you don't have the resources or know-how to carry out the job?'

'I see your point, but I'm going to have to take that chance.'

The use of hand sketches was entirely compatible with such a hand-made building, Alex told himself, and if he complemented his sketches with up-to-the-minute computer renderings, that would surely add to the sense of the time continuum. A continuum which spoke of the site's geological evolution, the coming of life in all its forms, the original human inhabitants—the Gudabanud people, European settlement, right through to the present day.

But enough of the serious stuff, off to the footy.

* * *

It was a Friday, later in the football season. The work day had set, and the friends were enjoying a drink and a quick meal at Federation Square, before joining the dark, murmuring throng that was bumping purposefully along the riverside walkway towards the lights of the 'G', Melbourne's famous MCG stadium. A night game, Demons v Pies.

'I read that The Turret is going to be an iconic building,' Karl said.

Alex looked at his friend with suspicion. Karl was surely setting him up. Taking the piss.

'It'll certainly be a landmark,' he responded.

'Not iconic?'

'Define iconic,' said Alex, attack being the best form of defence.

'The Sydney Opera House.'

'That's an example, not a definition.'

'Here's another,' something on his folded newspaper had caught Karl's eye, 'says here that Sorbent is an iconic brand.'

'So we're worshipping toilet paper these days? This is the kind of thing that gets Vin going,' Alex said, 'she hates the dumbing-down of the language.'

Karl looked up from his fettuccini and smiled. 'You two really are a couple now, aren't you? For better or worse?'

'For better.' Alex gave an apologetic smile, a little embarrassed that he had risen to the bait.

Reflecting on the so-called iconic buildings and their hero architects, it occurred to him that he did not have on his personal list of heroes the big international names like Libeskind, Hadid, Gehry, and their ilk. Was it because the work of these stars was so far removed from his own experience and aspirations? Or because of his unease at the sheer extravagance of some of their creations?

For Karl, who in Alex's view would have made a great modernist, good buildings were about bringing together the latest materials and technology and integrating them seamlessly, finding satisfaction, perhaps beauty, in their resolution. For Alex, it was the rightness for the place that he looked for first. What title should he hang on that? Site-responsive? Contextual? Some academic somewhere could answer that for him.

But you didn't always need clever words, did you? His dad just seemed to know this stuff. *Feel it Alex?*

Alex's finger traced the curve of his glass, leaving a little clear trail. Vin he could tell, but it would be sentimental nonsense if said out loud to Karl: his real hero, still the source of so much of his inspiration, was his father.

* * *

'Are we just followers of fashion, Karl?' Alex was looking enquiringly at his friend, across their table at a Causeway Lane café, taking in his trendy spectacles, his carefully chosen retro button-down shirt and modish hairstyle, short around the sides, long on top, streaked where it fell boyishly over his brow. 'Shouldn't we be setting new directions, finding better ways of doing things? Rather than being led by the architectural magazines?'

Did Karl's little smile into his coffee say *Here we go again?*

'You think too much, Alex', said Karl, dabbing a little line of froth from his top lip with a neatly folded napkin. 'If you think too much you'll never get anything done'.

Alex knew there was some truth in this. They both knew from their Uni days that there were people who deliberated so long over every step they took, researching so thoroughly every choice, that in the end they had little or nothing concrete to show for it. Time and the necessities of life defeated them.

But something else gave him pause. Depressed him sometimes. Was it possible that his own design approach, his design philosophy—one of simplicity, logic, sustainability and respect for place—was in reality no more than *an aesthetic*? The aesthetic that he was struggling with on his Otway design? And what distinguished that from *fashion*?

Alex felt the need to return to the place where this thing inside him, this philosophy, this aesthetic, whatever it was, was conceived. The bush.

rightness

SHORTLY BEFORE BOARDING his flight across the strait, Alex decided that, this time, he would not go to the Tarkine. There, he reasoned, his mission to search for signs of his father would take over. This time he felt the need to just be in the bush, just be with nature, to *feel* the answer to the questions his uncertainties were asking.

He had called his mother from Tullamarine and suggested that they spend the weekend at Green's Beach. She had quickly agreed and had booked them for two nights at a holiday cabin within a short walk of the beach.

The mild spring weather was kind to them. They had both donned shorts, usually confined to their drawers until later in the year. Mary had brought a thick novel with her as well as a briefcase stuffed with papers. She now sat in the welcome sunshine on the cabin's small deck, taking in the sea air and reading. She had kicked off her sandals and tugged up the hem of her shorts to allow the sun to warm her legs and help along her light tan.

'Mmm, this was a good idea, Alex.'

Alex walked barefoot to where the beach met a rocky headland. Between ragged ridges of rock emerging from the placid sea, he found a narrow wedge of beach. The apex of the wedge was filled with a dense accumulation of tiny, shining shells. He sat on the smooth sand and bent close to the shells, marvelling at the beauty and consistency of the miniscule beads. *The sea sorts them out for you*, he remembered his father saying.

Perhaps he should be content to allow himself to be sifted and sorted by forces bigger than himself, to accept his own ideas and ideals as worthy and legitimate, but neither better nor worse than those other clusters washed up into other coves elsewhere on the ever-changing shores of his profession.

Later, before the air began to chill, Alex followed a thin track through the bush around the headland, seeing through the greenery the incursion of some substantial new homes higher on the rise. Leaving them behind, he quietly made his way through the native grasses, between banksias, she-oaks and acacias, all the while the expanse of Bass Strait flashing its presence to him.

A mountain lizard moved out of his way. The breeze brought the scratchy cry of rosellas and the trill of a wattle-bird. The many grass tunnels told him of the presence of other creatures, creatures of the night: wallabies, potaroos, wombats, devils. And, look…was it? Yes, an echidna. A treasured sight to warm any jaded heart, it snuggled into the ground, leaving just a little hillock of spines to be seen.

On the wooded slope overlooking the strait, neither wild bush nor suburbia, Alex found that his mind had stilled. The strident questions had ceased. There was a rightness in what he did. A rightness for him. And that was enough.

peace

THE PRAHAN HOUSE was quiet, deserted but for them.

The peace he had found in the bush had stayed with him.

From outside came fragments of noise from a summer Sunday. Inside the cocoon of Alex's bedroom they lay, languorous, in a creamy light.

Alex moved a lazy arm under the love-twisted sheet. He gently curved his hand over her softness and felt again that intense sense of belonging, of completeness.

Vin smiled a drowsy smile, her eyes still closed. And in a while, in the un-measured drift of time, she moved her legs a little, and Alex's fingers moved into her dream.

She lay on her back, partially covered, her dark hair forming a swirled corona on the pillow.

Vin opened her eyes. She looked at him now with a gaze whose meaning he had come to know. He felt himself grow in response. He would be her man; he would enter her world, be part of her.

a pitch

'THANKS FOR THIS, PAUL.'

'No worries, Alex. What have you got for me?'

At Sonia Wong's suggestion, Alex was to pitch his Otway design to Paul Turner, BNG's fiftyish and fit director in charge of the Turret Project. Alex had encountered Paul on occasions and had been impressed with his ability to quickly size up a situation and make a decision. An ability which seemed to match his trim physique and neat, business-like attire. Alex looked forward to the day when he himself possessed such confidence, and hoped it would come before he reached Paul's advanced years.

The pair settled down in a compact meeting-room adjacent to the main drawing office.

'You'd be aware of the Otway competition, Paul?'

'Yes, I am. We briefly considered putting in an entry, but with everything that's going on, decided against it. Too busy with paying work. In any event, that sort of project is not really our strength.'

Alex took a deep breath as the director looked at him expectantly. He decided that, with Paul, he should be succinct and direct.

'I've prepared, in my own time, an entry for the competition. Since I'm not quite registered and don't have the experience or resources to carry through such a project, I'd like to be able to submit it in conjunction with BNG. If you think it's good enough.'

Paul looked at him closely through clear, grey eyes, his tanned features giving away nothing. Eventually he said, 'good for you, Alex. I like your initiative.'

Alex relaxed a little as Paul continued. 'I think it's unlikely that BNG would join you, but there's no harm in having a look at what you've done.' He smiled and looked at the A1 size portfolio that Alex had placed on the table between them, then glanced at his watch.

For the next fifteen minutes, the director gave Alex his un-divided attention, his initial curiosity appearing to give way to real interest as Alex talked him through the competition brief, the site and his design. Alex showed his sketches made at the site, his hand-drawn design concept, comprising thumb-nail sketches, schematic plans and cross-sections, and some of his intended construction details. Then prints of several preliminary 3D computer images, which Paul's glance indicated he knew must have been prepared on BNG equipment.

'I like it Alex. It's original, simple and elegant. It shows a rare feeling for its place.'

Something welled up in Alex at these words. If he did indeed possess a rare feeling for place, he knew where it had come from. He was silent.

'Impressive. You obviously have some real design skills.' Paul sat back and steepled his hands.

Alex shuffled the drawings back into order while he waited. The incriminating computer images disappeared to the bottom.

'Alex, I'm going to stick my neck out and say we'll go with you. There'll be conditions, though, as I'm sure you would expect. 'I should run it past the other directors, but that's a formality.'

Alex felt a little stunned. Making the approach had felt like pursuing a boyish dream. He hoped he could keep his composure until he left the room.

Alex's sky was a bright blue field occupied by a flock of happy, sun-tinged possibilities as he left the office that day, but, unseen to him, dark, wolfish storm clouds were gathering on the horizon.

shock waves

BEAR WHO?

That week, the talk in the office was as much about the growing financial crisis as it was about the footy. Did the Saints have any chance, or was the race to the premiership going to be between the Cats and the Hawks? Could the Macquarie Bank, the 'millionaires factory', really be in trouble, as its plummeting share price seemed to indicate? Alex had not previously heard of Bear Stearns or Lehman Bros, but it was becoming clear to him that the collapse of those entities on the other side of the world was sending shock waves even to these shores.

The Macquarie Bank gossip gained rapid momentum when somebody up the line at BNG let slip that Macquarie was one of the potential backers for the massive Turret project. The ripple of anxiety, as it radiated through The Factory, reflected the impact of that unwelcome little brick-bat.

America's financial crisis was going global. A new acronym would be coined: GFC. The BNG Factory had always been known for hiring-and-firing as its workload fluctuated, but this time was different. This time no-one was safe.

Two weeks later the worst fears of the BNG staff were realised. It was BNG's chairman, Sylvester Bakker, who addressed the assembly.

The entire complement of the BNG practice was gathered in the main drawing office, the largest space in the twelve hundred square metres of floor space over two floors occupied by the firm. Some were seated, some stood against the walls, others were perched on benches. There was an air of quiet apprehension.

Bakker cleared his throat and the room fell silent.

'By now', he said, 'you will all be aware that BNG has been heavily impacted by the current financial crisis. What you may not know is that our largest project, The Turret, has been shelved indefinitely, and a dozen other projects in the office have been halted. This is quite unprecedented in the experience of the directors.'

As Bakker spoke, his normally strong voice quavering, Alex felt his heart sink. He had hoped that the rumours had exaggerated the situation, but the tone of the chairman told him that was not the case.

He looked around the room. There was the spirited, talented Sonia, who had become a friend to him, clearly struggling to maintain her usual cheer. There was gentle, thoughtful Phillipe, an amazingly skilled CAD technician whom Alex knew to be supporting a young family, now looking sick with apprehension. And Brian, whose age would surely be a factor. And Aiesha, a single mum, now subdued. And earnest Eric. And all the others ... Alex was suddenly glad to be young and un-attached. Glad, too, that his registration as an architect was in the mail.

When the moment came, when it became clear that Alex's position was one of the many that would be terminated, the implications crowded his reeling brain.

Oh God, his Otways design. The disappointment of the lost opportunity, the opportunity which had so excited him, hit him like a physical blow.

And his mind raced through the list of his financial commitments. His share of the rent in the Prahan house was the first and most pressing. And how, he wondered, would his housemates fare in the unfolding circumstances?

Alex himself was frugal by nature and had put aside a little since he joined BNG, so he could pay his way for a few months, but beyond that?

The unwelcome meeting wound up and the room began to empty. To Alex it felt as if the very life-blood of the proud firm was leaking out onto the street.

As he made his way back to his desk, exchanging quiet commiserations with others, Alex experienced a growing sense of standing at a crossroads in an unknown land. Should he take the first ride he was offered, no matter where it was headed?

He found himself see-sawing between fear and a heady sense of freedom. Fear that necessity might see him take a road that lead to mediocrity and compromise, freedom that came from having the world open to him, nothing impossible. Fear of one day finding himself fifty years old and holding down a mundane job in a middle-of-the-road suburban practice, bending to the demands of unimaginative house clients. Freedom to seek out a path which could one day see him producing real architecture, buildings that his father would be proud of.

A series of sombre one-to-one meetings took place at BNG in the following days. The outgoing staff were formally given two weeks notice, told of their entitlements, had references arranged, and commiserations delivered. Alex was pleased to learn that Sonia had escaped the cut. She sat in as Paul Turner farewelled him from The Factory.

'You'll get a good reference, Alex. Someone will be lucky to get you. Don't hesitate to offer my number.' Paul handed Alex his business card, and Sonia followed suit.

'Good luck Alex,' she said. 'We'll miss you.' She embraced him quickly, her eyes filling.

'If and when things return to normal,' said Paul, grimacing as though thinking that prospect a forlorn one, 'you would be welcome back here.'

They both knew he wouldn't be back.

'I'm sorry about your Otways design,' said Paul, as he shook Alex's hand, 'but who knows, maybe you can still find someone to partner you.'

Fat chance of that. I'll be lucky if I can find a job.

arrivederci

'ALEX, I NEED TO talk to you.' Vin's voice was strained. 'Can we have dinner tonight?'

They settled on a little Thai restaurant in Chapel Street, not too far from Alex's house; it was a place they had come to enjoy. Alex had been apprehensive—I need to talk had ominous overtones—but was reassured by Vin's warm, welcoming embrace. Both rugged up against the cold winter's night, they hurried inside and chose a secluded corner table.

There was no small talk tonight. No *how's the job-hunting going?* No *how's life with Adrian?*

They ordered, touched glasses and Vin began. Putting her hand over his, she said 'Alex, I'm going to Italy'.

As her words sank in, he felt an ache take hold of his insides. *What does she mean?*

'I'm not going away from you, Alex; I'm going to Nonna.'

'Has something happened?'

'She's in the early stages of Alzheimer's, and needs someone to be there for her.'

'Couldn't you bring her home? I mean, back here?' *Wasn't there some other way, a way which didn't involve Vin going away?*

'The village means so much to her, Alex. She still has good friends there. And grandpa's grave is there. We think it would be wrong to bring her here, to add to her confusion.'

Family ties. Ties to place. Had Alex not been bound to his island home by the call of his father, he would have gone with this girl in a flash. This girl who had come to mean so much to him.

They fell silent as the spicy fish entrée arrived.

'Alex, I'd never forgive myself if I didn't go to her.' Her eyes asked for understanding.

Alex met her eyes and nodded, for a moment unable to speak. Through his misery he admired Vin for her readiness to make such a sacrifice for her grandmother, for her family.

'Where's her village?'

'It's a small town called *Buti*, close to Pisa, in Toscana—Tuscany. I've only seen photos. It looks lovely. Beautiful countryside.'

Alex only half heard as Vin explained her grandmother's situation and talked about passports, work permits and airline timetables. *How can she be so matter-of fact?*

'Alex,' she reached over and took both his hands in hers, 'I'm releasing you.' She held his eyes with her own. 'But with a warning: if you're still about when I come back, I'll snavel you up.' At which they both laughed, the laughter curdled with tears.

They were setting out into a new chapter of their lives; he, a new job somewhere, she, a new country.

Apart.

escape

THAT FRIDAY, at the end of a pummelling fortnight, Alex met Karl for a drink and a meal. Karl was one of the survivors; his small firm was impacted only slightly by the financial crisis, just one extravagant house extension parked on a Toorak shelf until better times.

Alex was sorry the footy season was over; he would have welcomed a night at the 'G', having a few beers and yelling his lungs out. Yelling at the greedy perpetrators of the GFC. Yelling even louder at the insidious condition stalking poor Nonna and grievously wounding him in the process.

Instead, over a gourmet pizza in High Street, he was asking for Karl's input to a mailing list he was putting together. He intended to email to a list of prospective employers an enquiry about employment prospects. It needed to be done, and it would take his mind off Vin.

'WD Design?'

'Yep.'

'Lyons?'

'Yep.'

'DCM?'

'Yep.'

'P&W?'

'Yeah.'

'Any small practices?' Karl refilled his chianti.

'I'll do them in the second round.'

'Fullertons?'

'No, but good idea. I'll add them.'

'Snoopy?'

'Yeah' (a chuckle).

'Who are you leaving out, then?'

'All the firms that we know for sure are laying off. And the sole practitioners, at least for now.'

'What about interstate?'

'Maybe Tassie,' Alex wiped his fingers on his napkin and picked up his pen, 'Yeah, I'll add a few of the better firms there. A long shot though.'

* * *

Looking at his in-box became a dispiriting activity. *These practices have other things on their minds, other priorities.* That was Alex's explanation for the scant response to his emails. Only a few replies straggled in to his in-box. Polite but negative. At least they answered.

His innate optimism was under siege. His reserves, both financial and emotional, were being depleted. A laboring job would do for a while, be good in fact. But those poor buggers are out of work too.

He sat in a local bar reading the employment pages and nursing a tall beer, his third. Or maybe it was his fourth.

The pub was a dangerous place; the room lurched as he stood to seek out the bathroom.

Shit. Shit. Shit.

* * *

It was inevitable that Alex would go bush. If he couldn't lose himself in the tumult of the stadium, then maybe he would find his equilibrium in the quiet of the bush.

I get it, dad. Your lone trips to the bush. But what devils drove you there?

* * *

It was an area he'd not been to before. In the island's north-east, overlooking the strait. Between the trees, the water shone. Shadows were beginning to lengthen; he must find a place to camp.

On the walk in he had not managed to outdistance his nagging thoughts. The air fares for this little escapade had pushed his credit card to its limit; his savings account was under threat; obviously no-one wanted to hire him; and would the dole be enough to pay his rent?

This spot might do for the night. Yes, it was a good site. Sheltered, backed into a rise, outlook towards the water

Hello, someone had been here before him—a long time ago, by the look of it. That had surely been a fireplace.

As he began to clear an area close to the bank to pitch his small tent, his hand encountered a tangle of branches. A tangle whose pattern he

knew. He looked with new eyes. Here, against the rising ground, against all odds, was surely the handiwork of his father.

What irony, that he should find this place now. Now, when he was not looking for it.

But perhaps that was the answer. Perhaps some replication, some echo of his father's emotions, his need to escape, had led him here. Led him to this place where the comforting enclosure of the bush encountered the wide, blue-grey mystery of the ocean.

Perhaps, instead of relying on a rational reading of his map, he should have allowed his feelings to point the way. Could that be how he would find the final place? The place in the Tarkine?

homecoming

AMONG THE messages, a sender's name stood out: w.carey@abcarchitects. It would be a polite *How are you? Love to have you back, but unfortunately...* sort of message. To Alex's surprise, it was not.

Alexander Gardner

From: w.carey@abcarchitects.com
Sent: Friday 30th October 2008 11:14 AM
To: Alexander Gardner <alex.gardner@quickmail.com.au>
Subject: Employment

Hello Alex

Good to hear from you, but sorry to hear about your lay-off from BNG.
Tassie is certainly not immune from the effects of the GFC, but our circumstances here at ABC are a bit unusual. You'll probably be surprised to learn that we're actually looking for a young architect at the moment. Woops, not allowed to say young.
We could only commit for twelve months, after that, who knows?
I think you would probably fit the bill, but the directors would need to meet with you to hear what you've been up to since you were last here.
We could pay your way over for an interview. If you're still interested, give me a call and we can set things up.

With warm regards
William

Alex re-read the message, allowing his feelings to settle. Vin's absence from Melbourne, perhaps from his life, would certainly make it easier for him to accept William's offer. And after all, he'd always intended to return to Tassie some day. Now fate, in the guise of the Global Financial Crisis, was nudging him back home sooner than he had expected.

* * *

The flight to the island was smooth; the skies were clear, with no hidden bumps. Below, the strait gave way to the familiar coast, where the low morning sun cast the rolling terrain into sharp relief. Even the sadness he carried for Vin could not entirely banish Alex's keen sense of anticipation. He was coming home. A different person, but coming home.

The sky over the state's capital was also clear. As Alex's taxi crested the wooded Tunnel Hill, the mountain appeared, standing above the city on the far side of the river. A snug-fitting glove of white cloud was easing over its crest, to then slide down its steep face as huge pillowy fingers, fading at the foothills into a disappearing vapour—the spirit of the wilderness carried in on winds from across the world.

Through his work experience stint and some holiday contract work, Alex had come to know the Hobart–based firm of ABC Architects pretty well, he thought, as the taxi headed to their offices in Salamanca Place. It was a mid-size practice, usually numbering a dozen or so people, sometimes reaching twenty, directors included. He knew that in the Tasmanian context that made it one of the larger firms, and the practice appeared to enjoy widespread respect.

Winning the occasional design award, the work of ABC ranged across a wide spectrum of projects, from house alterations to large and complex developments, from cafés to courtrooms, from holiday homes to hotels. Alex liked that about the firm; he liked that ABC gave those who joined it the opportunity to work on many different kinds of projects. A far cry from months of detailing the most mundane parts of a huge, impersonal office building.

William, never Bill—although his wife had on occasions been heard calling him Billy—gave the business gravitas and direction. The other directors were Peter Gregory, a quiet, intelligent man with a polished sense of design and a wealth of experience in the cut-and-thrust of administering building contracts, and Sarah Devine, *Divine Sarah*, unflappable and supremely competent—he had seen her in action.

Alex's interview with the directors—a chat really—went well, despite his anxiety for the outcome. If this didn't come off, what would he do? Go back to Lonnie? Go on the dole? Help his mother with the house?

When the directors exchanged looks and smilingly offered him a position, Alex felt the weight drop from his shoulders. Then a surge of pleasure and pride. An honourable reprieve, at least for a year.

'Thank you very much, That's fantastic. I accept your offer. I'm looking forward to coming back to Tassie, and back to ABC.'

It was only as he reached across to shake hands with each of them in turn, that Alex remembered the Otway project. Should he mention it now? He hesitated, considering how to broach the subject.

'Um, a thought has come to me, which I'd like to raise with you, if you have a few more minutes.'

'Of course Alex, feel free.' William settled back on his chair and looked expectantly at Alex across his steel-framed glasses, the late morning sun catching the silver in his hair. The others appeared curious, too.

The significance of the moment did not escape Alex. Three directors of an established practice were paying him the respect of giving him their full attention. Treating him, an out-of-work P–plater, as a professional colleague. This, on top of the previous week's arrival of his certificate of registration, felt to Alex like the real beginning of his professional life. A beginning ushered in by a feeling of profound relief, then excitement tempered with trepidation—he was keenly aware of how much he had yet to learn.

'I hope this doesn't sound too presumptuous, he said, 'but it's a now-or-never opportunity. You may be aware of the Otway Ranges visitor centre design competition?'

Peter and Sarah nodded; William said: 'We toyed with the idea of preparing an entry, but gave it a miss. Too much effort for such a slim chance of success.'

'Well, off my own bat, I prepared an entry for the competition—for the experience, really,' said Alex, 'BNG had agreed to submit it jointly with me, but clearly that's not going to happen now. I can't enter on my own, as entrants must be able to demonstrate that they have the experience and resources to carry the design commission through to completion.'

Alex paused. He couldn't read the expressions around the large table. They all looked thoughtful though, no shaking of heads.

'I'd love it if ABC would join with me to submit the entry. I'd hate to see my work just abandoned.'

This brought a little smile from all three. *Get used to it.* Courtesy rendered the common thought unspoken.

It was William who spoke first. He took off his glasses and rubbed the bridge of his nose. 'Alex, why don't you present your entry to us as soon as you can? Then we can decide if we should put our name to it. With yours, of course.'

That night, Alex phoned his mother and emailed Karl and Vincenza. He pondered briefly on how small was the number of people in his world to whom he felt close enough to tell his happy news.

Mum, I'm coming back to Tassie. I've got a good job in Hobart. Back at ABC. I'll be able to get to Lonnie much more often.

Karl, ABC wants me back! They might even join with me to submit my Otway design. Fingers crossed.

Hello Vin. A quick note: I want to share some news with you. I've accepted a job in Tassie, in Hobart. I think it will get me closer to the sort of work I want to do. You'll remember. I hope things are going ok with your nonna. Love, Alex. PS I'm registered as an architect now. (So is Karl.)

* * *

The directors and staff of ABC were gathered in the spacious conference room, whose two classically-proportioned windows looked out through the heavy sandstone façade on to Salamanca Place.

'Most of you will remember Alex Gardner; Alex is joining ABC— or perhaps I should say re-joining—as of now.' William was leading proceedings at the practice's weekly after-work professional development session. 'Tonight Alex is going to take us through a design he prepared while in Melbourne. Don't give him too hard a time,' William smiled, 'I'm sure Alex would be interested in any comments we may have, but let's save them until he's finished.'

Alex had loaded his electronic files into the room's audio-visual system and, as he spoke, he brought up the images on the room's large screen.

Referring frequently to the images, he described to his new colleagues the Otway competition brief, his analysis of the location and site, and his carefully documented design proposal.

Alex had found the moody, layered hills beautiful. He saw the bush and its creatures through the eyes of one who loved these places, and he was quick to pick up on those things which made this place special. His challenging task, as an architect, was to open the eyes of visitors to the centre to those same things.

What Alex hadn't revealed to the directors until that evening, was the fact that his design was not for the site nominated by the Shire Council, but for an alternative site nearby. He explained to the gathering that his preferred site was located at the head of a long valley, at the end of which the sea—Bass Strait—could be seen.

'That glimpse of the sea gives this location a quality that cannot be built. It establishes where this place is in the world. It orientates; it connects. And,' he clicked up a diagrammatic map, 'not only is the panorama superior from this location, but the site is more conveniently located in relation to walking and bike trails. See?'

'I'm not concerned that Alex's design is for an alternative site,' said Peter Gregory, rolling a slim black pen between long manicured fingers, 'I think we all know that it is often the entry that breaks the competition rules which wins the day.'

'Quite,' said William. 'Thank you, Alex. Well done. He glanced at his fellow directors. 'We'll have a chat about it and let you know.'

* * *

Alex had found a flat to his liking, where most of his belongings were yet to be unpacked.

The flat was on the north-eastern side of one of the hills which made up the inner suburb of West Hobart. The first rays of the sun lined the walls of his living room with brilliant bands of gold. On the back wall, a square window offered an oblique view back to the mountain, whose proud brow was just visible above the forested outline of the looming hill, Knocklofty. Alex was soon to discover that the many walking trails through the gum trees of the Knocklofty reserve were only a few minutes walk from his chosen new address.

The decision to take this flat, the lesser half of a divided Federation-style house, had been an easy one. The rent was affordable, the flat was of adequate size, had its own quirky character, a bit of back-yard, and was within easy riding and walking distance of the centre of the city. But above all, Alex loved that he knew exactly where he was, on this hillside between river and mountain.

He came to enjoy the going-down and the coming-up, the free-wheeling descent to the city centre and the demanding climb at work-day's end. Together they somehow laced his connection to this hilly city, reminded him daily of the nature of the place where he now lived, and that the natural world would not be levelled for his convenience

* * *

'I can tell you all now,' William announced to the regular ABC team meeting, 'that ABC will be helping Alex to fine-tune his Otways design. We'll lend our weight to meeting all of the competition's assessment criteria—those regarding resources, for instance.' He smiled at Alex. 'There's quite a bit of work to do, but we will join with you, Alex, in submitting this entry.'

a practice

'READING THE BIBLE?' Alex hadn't noticed Peter Gregory standing in one of the aisles, a glass manufacturer's catalogue open in his hands.

'Yeah,' Alex smiled, 'I'm finding it quite absorbing.'

Peter raised an eyebrow and went back to his reflections on glass. He took the thick folder with him and disappeared from the ABC library.

Reading the practice's carefully maintained and up-dated history, *The Evolution of ABC Architects*, was a far from tedious part of the firm's orientation routine; it was, for Alex, a compelling insight into his chosen profession. And he enjoyed the informal style of the document, largely taken as it was from the transcripts of a series of commissioned oral histories.

Alex read that ABC Architects had its roots in the 1930s when young Harry Anders, financed by his proud mother and reassured by her wide network of quite well-to-do friends, set up a modest second-floor office in the centre of Hobart. In the fifties Harry took on a young partner, James Bradden, a hard-worker who slowly built up the client base and reputation of the practice.

To Alex, who harboured an ambition to one day set up his own practice, this was all good stuff. He had made himself a coffee—his own mug now— and had taken the document into the firm's small library, a space crowded with catalogues, samples, building codes and reference books, where he cleared himself some space at a half-buried table. For how much longer, he wondered, would an architectural practice need to keep its own library, in this increasingly connected, digital age?

Alex sipped at his coffee and went on with his reading. When, in the sixties, William Carey arrived as the office junior, Harry Anders was an imposing figure: a larger-than-life man who came and went to and from his business and community activities, and while in the office was usually seen perched precariously on his drafting stool, hunched over his huge drawing-board, moving with practised ease his set square and long wooden tee-square to draw lines on large linen sheets with his ink drawing pens.

'Still here?' Peter Gregory was returning the catalogue. He looked vaguely along the shelves and turned to Alex. 'Could you put this back for me?'

'Of course.'

Peter looked at Alex. 'This really interests you, doesn't it?'

'It does. I suppose it's a bit like a family tree. I like to see how things fit together, how generations connect, how it all comes about.'

A passing reference in the document to the time of the Vietnam war gave pause to Alex. Wouldn't William be about the same age as his father? Had he been called up too? Perhaps he was one of the lucky ones.

If reading the firm's history had not been a requirement of his induction into the practice, Alex would have felt guilty about spending so long sitting in the firm's library. He walked to the tea-room and made a fresh cup of coffee. Too much coffee, he would have to go back to green tea.

According to the *Evolution*, when in the mid-seventies, following the retirement of Harry Anders, James Bradden had invited William to become a partner, neither man thought of the happenstance of their initials: A, B, and C. In those days the promotion of architects, as with other professions, was strictly limited, both by the profession's own code of ethics and by law. Advertising was forbidden and, for architects, lettering on any sign was limited to three inches in height—just big enough to make out from the other side of the road, if you squinted.

Harry Anders had died of a massive heart attack only two years after his retirement.

It was much later, near the coming of the new millenium, after James Bradden had retired, that the company took on the trading name of ABC Architects. The opportunities for marketing catch-cries were endless. Beginning with: *Choosing your architect: easy as ABC.*

Alex closed the *Evolution* volume and sat quietly for a moment. Did his future lie with this practice? Might he eventually become another name in the ABC family tree? Is that what he wanted?

Well, for now he would savour being back on his home island, give his best to the ABC family, and see what opportunities arose.

postcards

A POSTCARD. It was the third that Alex had found in his West Hobart letterbox since Vin's departure. On the first two, every square centimetre had been tightly patterned every–which–way with Vin's neat hand-writing. This was a much larger one, posted in mid-February 2009; it portrayed a collection of photographs of a place called Lucca. Again, Vin's message roamed around both faces of the card, becoming tiny as the available space failed to measure up.

Hello Alex. I've discovered that my Italian is not as good as I thought. A broad Australian accent, apparently, and I often get the colloquialisms quite wrong. Scema! Nonna is not too bad, but her memory lapses are getting more frequent and I know there will come a time when she's lost to me. That's really hard. Congratulations on your new job at ABC. I remember how you liked the people there. Alex, I've got a job too. I've landed a part-time job in Lucca, about twenty minutes away by bus. Lucca is amazing, stupefacente. You'd love it. It's a beautiful mediaeval walled town (as you can see) packed with character and history. I'll send you some of my photos. Maybe by email, whenever I can get that up and running. This whole region gets busy in the warmer months, with tourists coming to visit Pisa and Florence in particular. Haven't seen those places yet, but I will. Alex, guess what! I'm buying a motor-scooter! A second-hand Vespa. Of course you'll want to know the specs: 2000 model, ET4 125cc. Red, importantly (red is faster). Now I won't have to rely on bus timetables. And how about this, Alex: when I took nonna outside to show her the scooter, she climbed straight on the back! No kidding. Nonna's mind may be going, but she's still remarkably nimble for one her age. I must ask Papa, but I'm guessing that she rode pillion as a young woman. Passeggera. Alex, lest my chatty messages may cause you to think otherwise: I really miss you. Love, Vin

a butler's pantry

A SCATTERERING of lozenge-shaped shadows rose and fell across the sunburnt musculature of the mountain's lower slopes. Above, the parent clouds hurried as one across a cerulean sky. A warm, breezy February day in Hobart.

'Alex, we'd like you to take on the role of design architect for an apartment project in Sandy Bay.' William and Sarah were seated at a table by one of the windows overlooking Salamanca Place. The morning sun streamed in.

'Sarah will be the responsible director,' said William.

When Alex had first heard Sarah referred to as Divine Sarah, in an earlier chapter of his life, he had conjured up an image of a lovely woman with an hour-glass figure and long blond hair. (So much for his liberation from dumb male pre-conceptions. But he was younger then.)

In fact, Sarah lived up to her whispered sobriquet. A pleasant-looking but unspectacular woman of indeterminate age, generously put together, with short, dark hair, Sarah was a giving, good-humoured person who oozed competence, was comfortable in any company, and for whom no favour asked was too much trouble.

'That's great.' Alex was delighted that he would be working with her. And the project sounded both interesting and challenging. He was mentally rolling up his sleeves already.

Sarah introduced Alex to Crichton and Felicity St John-Hall in the ABC meeting room a week later. Alex couldn't help but feel that he was being paraded for inspection, but perhaps that was just his own insecurity, his consciousness of his professional P plates. So he adopted what he hoped was a confident, assured manner, attempting to allay any misgivings that the client couple might otherwise have had.

The clients were a striking couple. The man's handshake was strong, his hands manicured and tanned, as was the man himself. A fit-looking fifty-something with distinguished silver-grey flashes to his dark hair, his glimpsed gold watch and immaculate clothes whispered *wealth*. The woman's grip was firm, and as warm as her smile. An attractive woman who clearly took care with her appearance, she had long blond (blonded?) hair with just a hint of soft wave, and wore a jaunty designer dress with a hard-to-ignore clutch of cleavage, and statement shoes.

Alex had already been told by Sarah that the St John-Halls wanted to dispose of their old house with its large grounds and move to an apartment specifically designed to their requirements—'bespoke' as Felicity and other viewers of the British *Grand Designs* television series had learned to say.

'Crichton's business takes him overseas a lot, and sometimes I go with him,' Felicity directed this at Alex, with a conspiratorial smile, 'so a big house with a big garden doesn't make much sense for us anymore. If it ever did.'

Crichton smiled faintly at this, and Alex thought his eyes held a hint of *here we go again*. 'The grounds are nice for entertaining, darling,' he reminded his wife. His voice was as smooth as his attire.

'Have you seen our new block, Alex?' Felicity asked.

The couple had acquired a large river-front lot in lower Sandy Bay and had approached ABC to design a group of low-rise apartments on the site. They would retain one of these and sell the others 'to the right kind of people'.

'No, not yet. Sarah and I plan to inspect it this afternoon.'

'I think you'll be impressed.'

Alex was indeed impressed. The large site rolled down from the road towards the river, where it fell away down an abrupt bank to a narrow, rocky beach. A plain, pre-war, weatherboard cottage sat defiantly in the middle of the block, its days clearly numbered by the advancing ideas of Felicity and Crichton St John-Hall.

'What an outlook,' Alex said to Sarah, as they stood on a dry, sadly neglected lawn behind the house, gazing out across the Derwent estuary towards the distant hills of Opossum Bay. Alex imagined watching the Sydney-Hobart yachts come up the river, cruise ships pass by, dolphins leaping, even the occasional whale. An image flashed into his mind of Felicity, alluring in filmy, flowing white, champagne flute in hand, captivating a colourful crowd of envious guests on a broad terrace overlooking the river.

'What does the planning scheme allow, Sarah?' Alex asked, pushing the vision to one side.

'There are strict limits on height, to preserve the views from other houses and to retain the prevailing scale, also constraints on setbacks, the number of dwellings and the aggregate floor area,' Sarah explained, 'but you should check all that for yourself, please Alex. Before you start drawing any lines.'

He would. But he knew already, because Sarah had said as much to the clients, that it was likely that the site could accommodate five or six large dwellings—apartments or conjoined houses. The challenge for Alex, of course with help and guidance from Sarah, would be to produce a design which optimised the development of the site, making it work financially for the clients, and which included an apartment—a home—which would meet the no doubt demanding expectations of Felicity and Crichton.

* * *

Alex was using ABC's standard briefing checklist as he chatted with Felicity Saint John-Hall in the airy living room of her grand, Victorian house in upper Sandy Bay.

'I'll leave a blank copy of our briefing data sheet with you Mrs Saint John...'

'Felicity, please.'

'Felicity. This might look a bit bureaucratic, but it's important that we understand your requirements. Otherwise we'd be wasting your time and ours.' That was a line he had heard William say; he hoped it carried at least some of the same weight when he said it.

Felicity St John-Hall arranged herself languidly on the paisley patterned chesterfield, kicking off her shoes and drawing her legs up under herself in a manner which Alex found a little unsettling. How old would she be, he wondered. Mid forties?

'Felicity, as well as listing your room requirements and suchlike, we should talk about your lifestyle, how you will use the apartment.'

As they chatted, and he made occasional notes, Alex learned that Crichton and Felicity wanted an elegant, restful home which reflected their sophisticated tastes, allowed them to display their growing collection of artworks, and was well-suited to the entertainment of guests. And don't forget a secure garage for the cars: one Porsche, one RangeRover.

Talk of the kitchen and its role in entertaining made Alex think of his mother's small kitchen in Launceston: Formica benchtops and painted cupboard doors. He was on a steep learning curve. Was he up to it?

'And of course,' said Felicity, 'I will need a generous butler's pantry'.

'Yes, of course'. *Surely she doesn't have a butler? Of course not, don't be stupid. Don't embarrass yourself, Alex. Just note it down and check later.*

Back at the office, Alex grabbed the phone.

'Hi Karl. Quick question: what's a butler's pantry?'

He heard Karl click his desk phone onto speaker, and pictured him leaning back on his leather-and-chrome chair in the studio in leafy Hawthorn.

'Aha. You're doing a high-end house, aren't you?'

'Apartment actually, but yes.'

He listened while Karl explained that the term was a throw-back to earlier times, when a family's butler looked after the precious settings and tableware, etc, and oversaw some of the preparation in his own area, out of the view of guests, a kind of transition area between the kitchen—which of course was always out of sight—and the formal dining area.

'Nowadays, mate, the open kitchen is *de rigeur*, isn't it? But you still need to tuck some things away out of sight. So your up-market residence needs an area just off the kitchen to keep unsightly things and stuff that's not used often, and where a mess can be made without offending anyone's sensibilities. There are no rules, mate, it's just what you and your client work out.'

* * *

'Well, we've established the aisle width, haven't we?' Felicity smiled at Alex. They were meeting again in her Sandy Bay house, and were standing in its large but outmoded kitchen discussing her requirements for the butler's pantry in the new apartment.

Felicity was something of a puzzle to Alex: an attractive and clearly intelligent woman, apparently childless (no request for a nursery), with no sign of any employment (did she have business interests?). Her husband, Crichton, gave every indication of being a driven man, absorbed in his business affairs, but what of his wife? Perhaps Alex would learn more as the project proceeded.

'Lots of bench space, please. At least this much.' Felicity gestured as she walked along the kitchen. 'I think perhaps a pot sink. Washing up big things can be awkward, can't it? Lots of storage. I'm thinking maybe glass-fronted cupboards? So we can see where everything is. Especially useful when we have someone in to help. A wine fridge, so our whites and bubbles can be pre-chilled. Of course a food pantry, close to the kitchen and the main refrigerator.' Felicity opened the doors of their generous walk-in pantry cupboard. 'This size would be fine.'

She closed the door and looked down at a hand-written page fastened to a red leather clipboard. 'I've thought about what we need to keep in the butler's pantry. I'll give you this list,' she said, then proceeded to read it out.

'Our *Doulton* dinner set,' she opened a cupboard door and pointed.

'Our everyday dinner set. This one.

Our silver flatware,' opening a drawer, '*Christofle*, so gorgeous.

Our *Alessi* cutlery.

Our crystal glasses. *Orrefors*.

Our everyday glasses. Nice, aren't they?

Tea sets, we have several. You'd like this post modern set.

Coffee set; don't you love art deco?

Platters, various ; I love this *Carltonware* one.

Decanters.

Carafes, these two. Look at the *Orrefors* one.

Our pitchers, I love the *Starke*.

Ice buckets. Simple, but nice, aren't they?

Citrus squeezer. *Alessi*. Cute, isn't it?

Our condiment cruet sets.

And our everyday condiment sets. A bit of fun.

Our candelabra. *Georg Jensen*. Isn't it something?

Various trays. Under here.

And I think we'll keep our vases in here, too. I'll show them to you, there's quite a few.

The food processor.

Kitchenware accessories.

Egg-cups. *Alessi*. Aren't they lovely?

I think the coffee machine could be either here or in the kitchen. It'd be nice to have it on show.

And of course there are the usual appliances: electric kettle, toaster, sandwich maker, kitchen scales, mixers … oh, that reminds me, I'll be getting a *thermo-mixer*.'

As Felicity St John-Hall read through her list, it occurred to Alex that in days gone by the household butler would probably have maintained such an inventory. And that Leonard Hay, who had mentored ABC's founding father Harry Anders, probably planned a few butlers' pantries in the early twentieth century, when he designed grand homes for the wealthy merchants of Hobart.

From nowhere, images of the simple cooking arrangements in the village houses of India came to him, the few meagre pots and pans kept proudly polished. And, in a poignant recollection, he saw the simple implements that his father utilised in his bush shelters.

Not for the first time, he felt uneasy at such an extravagant display of wealth. It was something that he and Karl had talked about, his friend advising him to set aside any such misgivings and focus on his client's needs. Make that *wants*.

'Alex?' Felicity had reached the end of her list and was regarding him quizzically.

'Sorry, Felicity, I was, um, starting to think about the design ramifications.'

She graced him with a warm smile, and touched his arm. 'Good. We should also take an inventory of the artworks we'll want to display in the new place. Why don't we do that next time?'

success

Vincenza Genovese

From: alex.gardner@ABCarchitects.com.au
Sent: Tuesday 12th March 2009 8:10 AM
To: Vincenza Genovese <Vin.Gen@gmail.com.it>
Subject: Otway Success

Hello Vin,

Some good news at my end.

Do you remember that I put in an entry for the Otway design competition, with ABC? Well, I've just been advised that my entry has been awarded second prize!

Yes, I know you dislike exclamation marks, but at least I didn't underline it or, even worse, use caps. (My finger lingers over that cursed key even now…) Anyway, can you hear the excitement in my voice? I can't wait to tell William when he comes in.

The beauty of coming second in an architectural design competition (have I bored you with this before?) is that your entry remains a beautiful, seductive idea, never to be tested against the rigors of reality. Could you actually build the thing? Would it cost too much? Would it work? How would the real thing measure up against the vision?
Plus, Vin, you usually get some money for your efforts – in this case $20,000, thank you very much. Half for me! (Sorry, there's another one.)
And, your entry inevitably gets some exposure in architectural journals.
(Did you notice, Signorina Syntax, how I avoided the underline there, by using *italics* for emphasis?)
Think I'd better quit while I'm ahead…

By the way, the apartment job I told you about is getting underway, briefing and design, I mean. Interesting clients.

Trust all is well with you. What's spring like in Tuscany?

Love,
Alex

PS Karl is coming over for a visit next weekend. Usually it's me going to Melbourne .

Alex Gardner

From: Vincenza Genovese <Vin.Gen@gmail.com.it>
Sent: Tuesday 12th March 2009 11.05 AM
To: alex.gardner@ABCarchitects.com.au
Subject: Otway Success

How exciting Alex! Congratulations!

Alright, Mr Smartypants, maybe some things do warrant exclamation marks. And yes, this word nerd does approve of your use of italics.

I'm excited for you too, Alex. Please let me know how William reacts, and what exposure you get. And say hello to Karl from me when you see him.

Bravo,
Vin.

Spring in Tuscany? It's still quite cold now, but I'll get back to you on that.

Vincenza Genovese

From: alex.gardner@ABCarchitects.com.au
Sent: Tuesday 12th March 2009 1:35 PM
To: Vincenza Genovese <Vin.Gen@gmail.com.it>
Subject: Smart Alex

Hey Vin, my dad used to call me Smartypants.
He would have loved you.

Alex.

felicitations

'CONGRATULATIONS, ALEX.' Felicity had seen the local newspaper's report on the Otways competition, a happy William having alerted the press to the involvement of ABC, and Alex in particular. 'I'm very impressed. It seems I'm working with a talented designer.'

Alex, inwardly quite chuffed, mumbled a modest reply.

Alex and Felicity were again in the kitchen of her Sandy Bay home. They had been touring the big house, comparing her present accommodation with that which the new apartment was intended to provide. Felicity had some time ago kicked off her shoes and was padding around in little–girl white socks worn with bare legs and a fifties–style flared summer dress. On–trend, Alex presumed. Provocative, undoubtedly.

'The butler's pantry itself need not be very wide, Alex. Just wide enough for two people to use the space at the same time, if a particular need arises.'

'I'll allow one-point-one metres clear aisle width then', responded Alex, adding to the jottings in his stylish black notebook.

'Let's make sure, Alex.' Felicity took hold of the large pine kitchen table with her elegant, manicured hands and dragged it noisily across the quarry tile floor until it stood about a metre away from the bench containing the kitchen sink; she then straightened it up, parallel to the bench.

'You stand here', Felicity shepherded Alex to a spot with his back against the table, 'and I'll be working here'.

To Alex's growing discomfiture, she took up a position between him and the sink, turned her back to him, then bent over the sink as if working at it. As she did, the light material of her dress came against him and he felt the soft roundness of her buttocks press into him. As if to demonstrate the inadequacy of the space, she nudged gently against him.

'I think I'd like a little more,' she said, all businesslike.

'OK, let's make it one-point-three metres, then.' There was a strange croak in Alex's voice. He was finding it hard to breath. *His* particular need had quickly arisen.

Back at the office, he made himself a calming cup of herbal tea and took it to his desk, where he tried in vain to focus on matters architectural. God, he'd fantasised about a woman like that coming on to him. *Was* Felicity coming on to him? He couldn't misread those signals, could he? What were the ethical considerations?

* * *

Alex knew that he should have insisted that his next meeting with Felicity be at the ABC office, but she really was hard to say no to. And did he really want to say no?

This time they were meeting in the mansion's large formal dining room. The Lincoln green walls were adorned with gilt-framed paintings by early colonial painters. Alex thought he recognised a Haughton Forrest, and that was certainly a Glover. He had noticed some impressive contemporary works in other rooms, and was looking forward to inspecting them more closely, when he and Felicity made their inventory. The large painting just might be an Olsen, and that was surely a Ben Quilty he had spied, wasn't it?

Sunlight, dappled by the exotic trees outside, entered through a wide bay window, imbuing the dining room with a warm domesticity and providing more than sufficient light for the drawings to be closely examined. Alex spread out his developed design drawings on the huge mahogany table. He sat and turned them to where Felicity would be able to read them.

'Isn't it easier if I come to your side of the table, Alex?'

'No that's fine, thanks Felicity. I can read the plans upside down just as well.' Which was true, but Alex also thought it was better if he kept an appropriate distance between them.

As if not convinced by his reply, Felicity moved to his side of the table. Her simple dress wafted as she moved, its silky fabric caressing her form. She stood peering down at the large sheets of drawings.

'So, what's this area here?' she asked, leaning over and pointing, the light of the window reflecting on her red-painted nails and gilding her hair, which fell freely around her face. He was aware of her scent and her warmth. And, oh God, how her breasts moved with such disconcerting freedom under that dress.

'That's something I wanted to talk to you about. It's my suggestion for a gallery space, a sort of atrium, linking these other zones of the apartment without the need for constricting passages'.

'Mmmmm', it seemed to be an appreciative response. His client moved a little closer, all the better to see.

The room seemed suddenly to have closed in on the two people at the table. Felicity's side, her thigh and hip, so near under the thin fabric, now pressed lightly against Alex.

'There should be plenty of wall space for your paintings. I'll verify that when we do the inventory of your collection.'

'I can see it getting bigger, Alex. Our collection.'

As she leaned further over the drawings, a line was crossed. Alex's left hand moved, as if quite independent of him, and curved around Felicity's shapely calf. The skin was smooth, so smooth, and warm, so warm. She did not move away.

'You could use the gallery to display some of your wonderful artworks. The light quality should be ideal, with this orientation.' Alex's voice had taken on a little tremor. His hand moved upwards, examining the shape of her knee and gently kneading the soft flesh behind it. Discovering, savouring. She moved a little against him.

'I think it's a wonderful concept, Alex. You're very talented.' Her voice was soft. Distracted.

He dare not look, but from the corner of his eye he was aware that her painted index finger, no longer pointing, was absently tracing little circles around her left nipple, proudly evident through the thin fabric.

While the propelling pencil in his right hand continued to float over the features of the design, his left hand rose higher. The feel of her thigh intoxicated him. He was quiet now, not wishing to disturb her compliance, break the beautiful spell. His hand rose to where it closed the divide between her thighs.

'I'm pretty confident that this…can all be achieved…inside your…your budget,' he managed.

'That's good Alex. I'm getting quite excited'.

And with another incremental movement, he felt a little frisson of shock as his errant left hand arrived at the moist softness of her uncovered womanhood. *When did she dispense with her knickers?*

Un-noticed, his chaste pencil was wavering slightly above the word *bedroom.*

a sorry affair

HIS NEXT VISIT was pre-meditated. There was nothing spontaneous about it. Nor was there any professional purpose.

'Hello Felicity. Alex here.'

'Good morning, Alex.'

'Can we get together? There are some things…' *Was his voice shaking?*

'Yes, of course.' Hers was low and warm.

'Are you at home?'

'Yes. Can you come at eleven?'

'Uh huh.'

'And, Alex…'

'Yes?'

'Park around the back.'

* * *

Alex's phone was ringing. He picked it up from the bedside table and looked at the screen. It was Sarah.

Should he take the call? He looked at the bathroom door. Yes, he would answer it quickly.

'Hello? Sarah?'

'Oh, Alex. I need you; where are you now?'

'Um, Sandy Bay…'

'Can you be back here in an hour? Something's come up. We need to meet with the building surveyor.'

Alex was about to respond when Felicity emerged from the en-suite bathroom, wrapped in a towel and talking gaily. And loudly.

'Goodness Alex. How did you come to be so good in bed? At your tender age?'

* * *

'I'm disappointed in you, Alex.'

He recalled how these words, spoken by his mother, had cut into him, years ago. This time it was Sarah Devine speaking. Sarah, who he admired and respected. Again, the words found their mark. Puffed up with his own success, he had put himself beyond the petty bounds that held back lesser persons. Puffed up, he had become smaller.

Alex's face was aflame, his insides twisting with embarrassment and shame. Dismay and disappointment at his own behavior, at letting down his colleagues. *Did they all know?* He was a boy again, being admonished by his mother.

'I shall leave it to you to see that the personal liaison is finished. Any repeat, Alex, will see you off that project, and your position in the firm reviewed.'

Would Sarah tell the other directors? Tell William? *Mum, please don't tell dad.*

He emailed Felicity (copies to her husband and to Sarah) proposing a time and date for their next meeting, this time in the ABC conference room. He added a note: *Bearing in mind the stage we have reached, it is more appropriate that in future we meet at the ABC offices.*

Crichton was again unable to attend. He was still somewhere in China. Felicity was relaxed and composed. *She looked so good.* Sarah sat in for most of the meeting, allowing him to manage proceedings. Alex knew she must be watching them. Imagining, probably.

After discussing the preliminary design, Alex presented to his client an outline program for the project: design to be finalised by early April, development application to be lodged in mid-May, contract documentation to be completed by the end of July, the tender process to take place in August, commencement of construction in early September, with a target completion date in November the following year, 2010.

Felicity seemed content with the progress of the design, and accepted Alex's timetable.

Sarah excused herself and left Alex to wrap up the meeting. Left him, perhaps, to wrap up personal affairs.

The meeting over, Felicity shook Alex's hand. When she smiled and gave his hand a little squeeze, it was a silent acknowledgement of what had happened between them and confirmation of what they both knew: that it would not happen again.

As he saw her out, he glanced in the direction of William's office. William was watching.

* * *

Felicity was gorgeous. Seductive. He was young and male. They were adults. Was he being too hard on himself?

No, the guilt and shame were deserved. She was a client. A married client. He was an impartial professional consultant. Bound by a code of ethics to do nothing to lessen respect for and confidence in his profession. Well, he had certainly lost some respect, hadn't he?

Then there was Vin. Beautiful, clever, funny Vin. No longer with him. His thoughts always seemed to return to her. They had released each other, hadn't they? So why did he feel shame when he thought of her?

It had been quite a while since he had contacted her. He sat at the table in his flat and opened his laptop.

Vincenza Genovese

From: alex.gardner@quickmail.com.au
Sent: Wednesday 12th June 2009 8:31 AM
To: Vincenza Genovese <Vin.Gen@gmail.com.it>
Subject: G'Day Girl

Hello Vin.

Thanks for your letters and postcards. Keep 'em coming, I love receiving them. Perhaps one day I'll write you a good old-fashioned letter too.
I haven't got into Skype yet; Do you use it? Let me know and we'll give it a go.

Sorry to hear that your nonna's memory is fading. That must be so hard for you.

Is the scooter going well? I'm envious about that. Tootling around Tuscany sounds a bit more exciting than riding out to Richmond.
Have you felt the pull of Rome yet?

Anything more to report about your writing?

Mum is glad to have me back closer to Lonnie. I'm going up there next weekend, then over to the Tarkine for a few days. I won't stop looking.

Work at ABC is going well; I have felt very welcome there.

Vin, a confession: I have behaved badly. Been grossly un-professional. I'm too ashamed to give you details. I think perhaps the Otway success went to my head, but that's probably just my attempt to find some excuse. Be warned: sometimes I'm not very nice.

Love,
Alex

extremities

THE MOUNTAIN was pure white this morning, dressed in its best winter garb. Inside, in the ABC rooms overlooking Salamanca Place with its rows of naked plane trees, the peering morning sun was welcome. From here, the mountain was not visible, but its presence was always felt.

When, after six months at ABC, William ushered Alex into his office, Alex felt a surge of apprehension, echoes of his BNG experience. Was work running out? Or was this the moment of reckoning for his misdemeanour with Felicity St John-Hall? William had seemed a little distant of late. Or was that just his imagination? His guilty conscience?

As William began, Alex's apprehension soon evaporated; his breathing returned to normal.

'Alex, I've been very impressed with your work. You relate well to the others, and our clients seem to like you,' his eyes met Alex's. 'You make elegant design decisions quickly. That's a rare ability.'

'Thank you, William, but I'm only part of a great team.' He would not be puffed up again.

'Yes, we do have a good team. Alex, I'd like you to help us on the Greentree Lodge project.'

Alex's heart lifted. This is why he had become an architect. He had heard the directors talking about the challenging wilderness lodge proposed by their client, tourism guru Martin Greentree, through his business *Wild South*, and had assumed that the directors would hold such a plum job close to their chests.

'We suddenly have several new school projects in the office, each with a ridiculously short time frame,' William said. 'Kevin's money.'

Alex understood that William was referring to the 'Building the Nation' programme, an economic stimulus package hurriedly put together by Prime Minister Kevin Rudd and his government, intended to inject money into the country's economy and stimulate activity in order to limit the damage of the GFC.

William swivelled in his chair and gazed out at the bare trees. 'We have to spend this money as wisely as the limited time will allow and impress our government clients in the process. That will call upon every director and associate to bring his or her experience to bear.' He turned back to Alex. 'The Greentree project is new, fresh, and suited to your skills. Knowledge of the bureaucratic processes is not so imperative. And where it is needed, we can help you.'

Alex's excitement was mounting. 'It sounds great, William, I'd love to be involved'.

'Good, I thought you would'.

'What about Felicity ... the Riverbank Apartments? 'They're just about ready to go to tender.' Although excited by the prospect of the new project, Alex knew he would be unable to abruptly excise from his mind the job he had been so intimately involved with, come to regard as *his* project, if the truth be known. And Felicity and Crichton as *his* clients.

'Don't worry, we won't cut you out of that. I know you'll want to stay in touch with the project. And with the client.'

Don't blush.

'What do you think about asking Samuel to administer the construction phase of the job,' continued William, 'calling you in where any design decisions need to be made? If you like, you could attend the formal site meetings too.'

This seemed like a good idea to Alex. He liked Samuel Parata, whose misplaced vowels and hint of Maori in his appearance affirmed his Kiwi origins. Samuel was a clever technician with top-notch CAD skills and an excellent grasp of technical matters. Alex knew from their tea-room chats that Samuel's real interest lay in sustainable building practices, and his understanding of emerging technologies and changing building regulations was impressive. Attributes not really needed in this case, but such was life in a medium-size practice.

'Yes, certainly; if Samuel's happy to do that.' Alex replied, drawing a glance from William. Then a little nod.

* * *

Alex had set aside the sports pages—the Ashes series in England was not going well for Australia—and was doodling some initial design thoughts for the intriguing Greentree project at his kitchen table, when his mobile phone rang.

He looked at the screen.

'Hello mum.'

'Alex, Grandma Pauline has died.'

'Oh…' Alex pictured the straight but frail, white-haired woman in Ballarat. His father's mother.

'Apparently she died peacefully in her sleep.'

Pauline's humour, surprisingly naughty sometimes, came to Alex first. And her direct and giving nature. His idea of the archetypal CWA stalwart, which he knew she had been until recent years. Why hadn't he asked her more about his father?

'Who will arrange her funeral?'

'Her sister's family have taken that on; they've remained close to her. Will you come over there with me?'

'Of course.'

'How are things with you, Alex?'

'Really good, thanks, mum. I'm beginning work on a new project. A wilderness lodge down at Recherche Bay. But I can tell you about that when I see you.'

'Research Bay? Your father always wanted to go there some day. I remember he read about the French expedition and their impressions of the place.'

'I didn't know that,' said Alex, immediately moved by the sad coincidence. It felt as if his own connection to the place was meant to be.

* * *

Vincenza Genovese

From: alex.gardner@ABCarchitects.com.au
Sent: Thursday 11th July 2009 11.46 AM
To: Vincenza Genovese <Vin.Gen@gmail.com.it>
Subject: Grandmothers

Buongiorno, Vincenza

How are things going with your nonna? Is she still cheerful?
Have you made it to Florence yet? On the Vespa? Send me some photos when you go, won't you?

Over here, Grandma Pauline, dad's mother, has passed away. She lived in Ballarat, remember? A good innings, though; she was 95. She out-lived my grandfather, Duncan, by nearly a quarter of a century.

Mum and I will go over to the funeral. I imagine it will be a pretty small affair. Pauline wanted to be buried in the Connorville cemetery, out near where they had their farm, and where her family memories remained. Like your nonna, I suppose, at the end she just wanted to go home.

Oh, I have a new project. A very interesting one. At the southern tip of the island. Greentree. That happens to be the name of the client, but also fits the nature of the project. More on that later.

Love,
Alex.

* * *

The next month, Alex made the trip south to Recherche Bay, on the far south coast of the island. A colleague at ABC, who had been raised in the fishing and forestry township of Southport, which claimed the title of Australia's southernmost settlement, had told him of the beauty and solitude of the place. And of its history, for this was where an early French scientific expedition under Bruni d'Entrecasteau had in 1793 made friendly contact with the aboriginal inhabitants of this faraway place—the ancient Lyluequonny people. Then of course this island, which Dutch Explorer Abel Tasman had a century and a half earlier called Van Diemen's Land, was thought to be part of a great continent, a great south land.

Mary's reference to his father's interest in the area had prompted Alex to read about the expedition. D'Entrecasteau's own words, recorded for posterity, resonated with him and, he felt sure, would have struck a chord with his father.

"It will be difficult to describe my feelings at the sight of this solitary harbour situated at the extremities of the globe, so perfectly enclosed that one feels separated from the rest of the universe. Everything is influenced by the wildness of the rugged landscape. With each step one encounters the beauties of unspoilt nature..."

Alex elected to leave Hobart by the road that passed around the mountain. He had yet to give his new car—a well-kept, second-hand Forester—a good run, and looked forward to the drive.

The craggy mountain loomed above as he drove up the winding Huon Road between tall eucalypts, enjoying the positive feel of his car's all-wheel drive. How good it would have been to thunder the old BSA up this way.

High above the trees, scraggy vegetation surrendered to a rocky moonscape; splashes of snow flecked the mountain's pock-marked face. The rugged, columnar flutes of the dolerite 'organ-pipes' rose sheer from the slopes to the towering summit.

Driving south, Alex wound down to the Huon Valley where he passed through apple and wine-growing country to reach Huonville, on the Huon River. Weathered timber apple-sheds on the roadsides were stubbornly holding their ground against the influx of the new wineries.

Passing through the river-side village of Franklin, with its little flotilla of wooden boats, he arrived at Port Huon, on a river inlet dotted with working and leisure craft, then quickly reached Geeveston, where conservation and forestry came face to face, sometimes noisily. The road had left the water behind and was winding its way through countryside often depicted as quintessentially Tasmanian: rolling hills topped with thick forest, quiet green valleys with a scattering of modest farmhouses and sheds, rusting relics of farm machinery sharing leaning, cloud-chequered paddocks with Herefords and Jerseys. For Alex though, the true spirit of his island was elsewhere; it inhabited the wild bush.

At the town of Dover, the road briefly rejoined the water, this time at a wide bay near the river's mouth. Then it was off into the hilly country again, the twisting, forest-darkened road offering an enjoyable driving experience.

Southport proved to be a wide expanse of open rural land, a string of shacks and houses drawn out along its sandy edge, looking south across a sheltering bay to the untamed Southern Ocean.

The further south he drove, the more Alex felt the remoteness. Reaching Recherche Bay, he pulled in to a grassy parking area next to the beach at Cockle Creek, turned the engine off and stepped out of the car onto the sandy ground. *At the extremities of the globe.*

The silence was profound. A wallaby appeared from the long grass, apparently un-concerned by the intruder, and a pair of currawongs arrived to assess the prospects of a free feed.

Alex walked the few steps to the quiet beach and gazed out across the calm water, clear at his feet, a shining azure blue farther out, silver along the horizon. A tug of distant memory hinted at a rare, calm drawing of a bright horizon he might have seen his father work on, somewhere, some time.

Far to his left, beyond the edge of the bay, layers of serrated mountain ranges receded into the blue-grey mist of distance. And of time, it felt to him. To his right, closer, the view was framed by thick forest which came to the edge of the beach as it curved out towards a rocky point. A point on which, he had been told, he would find a sculptural monument to the whaling days of the early colonial years.

He saw two weather-beaten, wooden shacks, one darkly oiled, the other blue-painted, sitting nestled into the low dune amid grasses and boobyalla, on the very edge of the narrow, sandy beach. Just as so many modern-day visitors must have done before him, Alex marvelled at their enviable position; but he hoped that time would be allowed to erase them from the otherwise unspoiled landscape.

It was easy to imagine the time of whales breeching in the bay, dark figures moving on the beach and in the bush, wisps of smoke curling skyward from their cooking fires. He thought the wallabies would have been more cautious then.

This was why Alex had come here. To *feel* the place. And as he allowed the spirit of the place to enter his being, he became a little boy again, and his father was standing beside him, an arm across his young shoulders. *Feel it, Alex?*

giro

ALEX WAS SETTLING DOWN to watch *Grand Designs* when his mobile phone squarked. He muted the TV's sound and grabbed the phone, wishing he had thought to turn it off.

'Hello?'

'Alex? It's Vin.'

'Vin?' Alex felt the familiar warmth. 'Are you alright?' He pointed the remote control at the silent set and killed it. *Oh, she'll ask about my professional misconduct. What should I say?*

'I'm really well, thanks. And you?'

He could hear the smile in her voice. She sounded good, animated.

'Yeah, me too. It's so good to hear you.'

'Mmmm...I was sorry to hear about your grandmother.'

'Thanks. But as I said, she had a good innings.'

Alex put his feet up on an old vinyl poufe and eased back into the oversized couch which dominated his living-room.

'Guess what I saw today?' Vin said.

Perhaps she won't ask.

'Florence?'

'Not even close. I saw the *Giro d'Italia* riders go past.'

'Awesome.' Alex was envious. 'Whereabouts?'

'Stage seven went through Tuscany and came really close to our town. I went with a bunch of locals and we watched from the roadside just outside Ponteverde. And Alex, we took nonna with us.'

'Oh, excellent. Did she enjoy it?'

'Yes, she truly did. She seemed like her old self for a while; she was waving and cheering all the riders, especially any she thought were Italian.'

Alex smiled at the thought.

'The weather was horrible, though, really wet. Apparently some of the roads on this stage were atrocious, and the poor riders were covered with mud. It was hard to see who was who.'

Alex had seen some SBS vision of what the commentators were calling the 'mud stage', but kept that to himself as Vin continued. 'I must tell you:

Australia's Cadel Evans won the stage, and Richie Porte, from Lonnie, took the sprinters' pink jersey.'

'Fantastic. I hope you had an Australian flag, girl.'

'I certainly did. And I think it drew a grin from Cadel.'

'You'd make any man smile, Vin.'

'Careful, it might go to my head.'

lightly

JUST AS ALEX savoured the quiet of the bush, he hankered, though less often, for the swirl of the city across the strait. In the footy season, the 'G' called to him: the spectacle, the surging roar of humanity, the primal instincts, the thunderous affirmation of life. It was a contradiction that somehow seemed to make sense of being alive, of being human.

'There's no way that was a free kick,' said Karl loudly, as they bumped their way down the broad ramp, the vomitorium, the great stadium spewing out its human contents. Other jostling fans grumbled their agreement.

Alex knew that Karl was not happy; that didn't require much insight. Karl had, along with thousands of other Geelong fans, screamed his disapproval of the free kick given to St Kilda in the closing minutes of the tense game.

They caught a crowded tram to South Yarra where Karl now had a flat, and retreated to his favourite pub, where much of the talk was of the match.

'Have I told you that Gareth's talking about retiring,' said Karl, as the pair squeezed in beside a corner bench and manoeuvred themselves onto their stools.

Who does he play for? had been Alex's first thought, until he realised that Karl was referring to his boss, Gareth Dunlap. 'How will that affect you?' he asked, placing his tall cider on a coaster. 'What will you do if he does retire?'

'Not sure. Look for a new job, I suppose. Cheers, mate.'

'Cheers Karl.' They touched glasses and each took a long draught. 'Could you take over the practice?'

'No, mate. Apart from the fact that the office is in Gareth's own house, I'm not attracted to trying to set up a practice on my own, and there are no others to join me. If he retires, the office will certainly close down.'

'Right.'

'Might work out ok, though. Lately I've been feeling the need to do stuff other than houses.'

Alex nodded. He could understand that.

'Anyway, what about you? What about those apartments on the river? How did they finish up?'

Was there a note of envy in Karl's voice?

'They're coming up well. Hopefully they'll be finished by Christmas. That's this year, before you ask.' Alex grinned. It was a worn-out line, borne of many stories of construction nightmares, extended delays.

'All go smoothly?' asked Karl, wiping a line of Fosters froth from his top lip.

Smoothly? What was the answer to that? His relations with the client had been a crazy fair-ground ride that plummeted him from a heart-racing height to the depths of shame. Shame that would keep that part of the Riverbank story even from his friend.

'After a shaky start, yes, it went well.'

'What was the shaky bit?'

'We spent half of the contingency sum before we got out of the ground.'

'Tell me about it,' said Karl, rolling his eyes. He'd obviously been there, done that. 'And at the end of the day?'

'Samuel did a great job working back through our drawings and specifications and identifying where we could make savings with little or no adverse effect on the project. I have to take my hat off to him, he pulled the budget back on to an even keel.'

'Sounds like a good bloke to have on your team.'

'He is.'

Alex drained his glass. 'Another drink?'

'Thanks. Can you get out?'

When Alex returned, edging through the babble with two full glasses, Karl, apparently thirsting for details of projects other than houses, asked him about the Recherche Bay project.

'The Greentree job? Wild South, it's being called. That's under construction now. I told you we were looking at off-site prefabricated modules, didn't I?'

Karl nodded. 'How does that sit with your thing about solutions arising from the site?'

'Two answers, Karl. One is that these buildings don't really belong there; they will touch the ground lightly, as Murcutt would say, and be capable of being easily removed.'

Karl nodded.

'Two,' said Alex, 'simple economics.'

Answer Two brought a smile from Karl. Alex could see him thinking, *that's the real reason.*

It was a good question that his friend had asked, one which Alex had agonised over. Even though it felt like a betrayal of his father's values, the cost savings of prefabricating the modules off-site could not be ignored. In the end, he rationalized it with a simple analogy: he could take a tent to the wilderness or he could build a shelter there when he arrived. The tent could be taken away with him, leaving no trace.

What do you think, dad?

the right time

THE MONTHS ROLLED BY, filled with the routines and small crises of a design practice. And meetings: client meetings, design team meetings, consultant meetings, authority meetings, site meetings, office meetings…

The flurry of activity of Alex's multiple projects had receded and office life, for the past month or so, had been easily managed.

Felicity and Crichton were happily ensconced in their new apartment and, to their great satisfaction, the other apartments had all been sold and several were now occupied.

Wild South had been completed, more or less on time, and Alex had spent several weeks putting into order the contract administration records—site instructions, variations, the dreaded cost adjustments, progress claims and certificates, inspection lists, minutes of those innumerable meetings, and more.

* * *

The streetlights threw frantic shadows from the chaotic branches of the plane trees. A few hardy souls leaned into the wind on the wide footpath.

An agitated Alex had brought takeaway Chinese back to the warmth of the office. This evening, he was distracted and restless; an exciting and very recent development had set him thinking that this could possibly to be the final major clearing of his ABC desk.

Was this the right time?

He wondered what Vin would think.

Vincenza Genovese

From: alex.gardner@ABCArchitects.com.au
Sent: Thursday 11th July 2011 7.40 PM
To: Vincenza Genovese <Vin.Gen@gmail.com.it>
Subject: Greentree

Hello Vin
Trust all is good with you. And with your nonna.

A bit of exciting news from me. Remember that Greentree project I told you about last year? (Where does the time go?) Its official name is Wild South Wilderness Lodge.
Well, It's received a design award in this year's round of Tasmanian architecture awards. I'm stoked! Not just for myself, but for all the others at ABC who were involved.

ABC have been generous in their acknowledgement of my role as their project architect, and the building has received quite a bit of media exposure locally. I've attached a press clipping.

You know how I always wanted to have my own practice, be my own boss? Well, I'm thinking that now might be the right time. I'll keep you posted.

Thanks for sending the photos of Florence. I went quite green looking at them. I loved the shot of you on the *Ponte Vecchio*. Tuscany is definitely on my travel wish list, when time and money allow.

Love, Alex.

As Alex quickly scanned his email prior to hitting 'send', he saw with mixed feelings how the tone of his messages had changed, flattened, over the seasons from that of separated lovers to one of friends keeping in touch. *Love Alex*, no longer held the same meaning, the same message. Or did it?

Where does the time go? The banal and un-answerable query he had come out with suddenly seemed to hold real significance. Was this girl he had so treasured fading from his life? Did she have a romantic interest over there? Early on, they had sometimes made jocular reference to irresistible others, but it had long since become a subject they both avoided.

Vin's response was quick.

Alex Gardner

From: Vincenza Genovese <Vin.Gen@gmail.com.it>
Sent: Thursday 11th July 2011 11.05 AM
To: alex.gardner@AffinityArchitects.com.au
Subject: Greentree Award

Congratulations, Alex! You're making quite a name for yourself, aren't you? (Has your hat size changed at all?)

Yes, I can see that the timing might be right for you to set up your own practice. Perhaps you should go for it.

Love, Vin.

---

* * *

Two people were central to Alex's emerging plans.

One was Karl Fisher. Alex had been surprised and delighted when Karl had agreed to his proposal. Surprised, because he had imagined that Karl would remain in the big city; delighted, because he had come to greatly respect Karl's abilities, and saw them as complementary to his own.

The other person was Annette Marshall; Alex had met Annette through local professional development activities. She was an experienced and well-liked architect whose capabilities were well-known in professional circles and whose local network was impressive. Divorced, in her forties, the mother of a young daughter, she had for some time been working from her Taroona home, and had been open with Alex about her desire to no longer work alone, without back-up.

What would her response be? Could he really make this happen?

much to do

IT WAS WITH a mixture of regret at leaving his ABC friends and nervous anticipation of a wide-open, exposed future, that he sat down, the easy hubbub of the Salamanca market audible from below his window, to email Vin in this, his last month at ABC.

Things were happening so fast, and the pieces falling into place so well: was it all too good to be true?

Vincenza Genovese

From: alex.gardner@ABCarchitects.com.au
Sent: Saturday 21st August 2011 10.17 AM
To: Vincenza Genovese <Vin.Gen@gmail.com.it>
Subject: A New Adventure

Hello Vin

The new practice will become a reality. It's scary but exciting. I can't sit still at the moment.
Guess what, Karl is coming over from Melbourne to join with me!
Gareth Dunlap (remember?) has just retired and is closing down his practice, leaving Karl looking for a fresh start.
Annette Marshall, a very experienced local architect whom I've come to know and respect, will be the third partner. We have a big job ahead of us, but it's exciting.

I didn't relish the thought of telling William Carey that I would be leaving ABC, but he was ok about it. Quite supportive, actually. He wished me well and offered his help if we needed it. Within reason, he said, as we could be competing for work in the future!

Thanks for sending the material on Bologna. Those two leaning towers are amazing. Hopefully one day I'll see the place. And well done with the writing, that's fantastic. Sounds like just the thing for you. What other magazines are you submitting to? You'll tell me whenever you get something published, won't you? I expect to see your name in lights soon, so to speak, (no pressure).

Other news from me: my mother turns sixty next week. I'll be going up to Lonnie for her birthday of course. It'll be a small get-together with a few of her friends. I've done her a sketch of Green's Beach, working from an old photo, and I've had it framed. I'm a bit rusty with that sort of drawing, and I'll never be up to my father's standard, but I'm quite pleased with it.

So much to do.
Bye for now.

Love, Alex

a new start

FROM THE POPULAR dockside restaurant, the mountain loomed as a white-flecked backdrop seen through a grey gauze of misty snow-cloud which, high above, feathered to a cold blue sky. The sun-lit green-grey hills in the foreground stood in sharp relief. A bright fragment of rainbow arced heavenwards from Knocklofty hill. Alex's hill.

He looked across his glass at his two colleagues. The lights of the restaurant danced in his wine. This would be a good year.

'Here's to the new firm!'

In their little cubicle, all three raised their glasses: Alex, his pinot noir, Karl, his Heineken, and Annette, her sav blanc. And as they toasted their new venture, the trio knew that they would long remember this lunch, this moment; whatever the future held, this was a pivotal point in their lives.

'But who are we drinking to, Alex?' Annette had been pressing for the choice of a name for the new firm ever since the three had first come together. She pushed at the bridge of her quietly fashionable spectacles.

'Well', Alex responded, looking at his new partner, her swept-back, dark hair flecked with undisguised grey, 'whatever we choose, it shouldn't impose any boundaries on ourselves. Like Twentieth Century Electronics—how silly does that sound now?—or EcoArchitects, or even Gardner, Fisher, Marshall. Hopefully the practice will grow and change over its life but its name should be able to carry on.'

He watched as Karl put down his knife, took out a fine, felt-tip pen, and began to write on a white napkin.

'Ok', said Karl, 'we have Gardner, Fisher, Marshall; we have GFM in whatever order; we have Eco-Architects or Eco-Arc. What else?'

Annette took off her glasses. 'How about AKA? Would that be too flippant?'

'AKA? As in Alex, Karl, Annette?'

'Or Annette, Karl, Alex', smiled Annette.

Alex grinned at his new partner..

'Also Known As,' said Karl, 'I like it. Feels sharp.'

Alex, still musing: '*too* sharp, perhaps?'

Karl: 'Imagine a logo made up of just simple strokes – bold, decisive. Like the firm.'

Warming to the idea, Alex said, 'Pencil lines, perhaps. Maybe a little grainy, to hint at complexity behind the simplicity. Lines that are not rigid or perfect.' He took out his soft-lead clutch pencil and demonstrated on his own napkin.

'Of course', Karl tossed a little dampener onto the table, 'we'll have to check if the name is already taken'. He opened his brand new Apple iPad, a showy but pretty limited device in Alex's opinion. It was the first Alex had seen.

'Can you get the internet on that thing?' Alex asked.

Karl rolled his eyes. The table was quiet as he consulted his new device.

Minutes later he said, 'I'm afraid AKA is taken. A firm in New South Wales.

Shoulders slumped.

'Oh well, what are our other options?' asked Annette.

Alex saw that Annette had put the disappointment behind her quickly and was already moving forward, addressing the matter like the consummate problem-solver she was.

'Well,' he said, 'our name should say something about those things we have an affinity for. Those projects, or those values.'

Annette: 'agreed.'

Karl: 'say again, Alex.'

Alex: 'those things we have an affinity for. For which we have an affinity.'

Karl: 'never mind the grammar, what about *affinity*? *Affinity Architects*?'

Annette: 'didn't Louis Kahn use *affinity* in one of his famous quotes?'

Alex and Karl: silence.

Annette: 'I remember. It was: *Design is not making beauty; beauty emerges from selection, affinities, integration, love...*'

Alex: 'perfect.'

* * *

It was the fifth property the Affinity trio had looked at. The others had been either too small, of unmanageable floor plan, or just plain grotty. Alex thought this one, however, showed promise.

As he walked along Liverpool Street, heading out of the CBD to where the street began to rise towards the hilly residential area of West Hobart, he was thinking: affordable rent (out-goings included), hopefully only superficial fit-out work required, enough space to grow a little, easy access to the city centre, good parking options for clients *(now all we need are clients)* and an acceptable, while not salubrious, address.

'Alex? Michael Diprose'. The young, be-suited agent offered his hand.

'Hello Michael. Alex Gardner. Good to meet you. Let's see what's on offer.'

Alex was ushered through a narrow shopfront and a small shop, more like a wide passage, into a surprisingly spacious rear area which appeared to have been a work-room of some sort. It boasted a carpet-tile floor and an open truss ceiling with an array of suspended fluorescent lights. The accumulated dust and musty odour told him that the space had been vacant for some time.

A design studio in the making, he thought. A high triangular window in the truss zone, glazed with obscure wired glass, faced a little laneway on the western side of the building. *Mountain view potential there?* A separate staff room, kitchenette and toilet facilities opened off the large space. Through a window in the staff room, Alex could see a small, open light-well, its opposite side bounded by an un-adorned brick wall. *Potential there?*

Alex struggled to conceal his rising interest. 'It's a possibility, Michael. But I can see that we would have to spend some money on it, so I would be looking at a slightly lower rent than what you're asking'.

'Slightly lower might be acceptable to my client', said the agent, a little too readily for the owner's interests, Alex thought. But Michael's response had just confirmed that the owner was pretty keen to lease it.

'I think it's worth bringing my partners to have a look'.

* * *

Alexander Gardner

From: Vin.Gen@gmail.com.it
Sent: Sunday 9th November 2011 11.05 AM
To: Alexander Gardner <alex.gardner@AffinityArchitects.com.au>
Subject: Affinity

Affinity? I like it.

Your mother must be proud, Alex. And I imagine that your father would have been, too. I know that would be on your mind.

Please give my regards to Karl. Would I still recognise him?
Is he still shopping at Vinnies?

Love, Vin

PS Hey, I had another article published in *TurisItal*, the Italian travel magazine. An Australian's view of Tuscany. I think it could lead to more work from them. Fingers crossed.

a plan

UNABLE TO SLEEP, Alex had come in before dawn. His excitement was tempered with trepidation. Were they really ready for this? Why was he doing this, really? The task ahead of them was daunting; so much to be done, so little certainty.

Their modest but artful alterations to their leased space, which had earned from their landlord a three-month rent holiday, were almost complete. Alex found a plastic chair, one of several left behind by the previous occupant, uncovered a large desk which a friend of Annette's had sold to them for next to nothing, and sat down to draft an action list.

The three had already talked through the steps they needed to take to get their new show on the road, and Alex, amid the drop sheets, step-ladders and paint cans, listed those steps now on his lap-top, occasionally adding his own thoughts.

These were the beginnings, he supposed, of a business plan of the sort that the bank's business manager had spoken of.

Legal structure: *partnership (for now, at least)*
Partnership Agreement: *action reqd*
Accountants: *Swanston p/l*
Bank: *Affinity account opened*
Finance: *bank loan underway, to be signed off asap*
Property lease: *executed (3+3+3)*
Management: *discuss. (can we share leadership?)*
Fitout: *underway.*
Furniture: *list and procure asap. finance?*
Equipment: (computers, etc): *itemise, arrange finance*
Vehicles? *discuss approach*
Library: *list and procure*
Insurances: *(esp professional indemnity!) action asap*
Staff: *discuss; (recept/admin person first? Technician?)*
Office systems: *(a big job!) discuss*
Marketing plan: *discuss*
PRODUCING INCOME: *top priority!*

As Alex looked back over the list, two things seemed to come to the surface. First, management. They probably should give one person the responsibility of management leadership. Or perhaps they could rotate that role? Second, but of paramount importance, was the need to be getting work, producing income.

Alex was turning his mind to this when he heard the entrance door on Liverpool Street being unlocked. Moments later, Annette appeared through the painter's shrouds, a reassuring figure in torn blue jeans and a bulky jumper, her hair tied back, clearly ready to pitch in with the tidy-up.

'You're here early, Alex.'

'Just trying to get my thoughts straight. A lot to do.' He smiled at his new partner.

'Did you bring Olivia?' Alex looked past her. Olivia was Annette's eight-year-old daughter.

'Not this time. She's at soccer practice.' Annette dumped a battered carry-bag on the floor. 'Shall I make us a coffee?'

When she returned from their small kitchen, which was already equipped with a hot water urn and the essentials for making tea or coffee, she placed two steaming mugs on the desk and found a chair.

'What are we looking at?'

'Work coming in. These are the jobs that I've noted down from our discussions.' Alex picked up a separate sheet of paper. He could see Annette's eyes going to it, probably registering the shortness of the hand-written list.

1. *South Hobart consulting rooms – confirmed. (Annette)*
2. *Kingston restaurant fitout – confirmed. (Annette)*
3. *Battery Point B&B alterations – proposal. (Annette)*
4. *2 Houses, Sandy Bay – to be confirmed. (Alex)*
5. *Cellar door complex, Huonville – to be confirmed. (Alex)*
6. *New house, Taroona – probable. (Karl)*

Anette had brought three live projects into the new practice, Karl was optimistic of procuring commissions for two jobs, both 'sea-change' referrals from Gareth back in Melbourne, while Alex felt reasonably sure that a Sandy Bay residential project would come his way. He didn't know for sure, but he suspected that Felicity St John-Hall may have had a hand in that. He knew already that word-of mouth was the most effective marketing medium in this small city.

'Hi guys.' It was Karl, managing to make a fashion statement even dressed for manual labour: grey bib-and-brace overalls probably courtesy of the OpShop, a crimson flannel shirt, ditto, and green sneakers. 'With you in a minute.' He disappeared to make himself a coffee.

When Karl was settled, Alex handed him the job-list and asked, 'Can you think of anything else?'

'Ok. What's *not* here is important, too.'

His partners looked at him. Karl brought his mug to his lips and grimaced. Alex could see that he was making a mental note to get some decent coffee.

'Alex, your award for the Wild South project—ok, I know it was an ABC job, but everyone knows who designed it—that award is one of our greatest assets right now. We need to capitalise on it. We need to be, you need to be, working on getting more work of a similar nature. Fronting up to potential clients, including the government departments who look after national parks, tourism facilities, etc.'

Annette was nodding. 'He's right Alex.'

'In the meantime, 'Karl said, 'while we're madly marketing, we should all be pitching in to get Annette's jobs moving and fees rolling in. Some cash flow, the bank will want to see that. And on that score, I've had a go at drafting our first year budget...'

The other two looked at him, then at one another, with one thought in mind: *here is our managing partner.*

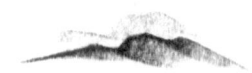

a hug

Alexander Gardner

From: Vin.Gen@gmail.com.it
Sent: Tuesday 23rd February 2012 7.31 AM
To: Alexander Gardner <alex.gardner@quickmail.com.au>
Subject: Nonna

Hello Alex

The chianti is making me feel a bit homesick. Dad always drinks it, either that or his grappa. Would you remember that?

Poor nonna's mind has drifted away for good, now. We (her friends and I) can no longer reach her at all. It's so sad, Alex. I've been talking to mum and dad about what to do. I just don't know.

Sometimes I just need a hug. You know?   V.

Poor Vin. Alex was saddened by the email that pinged into his lap-top as he was tipping muesli into a bowl on his kitchen bench.

Her message tugged at his heart. He looked at the time. What time would it be in Italy? About nine-thirty in the evening, he reckoned. *Sometimes I just need a hug.* Did she have someone there to hug her? Is that what Vin was trying to tell him? Or was she saying that he still held a place in her heart, that she needed a hug *from him*? Either way, he was going to call her.

'Hello Vin?
'Alex?'
'Yes, it's me. I just opened your email...'
'Yes, sorry about that,' Alex could hear the sorrow and the wine in her voice. 'I was just feeling a bit low.'

'I'm hugging you, Vin. Can you feel it?' His own voice was husky.

'Oh Alex...' He could hear her quietly sobbing. His heart ached for her.

a new client

THROUGH THE OFFICE'S newly re-glazed high window, Alex looked up to the west. Against an icy blue backdrop, the mountain wore a fat, white boa draped along its uneven shoulders, feathering away delicately at the ends.

'Alex, this is Roderick Harding.' Karl had called him into the firm's conference room, where a tall, well-dressed young man was holding out his business card. A prospective client, Alex thought. *Why us?*

```
Roderick Harding
Harding Associates
Property Development
HA
```

Ha. I quite like that. A shorter version of 'aha', the little exclamation that signals the finding of a solution.

Alex looked back from the embossed business card to the man who proffered it. The man had an even tan (ski or solarium?), carefully trimmed dark hair and perfect eyebrows. His confident smile revealed a set of improbably white teeth. Alex was no connoisseur of men's clothing, but the dark, tailored suit said *expensive* and the tie-less white (silk?) shirt said *not just an ordinary businessman*. Hang on, there's a little logo; is that *Versace*?

'Hello Roderick'.

'Call me Rick, guys.' His smile was immaculate, too.

'I'm impressed by Martin Greentree's project. And I'm aware of your role in it,' he said, looking at Alex. 'I'd like to talk about a project I have in mind.'

'Let's sit down. Coffee, Rick?'

Alex saw Rick's eyes appraising Andrea's young bottom as their receptionist left with the order: one short black (the good-looking visitor), one green tea (yuk, Alex), and one flat white (Karl). And biscuits, of course.

'Harding Associates, H,A,' Rick said the letters individually, 'is a small but very effective development company. We're Sydney-based but our reach is nation-wide. Our strongest asset is our pro-active entrepreneurship.'

Proactive: a word on Vin's hate list, Alex remembered, with a twinge of melancholy.

'We have established relationships with financiers and major construction companies. We see the opportunities and go after them. You may know some of our projects. Perhaps *The Sands* on Bribie Island? Or *The Elfin* at Port Fairy? *The Lakes* at Gippsland? All boutique resorts. They were all, one way or another, created by Harding Associates.'

'I know The Lakes', responded Karl, 'Very impressive.'

Alex nodded non-commitally. He knew of none of them, but that meant little.

'I'd like to see if we might work together on another select resort, this one in Tasmania. We've been tracking the increase in international interest in this state, and we think that the time is right. We've also done our homework on your practice, and as I said Alex, we really liked your design for the Wild South project.'

'Thank you for that, Rick,' Alex said, 'but that was an ABC project. Perhaps you should be talking to them.'

This brought a quick glance from Karl. *Don't give it away, Alex!*

'I want to work with your practice,' Rick's direct gaze took in both partners. 'I've considered several others, including ABC, but here I am.'

Rick graced Andrea with a brilliant smile as she set down the carefully-chosen designer mugs, short black Mr Harding, then watched her leave the room.

'I feel sure that we can agree on some basis for progressing your ideas' said Karl, slipping comfortably into his managing partner role. 'It would certainly be appropriate for Alex to drive the design.'

'Excellent,' said Rick, I would want one of the partners to be ultimately responsible. No handing it down the line.'

'Of course,' said Alex, thinking that there wasn't much of a line for it to be handed down.

'Once we understand your brief,' said Karl, 'we will submit to you a draft agreement which would set out the scope of service, deliverables, timelines, personnel, etc. And of course our proposed fees.'

'Haa,' breathed Rick.

So is this what the HA really means, thought Alex. *Ha well, that's something we need to talk about. Ha, you'll be lucky.* He guessed that Karl was thinking the same thing. At ABC, William had told Alex more than once about those clients who, having a nice job to offer, endeavoured to get free services out of the architect—and the architect's secondary consultants, to boot. *Just to get the project started, you understand. Just share a little of the up-front risk with us and reap the rewards later. Code for: lock yourselves in and we'll screw you later.*

Alex watched through the office shopfront as their new client left. He saw Roderick Harding glance at the mountain, ease out of his designer suit jacket and carefully hang it behind the driver's seat of a large black BMW with interstate plates.

By the time Rick returned to Affinity the following week, he and Karl had come to an understanding about fees. Affinity would not do any work for nothing, but the firm would not send any invoice to HA unless and until they had secured from the local Council a development permit for the project. After that, services were to be provided in accordance with a fee schedule set out in the agreement.

On entering the Affinity offices, Mr Harding—*call me Rick, please*—had slipped a little sheaf of parking tickets into Andrea's hand, with an intimacy that suggested they might be love notes. His conspiratorial smile said, *You'll be able to look after these, won't you sweetheart?*

'So, Rick, where do you propose to site your new boutique resort?' the question came from Karl.

'We've secured a site on the west coast, north of Great Boulder Cove.' Rick clicked his cup onto its saucer and opened his black leather briefcase. *Niemen Marcus.* He took out a silver USB stick and passed it to Alex.

'Can you put this up on the screen?'

Moments later, all three were looking at a satellite image on the room's large TV monitor. The resolution was impressive; both the images and the screens to view them had advanced in the years since Alex had first encountered Google Earth at BNG.

Rick moved the cursor to a small beach, 'here is the cove,' then tracked a wobbly outline around a shrubby area behind the dunes, 'and here is the property we have an option on.'

'That's a big property. I know the area,' said Alex. Something was starting to unsettle him. Alex had never heard the name Great Boulder Cove, but he knew the sandy cove where the cursor had settled, just as he was familiar with the area around it.

'Really?' Rick looked at him in un-feigned surprise. 'But there's no road in yet.'

'True, but you can get there by walking in. Or part of the way by trail-bike. I've covered a lot of that coast.' Alex wasn't about to tell a stranger about his personal quest. Karl knew of it, but kept silent.

'That's great.' Did Rick's thoughtful expression belie his words? 'I didn't expect to find someone with knowledge of that locality.'

'So,' Karl said, 'what's your intention, Rick?'

'Another boutique resort, Karl. This one geared towards international high-fliers who like the idea of spending a few pampered days on a remote, wild coast on an island at the bottom of the world. I have an operator and investors lined up.'

'Sounds interesting.'

'We're excited about it.'

'Have you put your design brief in writing?'

'I have. I know how you architects like everything to be documented.'

'It wasn't always so, Rick,' Alex smiled ruefully, 'but the liability issues are much bigger nowadays.' He used Wiliam's words: 'Every instruction that's not recorded is like a forgotten land-mine waiting for someone to step on it later on.'

Rick arched an eyebrow. 'Very graphic. But I don't imagine we'll find ourselves in any explosive situations.'

But, as he watched Rick Harding bid a lingering farewell to Andrea, something was causing Alex to think that the entrepreneur would make a formidable adversary, should any conflict arise.

the cove

ALEX AND ANNETTE were to meet Rick and his colleague Steve Kosta at the small Cambridge airport, outside Hobart. From there, the group would fly by chartered helicopter to the Great Boulder Cove site—a trip of little more than half an hour, compared with more than five hours by road. Seats on the aircraft were limited and Karl had drawn the short straw.

At the airport they were met by their pilot, a disconcertingly young-looking man called Nathan. A fan of Tom Cruise, perhaps, dressed as he was in a leather bomber jacket and aviator-style sunglasses. Three years, was his answer when Steve asked the question on all of their minds: How long have you been doing this?

Nathan, at Rick's request, flew an indirect route, taking a wide arc out across the city and its mountain and over part of the state's vast World Heritage wilderness area. The rising sun behind them threw the ancient, rugged terrain into deep relief, the valleys dark, foggy and un-knowable, the ranges burnished a dull bronze, the snow-laden peaks flashing white, and here and there the steely gleam of a winding river or still lake. Occasionally, the pilot pointed and called out the name of some topographical feature: *Mount Anne. Lake Gordon. The Franklin River. Deception Range.* No-one else spoke.

For Alex, there were no words. His heart was filled with the raw beauty of this unsullied, timeless land. He wished that the well-meaning child-pilot would keep silent too. The names, applied only moments ago in the great span of time, seemed to Alex somehow to diminish the primordial place now passing beneath them.

Wheeling north, the young Top Gun flew them out over the expanse of Macquarie Harbour, where they spotted remote Sarah Island, dreaded by convicts in colonial days, then the thriving, post-card-pretty, tourist town of Strahan. Alex thought that Rick seemed more alert now, probably keen to understand the proximity of these established visitor attractions to his own project.

They followed the coast northwards, first over Trial Harbour then the sparse shack settlement at rocky Granville Harbour, and on to the place that Rick called Great Boulder Cove.

On the site itself, a contractor from the old mining town of Zeehan, forty-five minutes to the south-east of them, had cleared and levelled an area where the helicopter could safely put down.

As the small group stepped out onto the sandy ground and the flurry settled and the clatter of the machine died, a quiet embraced them, visited only by the sighs of the unseen surf. They had flown over the cove just a few minutes ago, but from here it was not visible, hidden by a continuous line of sand dunes.

Rick quickly took the lead. 'This is the area where we would like to build the resort.' He threw his arms wide—arms clad in an expensive-looking mohair overcoat. His words came out as puffs of vapour in the cold, still air. 'There will be road access of course, but we intend that most guests will arrive by helicopter,' he said, pointing a leather-gloved finger to the sky. 'Let's have a look at the beach, shall we?'

The small party walked to the dunes, Rick making occasional remarks, Alex and Annette busily taking photographs and making notes as they went, opening their every sense to the place. Their task today was to get the feel of the site, to understand it. Questions could wait until their return to Hobart.

Rick stifled an expletive when sand found its way into his shiny ankle-boots as they trudged up the dune. Alex glanced at his own well-travelled Blunnies and grinned to himself.

From the top, they could see that this was part of a second row of dunes, behind the primary dunes edging the beach. No surprise, the satellite image had portrayed this clearly. They made their way across to the top of the frontal dune, by which time they were much warmer, despite the chill air. From here, the small cove lay before them.

Alex caught his client looking at him and nodded in response to the question asked by Rick's raised eyebrows. Yes, this was indeed a special place.

Alex savoured the salt tang, coloured by the faint odour of seaweed; he enjoyed the cries of the sea-birds above the rhythmic sound of the surf; he welcomed the feel of the sand moving beneath his boots, the gentle brushing of the grasses against his legs. He took in the arc of beach, the rocky point with its dominant boulder formation, and the embracing dunes—surely middens, evidence of other lives, other times.

Can you imagine, Al, how many lives…?

a hero shot

A FAINT FLORAL scent lingered behind as Andrea left the meeting room.

Rick stirred his coffee and turned to the purpose of the meeting. 'Now that you've seen the site, I'm sure you can understand why we're excited about this project.'

Alex and Annette obediently nodded and smiled.

'We've done some preliminary work on areas, so we can be sure that the site can meet our needs.' Rick opened his sleek lap-top and looked at the screen.

'To give us the area we need for the buildings, subject of course to your final design, we will have to carve out part of the secondary dunes. This will not be visible from the beach. Related to that is a concept which we think can become the key marketing point of the resort.' Rick paused, as if for dramatic effect, while Alex experienced a growing unease. No architect liked to have a client impose ideas on him, but was that all that was troubling him?

'Alex, thank you for pointing out that these dunes may be aboriginal middens.' Rick must have seen Alex's hesitation. 'We hadn't been aware of that. But our scheme involves very little interference with them.' He continued with his explanation. 'From the resort complex behind the dunes, we will cut a direct, near-level connection to the beach. An access through the frontal dunes, a tunnel, if you like, bringing guests directly onto the beach.' Rick looked at his small audience. 'Imagine the drama, emerging into the cove in that way.' He paused for the approbation that this concept clearly deserved but, receiving only thoughtful looks, continued.

'We've run this past our marketing people, and they're excited about it. *The hero shot*, they're calling it. Imagine an aerial view of the cove taken from out over the sea,' Rick's hands became an aeroplane, 'the camera slowly zooms in,' his aeroplane hands banked and lost height, 'and we see on this beautiful secluded beach, a secret opening …'

But Alex, far from being excited, was experiencing a sinking feeling. His mind raced. *Don't be negative. Look for solutions, not obstacles. This is a rare opportunity for a new firm like ours; don't throw it away. Remember the overdraft.* He looked across at Annette and could see that she too was unconvinced by Rick's enthusiastic spiel.

Adopting what he hoped was an appreciative smile, he said to Rick and Steve, 'That's quite a concept...'

But even as he spoke, his father's words, said to a small boy in another lifetime, came back to him. *It's for time and the elements to do that, Al, not us.*

'These dunes, middens, or whatever, are not on any official list of significant aboriginal sites, right?' Rick demanded.

'That's right,' responded Annette, 'but...'

'Then here's what we do. We prepare our planning application, lodge it with council, and let them make their decision. We're not obliged to make any reference to what might or might not be aboriginal middens.' He looked around the group. 'Now let's move on...'

'Rick, we should talk about the application process.' Annette was surprisingly calm. Alex admired her for that, and was again glad that she was part of the Affinity team. 'The proposed use will require an amendment to the current planning scheme...'

'That'll be fine,' put in Steve, 'We've spoken to the mayor and he'll push it through, no worries. He's keen as mustard.' He leaned back and folded his arms across his chest. Case closed.

'It's good to have his support, but it's not his decision though, Steve.' Annette's quiet tone was that of an impartial adviser fulfilling her responsibilities. ' Under our state planning laws, any planning scheme amendment, once recommended by the local council, must go to the state's Planning Commission. Their review of it is a very thorough and very public process. And unfortunately it can take a while. All aspects will be scrutinised. We would recommend that you engage a local planning consultant to guide you through the whole journey. We can give you some names.'

Alex could no longer keep silent. 'I think it only fair to say, Rick, that so far as the middens are concerned, we have an ethical *and moral* duty to reveal their presence, so that a properly informed decision can be made.'

Rick stared at him.

Oh Christ, Alex was thinking, *I've gone too far.*

The room was deathly quiet.

Rick very deliberately gathered up his papers from the table and began to silently pack his designer briefcase. Steve watched him, then followed suit. The pair stood and wordlessly left the meeting room.

   Alex and Annette, and probably the others, heard Rick hiss two words as he left. *Arrogant prick.*

   After muttering an apology to Karl and Annette and quickly checking his diary, Alex fled the office. To the bush track on Knocklofty. To think.

damage control

'I DIDN'T TAKE to him anyway,' Annette offered in her calm manner, as though spurning a new client were no more weighty a matter than choosing a new brand of coffee for the meeting room. The three sat there now, in the meeting room—*conference room* when clients were in earshot—on a new day.

Grateful, as always, for Annette's impeccable sense of proportion, Alex said 'I owe you two an apology.'

'Forget it Alex. You're bringing in more work than you're scaring off.' Karl said with a smile and a macho shoulder-grab.

But his partners' outwardly relaxed attitudes to his foolhardiness were not wholly convincing to Alex. It could have been a wonderful project. And he was concerned that his actions may have been unprofessional, even left the firm open to a formal complaint.

When he put this to the others, Annette said, 'Alex, I'm satisfied we've done nothing unprofessional. But if you're still worried about that, why not talk to William Carey about it. William has had a lot of experience with handling disputes and complaints. I think he'll set your mind at rest.'

* * *

Alex was sitting with William at an outside table in Salamanca Place. He would normally have been allowing his mind to wander deliciously in the morning sunshine, but today he was anxious. Had he behaved unprofessionally? (Again?) Had he left himself open to a formal complaint to his professional body—a complaint which could potentially damage the fledgling firm? These were the questions he had, without naming the estranged client, put to the man who he had come to regard as his mentor.

William looked thoughtful as he set down his coffee and leaned forward, speaking quietly. 'It sounds as though you might have gone a bit too far, Alex. From what you say, I think you could have handled it better, more diplomatically.' He smiled up at a passer-by, and continued. 'I've always found it better to try, shall we say, to *educate* one's client on such matters. Very diplomatically, of course. It can take time; you need to gain their confidence first,' he looked at Alex, 'and their trust.'

Trust. Crichton St John Hall had probably trusted him. Was William alluding to that episode? Did he know about it?

'Yes, I was probably a bit silly,' said Alex, after a moment. 'If the truth be known, William, I didn't much like our client, and his implication that we should turn a blind eye to something important to me tipped me over the edge.'

'I admire your integrity, Alex, but perhaps you could have allowed a little cooling-off period, even just a break in the meeting, to get your thoughts together.'

Alex nodded.

'You may still have chosen to advise him of your obligations under the profession's code of ethics, but dispassionately, just as you would advise a client of any other constraints. You probably went too far when you referred to a *moral* duty. Your client might infer that you regarded his position as immoral. And he'd be right, wouldn't he? I'm not surprised he walked out, Alex.'

Alex coloured. He had wanted William's honest opinion, but had hoped that he might be vindicated by it.

'Your client probably thinks you've wasted his time, but if you didn't yet have a formal agreement then I don't think he could pursue that, and I don't see that you've done anything unethical. Except for the bit about not liking your client—I wouldn't be repeating that—your motives seem to have been pure.'

* * *

'It's a good letter, Alex.' Annette was perusing a draft of a letter that Alex intended to send to Roderick Harding.

'I think it covers it well,' she said, passing the draft to Karl. 'You've recorded the fact that there was no formal agreement in place; you've confirmed that our involvement has ceased and that no fees are due; and you've offered an olive branch without hint of any professional misdemeanour.'

'Yeah, mate, I agree,' offered Karl, as he finished reading and handed the letter back to Alex. 'Send it off and let's be shot of the bloke.'

So the draft was firmed up as an old-fashioned letter and snail-mailed to HA.

Harding Associates Pty Ltd
PO Box 753X
North Sydney
NSW 2060

Att Mr Roderick Harding

Dear Rick,

I regret that our meeting of 7th July regarding your Great Boulder Cove project concluded so abruptly, and on reflection feel that I owe you an apology. If I had reservations about any aspect of your project, I should have been more ready to engage in a reasoned discussion, rather than respond as I did.

We infer that you will no longer be requiring our services. The draft terms of engagement will therefore not be executed. We confirm that no professional fees have been accrued, and we will do no further work on the project. Naturally all of our discussions will remain confidential.

We hope and expect that any issues with the project can be satisfactorily resolved and we wish you every success with it.

Yours Sincerely

Alex Gardner
Affinity Architects

---

* * *

It was in early November that year that Annette brought some news of HA to the other Affinity partners. Alex and Karl were standing at the sink in their kitchenette, doing their best to achieve peaceably in the small space the simultaneous preparation of a green tea (Alex) and a black coffee (Karl).

'I hear on the grape-vine that HA are now registered as architects in Tasmania.' Annette said, while reaching across them for the jar of vile de-caf coffee. 'I'll ask Andrea to check that out; it's public information.'

She had Alex's and Karl's full attention as they backed away from the sink. Alex was frowning thoughtfully; Karl looked at her enquiringly, his impressive eye-brows raised.

'I heard that they've taken on one of the architects who has done work for them previously in Victoria. Paul Abernathy, I think the name was.' Alex and Karl looked at each other, but the name meant nothing to either of them.

'Oh well, good luck to them, I suppose,' offered Alex. The loss of the Great Boulder Cove opportunity still hurt and embarrassed him.

I mucked that up, dad.

nonna

IN LATE NOVEMBER Alex heard the burble of an incoming Skype call.

'Hello Alex.' It was Vin.

The picture was poor, but Alex could see immediately that something was wrong. Against the backdrop of the cosy, softly-lit living-room, *soggiorno*, of her nonna's cottage in Buti, Vin's face was a dim cut-out. But he could see well enough to know that she was tired and unable to smile.

'Hello Vin.' His voice softened. 'Is everything alright?'

'Have I caught you at a bad time, Alex?'

Alex had been about to boil an egg to round off his breakfast. He stepped across and turned off the hot-plate, out-of-shot for only a moment, then returned to his lap-top.

'No, no, not at all. What is it?'

'Alex, nonna has died.'

'Oh Vin...' He looked at the empty armchair, burnished by the light of a standard lamp, in a corner behind Vin. His own pathetic troubles fell away.

'She had a massive stroke, an embolism they called it, and she died in the ambulance.' Vin seemed calm and matter-of fact, but Alex could sense the strong emotions pressing behind her stoic exterior.

'Mum and dad are coming over. Nonna...' the name caught in Vin's throat, 'Nonna will be buried here in the village cemetery. With nonno. Grandpa.'

'Oh I'm so sorry, Vin.'

'It sounds terrible, but I think it's better this way.' Vin spoke quietly, as if lacking the energy or will to keep talking. 'We'd already lost her, and she'd lost us.'

ritorno

IN THE DAYS following Vin's call, Alex felt stricken with helplessness. As much as he wanted to give comfort to Vin, he could see no way that their physical separation and the passage of time would allow it to happen. After all, he was no more than an ex-boyfriend. He had no place in the family's grieving. He sent brief but heart-felt notes to Vin and to Mr and Mrs Genovese, and hoped that each would see the sincerity in his struggling words.

The days became weeks. Alex immersed himself in the day-to-day stuff of the practice, trying not to think of what was happening in Buti and what Vin's plans might be.

* * *

In December, Andrea routinely passed a telephone call through to Alex.

'I'm back, Alex,' a cheery voice announced.

It took Alex a moment to register the reality. He felt his face crease into a broad smile and, good heavens, his eyes fill up.

'Hello Vin.' He swivelled his chair away from the eyes and ears of the drawing-office. 'Back where?'

'At home in Melbourne. We all came back together, yesterday.'

Alex was having trouble finding words. He just wanted Vin to keep talking so he could listen to her voice.

'It's so good to know you're back, Vin.' *Did she realise how much he meant that?*

'Yes, it's been a long time, hasn't it?'

Alex thought he could hear her parents in the background: her mother's sing-song voice punctuated now and then by her father's deeper tones, the clink of crockery…morning tea perhaps?

'How did the funeral go?' he asked.

'It was lovely, Alex. There were so many people there. Nonna was a popular figure in the village. She had a wonderful send-off. And mum and dad had a great time, all things considered. Especially dad, who caught up with a couple of his old school-mates. He had great fun trying to explain Australian Rules football and his beloved Bulldogs to his friends.'

Alex smiled at the image of Vin's father Sergio miming a punt kick or handpass to his laughing mates.

'I must come over and see you,' he said.

'That'd be lovely.'

'I'll ask Andrea to book me a flight.'

'Oh, and who would Andrea be?' There was a playful note in Vin's voice. It was so good to hear her happy again.

'Ha. Our admin person. Receptionist, book-keeper, everything. But you knew that.'

'Yes, of course I did. Perhaps I shall meet your team some day?'

'I hope so. But first things first: Why don't we meet for dinner at our place?' *Was he pushing too hard, too soon?*

'You mean in Hardware Lane?'

Alex laughed. 'No, Tim's Tucker was our *lunch* place.'

'*Tony's Tucker*,' she corrected. 'Table six. I wonder if it's still there.'

A warmth spread through Alex as Vin spoke of their special places. 'I don't know. I hope so. But I meant the Golden Dragon.'

'Oh yes, good idea. And if that's not still there we'll have a spring roll on the doorstep of whatever's there in its place.'

Vin was sounding so much better, so much *closer*.

* * *

The Golden Dragon was still at the same address. When Alex had the temerity to enquire, an indignant young female voice with no trace of accent assured him that the family-run restaurant had been there for twenty-five years and would still be there in another twenty-five. He had apologised and made a reservation—a table for two in that secluded alcove upstairs near the front corner, please.

The voice had become more friendly. 'I know the table you mean; a romantic choice, sir. And, yes, you're in luck, we can give you that table tomorrow night.'

His flight over was uneventful. He had made his excuses to his partners and was touched by the warmth of their encouragement. *She'll be plump now, Alex*, Karl had joked, while Annette had said how she was hoping to meet this Italian beauty someday.

As was his way, Alex arrived early at the restaurant. Outwardly, the Golden Dragon looked the same. Alex was uncertain whether to go inside or wait out on the narrow footpath, weathering China Town's constant stream of humanity. He stepped into the recessed doorway and made a show of studying a menu in the window while he decided what to do. The writing may as well have all been in Mandarin, such was his state of mind.

'I'd have the Char Siew if I were you,' said a familiar voice at his shoulder. And the hug that he gave Vin was spontaneous and from the heart. When they came apart, they looked at each other for a long moment. *No, Karl, she's not plump.* The Italian beauty reached up and gently adjusted his hair.

They were led to their table by a dapper, smiling, Chinese gentleman of indeterminate age, Alex carrying his briefcase, Vin sporting a soft Italian leather shoulder-bag— acquired at Lucca, he was to learn.

Vin whispered, 'it's our table, Alex.'

They were facing each other across the white table-cloth. A small, elegant, white porcelain vase contained a single orchid. Alex couldn't take his eyes off the poised, dark-haired young woman opposite. He searched her face for some evidence of the passage of time, but found only a few more fine lines, visible when her amazing smile appeared.

Their wine arrived, a Tamar Valley pinot grigio, a Tasmanian product graced with Italian style. It had seemed the only possible choice.

'Cheers. Welcome back, Vin.'

'*Cin cin.* Thank you.' They touched glasses. 'Do you remember what you had when we came here before? On our first dinner date?'

'Um, wonton soup, I think. Then my main was satay chicken, wasn't it?' Alex knew that Vin would remember every detail, as she always did.

'That's right. I'm impressed.' And what did I have?'

'You had a short soup. And I remember that your main course involved beef. And we both had steamed rice.'

'And that's what I'll have tonight. Sichuan beef. It'll be a *Sliding Doors* moment.'

'Not *Ground Hog Day?*' asked Alex.

'Ok, a *Sliding Ground Hogs* moment.' They both laughed.

It was the strangest feeling. Part tentative first date, with all the excitement of exploration and discovery, and part homecoming.

'Tell me all about Affinity, Alex.' Vin brushed a strand of hair away from her face, using her little finger in a manner which Alex found so feminine and so exquisitely familiar. She was lightly tanned from the Italian sun and wore lipstick of a soft ruby colour. He could feel his heart swell.

'Things are going quite well. Work is flowing in and we now have three staff, Andrea and two others – Samuel, a technician, and Caitlin, a graduate architect.' Alex could see that Vin was taking real pleasure in hearing of his modest successes. Between spoonfuls of soup and skirmishes of chopsticks versus wayward wontons he fleshed out the Affinity story with the day-to-day details that he knew she would be interested to hear.

'Enough,' he said, placing the china spoon in his empty bowl and dabbing his napkin to his lips. 'I want to hear about you. Especially about your writing.'

As Vin told of her journey into the erratic realm of the free-lance writer, of her successes and disappointments, of her published articles and short stories, Alex experienced a growing pride, tinged with regret that he had not shared those times with her.

Neither spoke of significant others. It was inconceivable to Alex that Vin had not encountered romance in the time she had been away, but he took her silence to mean that there was nothing important to tell. Did she understand that it was the same for him? That no-one else he had met had affected him as she had?

As the evening passed, he felt the need to tell her as much. Taking the opportunity afforded by a comfortable lull in their conversation, as they disposed of the last few grains of rice, he looked directly at her and said: 'Vin, I'm still un-attached.'

There was a moment of silence, invaded only by the muted sounds of the restaurant—chopsticks on china, the clink of glasses, soft music and the lilting hum of conversation. He saw her eyes fill and her face crinkle into a smile that betrayed a complex of emotions. He thought he read *relief*. Did he read *love*.?

'So am I, Alex.' her voice wavered. She reached over and took his hand.

'I didn't think it would be like this,' he said, as they waited for their jasmine tea to arrive.

'Like what?'

'Like… well, as if you haven't been away at all.'

She nodded her understanding.

'When are you going back to Hobart?' Vin asked as Alex poured the tea. Two fortune cookies on a small white plate awaited their attention.

'I have a flight in the morning.'

'Come and stay at our place tonight. We have a spare room.'

Alex smiled his acquiescence. He had made no hotel booking and had a change of underwear and a clean shirt in his briefcase.

Standing to leave, he broke open his fortune cookie and unfolded the little note: *Follow your heart, it is your best guide.* He watched as Vin wrapped hers in a tissue and placed it in her bag.

The couple sat close together in the taxi. Alex spoke into Vin's ear, feeling her hair brush his lips. 'Do you remember what you told me just before you left for Italy?' Light from passing cars and streetlights gave him glimpses of her smile.

'Of course I do. I gave you a promise.' She squeezed his hand.

He was quiet for a moment. 'I took it more as a guarantee.' *If you're still about when I come back, I'll snavel you up.* He was conscious that she turned her head towards him in the darkness.

'Is there a difference?' There was a smile in her voice.

'You're the Word Girl,' he said.

'I don't know it all. And I'm not a girl any more, that I *can* guarantee.' She nudged him playfully, and like happy children they gently butted heads.

A porch light was illuminated at the Genovese house, but inside was in darkness. As Vin felt for the light switch, a dim figure emerged from the gloom, lit only by the light from the porch entering through the patterned obscure glass of the front door.

'You're still awake, Papa?' said Vin to the figure in striped pyjamas. Her father's face cracked into a smile as he saw Alex, and he advanced on him. Ignoring Alex's outstretched hand, Sergio took him into an abrupt bear-hug, then pushed him back and looked at him, nodding as if affirming some private thought, before retreating along the darkened hallway towards the parental bedroom, leaving the young couple grinning stupidly.

'I think he approves of you, Alex.' Vin laughed softly.

kunanyi

THE AFFINITY PARTNERS were settling into their chairs for their weekly partners' meeting. The outer office was quiet at this time of morning—the reason the partners chose to hold these meetings from 7.45am until 8.45, well before the office was due to open.

This morning Alex was having trouble focussing on practice matters. Vin seemed to have taken occupation of his mind; his thoughts were on her impending move to Hobart. He and Vin had been engaged in an intense frequent-flier romance since her arrival back in Melbourne, and she was soon to come south to see if life together in the southern city would work for them both.

Alex was remembering how, on her very first visit to Hobart, he and Vin had walked along the quiet bush tracks on Knocklofty, above his flat, laughing and touching each other often, talking of many things, and pausing occasionally to look through the gum trees out over the hilly city and its broad river.

He dragged his thoughts back to the meeting. The young firm needed his full attention.

* * *

Vin looked towards the mountain. Alex's mountain. It was nowhere to be seen this morning. A soft, misty sky had fallen before it, masking it, so that the city's backdrop was lowered to the height of the nearer hills. The still air was deliciously cool and moist after the heat of the last few days. Welcome relief for the sweating removalists from *Housemovers*.

'Where do you want this, love?' The grey-haired, grey-overalled man was squinting around the corner of a large cardboard carton he was carrying, his arms hugged around it. Vin thought it looked too heavy for a man of his age. Where was his younger colleague?

She glanced at the bold label: *clothes*. 'Just over there for now, thank you.'

She was overseeing the delivery of her belongings to Alex's flat. Well, not all of her belongings, but enough of them to get her started here. Plus a painting of Buti by an artist friend of her nonna. Her precious books were included of course; they waited now in the van at the kerb, huddled in their containers. Her other bits and pieces would remain at the house in Footscray until she and Alex had survived the test of co-habiting (she had no doubt they would survive it) and until they found more spacious accommodation—she looked forward to that shared adventure.

Dear Alex had done his best to make space for her, but what do men know? She could see that half of the shelf space in the bathroom was going to be hopelessly inadequate for her feminine requirements. And the wardrobe hanging space would never do. As for space for her shoes, well... But if a clever architect, *her* clever architect, couldn't solve these important little dilemmas then who could?

An altogether different concern had been settled with news that her application for a part-time position at Fullers Bookshop had been accepted, thanks in no small measure to an embarrassingly fulsome reference from dear Adrian Page. Her concerns about money, about paying her way, were calmed. And she was eager to plunge back into her free-lance writing, confident that her experience and her contacts, both within the country and abroad, would stand her in good stead. The Word Girl was back.

'What about this, love?' It was the grey man.

Alex felt ineffectual, a little redundant, as he watched proceedings from a safe distance. He eyed the new bookshelves he had constructed in the living room. Plantation Tasmanian Oak, *eucalyptus delegatensis*. Nice finish, well done there, Alex. Elegant connections. Fully demountable, so that the landlady wouldn't score them when he and Vin departed the flat.

He had seen that Vin was delighted with the shelves, and they were now both looking forward to seeing her books rubbing shoulders with his more modest collection, the more precious items of which were his shadowy Uncle Geoffrey's art books that had found their way to him.

With each carton that was hefted through the front door, the flat shrank. Alex's apprehension was mounting: would there be space enough for them both? As an un-attached young man, the small flat had suited his needs nicely, and besides, he had been too pre-occupied with the new practice to even contemplate moving. But now?

* * *

'Vin!' Alex called from the kitchen. 'The mountain is getting its name back!'

It was Australia Day 2014, several months after Vin had moved in. He carried the newspaper past unpacked boxes through to the bathroom, where Vin was doing things to her face—baffling to Alex, who thought she needed no enhancement. Her expression was comically contorted now, as she attended to her eye-lashes.

'Look,' he said, 'the mountain is going to have dual naming. *kunanyi* / Mount Wellington.'

'kunanyi,' echoed Vincenza, peering at the news report. 'Oh Alex, that's excellent.' She gave him an awkward hug, keeping her face and funny little brush well out of harm's way. '*Mount Wellington* conjures up images of invading redcoats, but *kunanyi* feels exactly right. To me, anyway. A bit mysterious, evocative. It alludes to secrets of the past, things unknown to us white people. The mountain must be so glad!'

Alex laughed.

As he went back to the kitchen, he thought of the inexorable passage of time. The mountain, nameless for most of its existence, had, at some time in the numberless years of the original human inhabitants, come to have meaning for those first people, and they had referred to it by names of their languages. *kunanyi* had been one of those names. The descendants of those ancient people must be glad too.

'I think there's a story there, Alex,' he heard Vin call.

He returned to the bathroom and hugged his squirming flat-mate; he loved her even more for the silly, everyday things, and because he saw how she shared his pleasure at the news about the mountain.

a gamble

FAR BELOW THE MOUNTAIN, in the streets of the city, the young practice was growing. For Affinity, the passing of time was marked by the excitement of new commissions, the disappointment of the ones that got away, the satisfaction of jobs completed, the pleasure of welcoming a new face to the team, and the erratic dipping and soaring of the firm's bank overdraft.

For Alex, there was a quiet satisfaction, and a healthy measure of relief, that the firm was surviving, and that he was sharing its inching growth with his cherished partners.

'Morning all', said Alex, as the team settled around the table for its customary Monday morning meeting. While Karl chaired the partners' management meetings, leadership of these whole-of-team gatherings was rotated around the partners. Today Alex was in the chair, and had seated himself in the middle of the group. The comforting aroma of brewed coffee was on the air, chairs shifted, a newspaper rustled, morning traffic murmured outside on Liverpool Street.

In accordance with the established routine, everybody was there. Samuel Parata had come across from ABC Architects, in response to an Affinity advertisement. Not head-hunted, Alex had assured a disappointed William. Caitlin, a more recent addition to the firm, was a graduate architect. She was a slender young woman with a freckled nose and wild, red hair, whose girlish appearance masked a formidable intellect and a serious commitment to her chosen profession. And bright, young student Helen Wong, come for the duration of her gap year. Andrea was there, too, alert for the sound of the telephone or reception buzzer.

Karl was last to sit, and this morning showed signs of a late night. Vanessa? wondered Alex. Vanessa: a new person in Karl's life. He saw Annette give Karl a knowing look.

Karl seemed to have settled easily into Hobart life. He had found a smart flat in South Hobart, from where he could walk along a leafy track beside the Hobart Rivulet directly to the city centre. Of late, he had been seen in the company of the same young woman on a number of occasions.

It had seemed significant to Alex when Karl had introduced Vanessa to his business partners. Like meeting the family.

Although a little blurred this morning, Karl was wearing the sharp uniform of his profession. Retro had given way to black jacket, black shirt, no tie, rimless glasses.

Sensing that this was not your ordinary Monday meeting, the group fell silent and looked expectantly at Alex.

Alex had spoken to his partners by mobile soon after he first saw the notice in the Saturday paper, and the competition had been uppermost on his mind ever since.

Tasmania's state government had announced it would select the designer for its much-vaunted and long-awaited network of new visitor centres by means of an architectural design competition. The competition would be open to all architects registered in Australia, with international architects able to participate only by associating with Australian architects, the latter to carry the responsibility for seeing the successful design through to completion.

There had been speculation in architectural circles for some time about the means by which the architect would be selected, and indeed whether the enviable job would be handed to a single practice or distributed among a number of firms. The announcement of a design competition was welcome news for emerging firms like Affinity, who might not otherwise be considered for such a commission.

'Did you all see the ad for the Government's visitor centres design competition?' Alex asked. 'In Saturday's paper?'

'Yes, I cut out the ad,' said Andrea, pushing a rectangle of newsprint onto the table.

Alex gave her a smile of appreciation.

On the government's website Alex had found a comprehensive brief for the project.

'It will be a two-stage competition open to all registered architects who can demonstrate the capability to carry out the project,' he said. Could Affinity demonstrate that, he wondered? Might they fall at the first hurdle? 'The final decision is to be made in eight months time.'

From the brief, he read: ' "The first stage of the competition is to be the submission of the firm's credentials together with a preliminary design concept from which a jury will select a short-list of five finalists. These will then be invited, for a nominal fee, to develop their concepts into a detailed design proposal. The prize for the successful architect will be fifty thousand dollars and the commission to carry out the project." '

Alex regarded his partners. He guessed that Annette would be up for it, but that Karl would probably be reluctant to gamble valuable time and resources on an entry into a competition against long odds.

'Fifty grand,' said Alex. He looked towards the drawing office with its cluttered desks bearing large computer monitors, and broad benches littered with drawings, models and material samples. Then at Karl. 'That would clear our overdraft.' He noticed Caitlin look up, and fleetingly wondered if perhaps he had been a little too open with their staff.

'Sure, Alex, but our chances would be small. And our debt will be bigger when we miss out.' Karl's slick silver pen doodled a distorted dollar sign as he spoke.

'It's not just the money though, is it?' countered Alex. 'By being in it we are putting our hand up to say that we care about this place and want to help shape its future. And that we can do this job as well as anyone'. The nods around the table heartened him, made him feel proud of the team. Annette was smiling.

Alex's eyes strayed to the mountain. How glad he was that they had installed clear glass in that window. Such a small intervention for such a reward. The mountain always helped him to find perspective, to see the big picture.

'Who are the judges, Alex?' asked Samuel, the pragmatist.

'There will be three on the jury.' Alex extracted from his papers a print-out taken from the web-site and peered at it.

'One: "a nominee of the national president of the Institute of Architects"; two: "a nominee of the Minister for Tourism, being a person with wide experience in the tourism industry in Australia"; and three: "a nominee of the Minister for State Development, being a person with recognised design credentials".'

'Competitions are a bit of a lottery,' said Annette, looking at Samuel. 'Juries are unpredictable; the group dynamics can't be foreseen.' She looked back at Alex and said, 'We'll need to come up with a strong idea that sets our entry apart from the others; one that demands attention.'

Karl pondered out loud: 'I suppose the exposure would be good for us. Even if or when we're not short-listed we could find some way to show our ideas out there. Maybe get the paper to pick up on it. Local firms ignored, that sort of stuff. They love that.' He looked thoughtful for a moment and said, 'All right, let's do it'.

* * *

The following Monday morning the competition was again the main topic of conversation.

That Alex would lead the small design team was never in question. This was his kind of project. He would bring a preliminary design concept to the other partners first, then present it to the full team for a robust critique—an excellent learning experience for them all. Refinement, modification or even abandonment might follow, everyone having the opportunity to contribute.

'These are my thoughts so far,' said Alex. 'Our first stage submission will need to make much of our credentials, which as a firm are fairly slim. An outline of the practice, a brief CV for each team member, a statement of the firm's philosophy... Yes, we do have a design philosophy,' he smiled at Karl, 'how many times have we talked about it? The challenge will be to reduce it to something clear, concise, and free of professional jargon.'

'A tall order for an architect,' observed Karl, causing the others to smile.

'We'll need to explain the firm's response to the competition brief: how the buildings will function, how their siting and design will contribute to the story they tell,' said Alex.

'I hope you'll make reference to some of the features of the Otway and Wild South designs, Alex,' said Annette. 'I like what they say about design quality and consistency of approach. That's surely relevant to this project. And, hey,' she raised a hand as a thought struck her, 'why don't you slip in some of those lovely drawings I've seen in your final year design thesis?'

'Mmmm, yes, If you think so,' said Alex. 'That would save us time and would certainly illustrate the design approach: crafted, site-specific.'

'Speaking of which,' said Karl, 'we need a design concept.'

The first-stage submission came together in the following weeks.

Karl compiled the details and attributes of the Affinity team, its recognition in awards programmes, its experience in the field of remote area buildings, and its capability of handling the project (fingers crossed). Annette wrote in her clear style of the practice's design philosophy, and was pleased when Vincenza offered to review her words. A friendship was growing between them.

Alex gathered an impressive array of drawings and images of carefully crafted buildings or building components, each of which appeared to have grown from its natural surroundings. He included preliminary free-hand design sketches from his Uni work, from the Otway entry, and from Wild South; Samuel helped him to merge these into a striking collage of ideas. Samuel also converted some of the sketches of their elegant construction details into impressive, state-of-the-art 3D computer models.

Caitlin dissected the functional brief for the proposed new centres and drafted for Alex a summary and a series of thumb-nail diagrams sufficient to show the assessors that Affinity understood the building requirements and would respond appropriately to them. Of course, if they were short-listed—a very big *if*—there would be much more work to do.

Alex could only hope that the Affinity team's local knowledge, their commitment to the place where they lived and worked, their brief but impressive record, the clear consistency of thought in their work, that all these things would register with the selection panel. *We are here. We know and care about this place. We are good at what we do.*

a list

IT WAS JUST ANOTHER email to alight on her screen at the Affinity reception desk, but when Andrea saw the title: *VisiTas Design Competition: Shortlist*, she grabbed the phone. 'Alex, we have an email about the design competition. I'm forwarding it to you now.'

Alex's heart fluttered. He was certain that they would have had a phone-call or special delivery letter had Affinity been short-listed. An impersonal email had to be bad news.

Opening the email, Alex's eyes went straight to the list of names he could see in the body of the message:

Venture Architects, WA
Bob Morris and Assoc, Tas
Danvers Gordon Wong, Vic
Harwood Mellors, NSW
Affinity Architects, Tas

Affinity Architects, Tas! Alex read the list again, then the full email and, finding that it had not been an illusion born of hope, let out a whoop and punched the air, turning heads in the drawing office and bringing the enquiring faces of Karl and Annette to the doorway of his office alcove.

But Alex found that he had to turn from them. His thoughts had tumbled into the place where his father still lived within him. Where a little boy so wanted to make his dad proud of him.

a line

THE AWAKENING MOUNTAIN was powdered with pink snow. A few blush-edged, flat clouds lay just beyond its rim, their languorous demeanour holding promise of a fine day.

Vin placed a mug of steaming tea on the table, the little noise punctuating Alex's thoughts. He smiled and looped his arm around her waist, then gently followed the shape of her buttocks with the palm of his hand.

'What are you doing?' she asked.

'I think it's called foreplay.' He felt himself stirring.

'Don't be silly.' Vin smiled. 'On the computer.'

Alex had been exploring a different kind of terrain. He nodded towards his lap-top screen. 'I've been looking at the locations for the new visitor centres, trying to identify suitable sites.'

The final sites for four of the proposed new visitor centres had not yet been pinpointed by the Government. These were in areas where an especially high degree of design (and political) sensitivity would be required: one on a wooded coast in the far south; one in the rolling green hills of the north-east; one in the high lake country, and another in the controversial Tarkine.

'Where's this?' Vin pointed at the satellite image on the screen.

'I'm tracking the Tarkine coastline at the moment.'

'Can you go in closer?' Vin seemed to be fascinated.

'Yes, the resolution is really good these days.' Alex zoomed in. 'I don't normally go so close, because you lose the sense of where you are. You can't see things in context.'

He seemed to remember his father saying something like that, a generation before the miracle of photographs taken from beyond the sky. *Sometimes when you get too close to things, you can't see them as they truly are.*

He began to track southwards down the beach to illustrate his point. The screen was filled with bright sand. Breaking waves, stilled by the celestial camera, lined the left side of the screen, and on the right the beach began to give way to grassy dunes.

Far too close to see where you were; the image could be any beach, any place, but he could see that Vin was fascinated.

He scrolled down a little further. Ragged areas of rock passed by, a cluster here, a scatter there, a little row...

A chord sounded somewhere in his memory.

A little row. *A little line!*

'What's wrong Al?'

Alex had frozen. The image had frozen. Helpless motes were trapped in the winter sun as the room waited. And, as if emerging from the timeless sands on the screen, his father's words came to him: *Sometimes I make a row of rocks, if I need a line to last a long time.*

Alex was peering at the screen. Not daring to breath, he zoomed in as close as he could. Three black objects, rocks, equally spaced and forming a perfectly straight line, between the dunes and the unmoving white edge of the blue-green sea. *Nature didn't do that, did it?.*

'Alex, you're frightening me.' It was Vin. In the real world. She hugged his shoulders and leaned forward to see what had taken him from her on this clear winter morning in the toasty embrace of their crowded little flat.

'My father. Vin, we may have found a sign.' Alex's eyes shone.

'Oh, Alex.' Vin tightened her embrace.

'Let's see where the line points.' Alex at first zoomed out to understand the location. 'I've never searched this area,' he said. His hands were trembling. 'But I can imagine him liking this place.'

He zoomed in again to the row of rocks on the beach, as closely as he could, then very slowly followed the direction in which the rocks pointed, just north of east. Over the dunes he moved, a vicarious explorer of unknown territory, onto an open, sparsely vegetated sandy area.

The shadows revealed to Alex the nature of the topography: here it was relatively flat, but further to the east the shadows suggested a rise in the ground. As the image inched closer to the edge of the open area, Alex became even more alert. For he guessed that somewhere on its edge, a little elevated and certainly sheltered, would be a spot his father might have chosen to build a campsite. He zoomed back out to quickly check that he was tracking in the correct direction, then back in.

Vin, too, was spellbound. 'What are you hoping to see, darling?' she whispered.

'Well, I've already seen that it's the kind of place my father would have liked. I think it's quite possible that he made that line of rocks. I'm looking now for where his shelter might have been.'

'Alex, where is this in relation to where you found the bike?'

Alex stopped what he was doing; he looked dumbly at Vincenza. He had been so caught up in the discovery of the rocks that he had not considered the question of the bike.

Feverishly now, he once again zoomed out, this time much further out, until the image on his screen took in both the bike location and the position where the line of rocks shrank to specks before disappearing altogether.

What he saw surprised and excited him. The long beach was the common factor. Near its northern-most extremity, what looked like a creek-bed traced its way from near the big tree to the beach. And, near the southern end of the beach: the now indiscernible row of rocks. It was much more distant from the bike than he had expected, and probably further than his father had intended, but it all made sense.

'Vin, I think we've found it!' Alex had to stand to relieve some of his tension.

The pieces were falling into place. Daniel had surely made his way to the beach, walked most of its length, then ventured inland, where he had found a place to build a shelter. Not just any shelter, his *final* shelter. The link with the place where the bike was found surely proved that. Didn't it?

Alex resolved immediately to travel to the Tarkine. He knew he would be useless for anything else until he had chased down this lead. He would drive up the next day, stay overnight at Corinna, then go bush early the following morning. And, despite Vin's offer to come with him, he would do it alone. Because that's how it had to be.

'Can I book you into the hotel at Corinna, Al?' Vin did not want him camping out in mid-winter.

'Yes, thanks, darling,' Alex looked up. 'Can't imagine there'll be any shortage of vacancies at this time of year.'

He was listing the items he would need to pack. The usual camping stuff, cold-weather gear, satellite photos with co-ordinates marked, GPS, spare batteries, phone/camera, charger leads, a few provisions... And would he load the mountain bike on the back of the Outback? Yes, probably.

'Would you like me to email the office and tell them that you'll be away for a few days?'

'Thanks, Vin. No, wait a minute, we'll be seeing Karl tonight, won't we? I can tell him then.'

'Oh, of course. You still want to go?'

Alex and Vin were to meet with Karl and his friend Vanessa that evening at the Winter Feast, a highlight of the city's winter festival, Dark Mofo.

'Yes, absolutely.'

* * *

The interior of the massive Princes Wharf Number One shed, PW1, was a scene of glittering activity and enticing aromas.

Outside, between the shed and Salamanca Place, in cordoned-off Castray Esplanade and on the lawns under the ghostly, naked plane trees, a tumult of chiaroscuro: crackling fire-pits and braziers sending sparks into the night sky, dark puffer-jacketed and scarfed throngs, jets of flame, and fiery jugglers in a dreamlike bamboo cathedral. Haunting music accompanied the culinary offerings.

The foursome, between them, feasted on barbequed octopus tentacles, wallaby curry, barbequed squid and scallops. Alex and Karl chose from a range of local ciders while Vin and Vanessa each had hot mulled wine.

Alex was pleased for Karl; it seemed that in the smart and funny young woman, her fair colouring a striking complement to Karl's shadowed darkness, his friend had at last found someone special.

Was that a spot of rain? Alex looked towards the mountain. But of course, in the moonless darkness, the mountain was not to be seen. At any rate, he realised immediately, from where he stood it would be obscured by buildings—the familiar wall of colonial warehouses which looked over Salamanca Place, a wall now reduced to darkness by the dazzling, living flames before him.

So there was no mountain to tell him what might be in store. Instead, as his eyes sought the mountain, he saw a patch of golden light. High in the dark floated a golden rectangle, shimmering in the turbulent air above the fire. And in that otherworldly window was the dark figure of a man, watching.

And the figure became his father, Daniel Gardner, watching from another time and place, watching his son's struggle to lay him to rest.

a dark river

ON A BEACH far below the mountain, in the comfortable suburb of Sandy Bay, hundreds of hardy souls shed their inhibitions along with their clothes, to brave the cold waters of the river in a dawn parody of pagan ritual to the winter solstice.

Alex had other things on his mind. As he headed north out of Hobart on the long drive to Corinna, he was asking himself: was he silly to keep going with this search? Had it become an obsession? All he knew for sure was that the weight inside him, the empty ache that all too often visited his gut, could not be ignored.

He knew his father must be gone. Dead. But to keep looking kept alive a *connection*. It was something that he could do for both his father and his mother. And he needed to know. *How he needed to know.*

Black swans moved slowly on the still water while a misty fog floated close above them, drifting silently downriver, as Alex crossed the old lift-span bridge to Bridgewater. Further north, with the sun in his eyes and the car's de-mister working hard, he passed the pretty historic town of Kempton. The hills up here, wheat-coloured for most of the year, were now green-tinged.

The sky was clearing of its misty indecision. A few thick but brief fog-patches later, he was nearing Oatlands. No time to stop, coffee would come at Ross, a bit further on, when he was more than half-way to Lonnie.

Approaching Ross, Alex turned in off the highway. Over the famous bridge, then a turn into the elm-lined main street.

He took his steaming plastic mug outside the shop, a newsagency-cum-café, and paused in the cold morning air, enjoying the weak sunshine. His breath, like that of the two rugged-up sheep in the small, frosty paddock opposite, came out in white billows. He strolled as he sipped the scalding coffee.

As he passed a stone cottage, the low morning sun momentarily shone its golden reflection back at him from a tall, small-paned window. He remembered another golden rectangle, that celestial window which last night had floated above the blaze and hubbub of humanity in Salamanca Place. He imagined his father in this gleam too, following his progress.

Back on the road his thoughts ran to another ethereal opening he had confronted. It had happened during his time at ABC. He had been inspecting a building under construction in the city's CBD, William having asked him to report on progress on the multi-story project.

He was on the ninth floor. A concrete pour had been taking place two floors above; this level was a forest of scaffolding, lit by daylight washing in from the perimeter of the thousand-square-metre floor. He had skirted the building's central core and approached a doorway, an opening, in the raw pre-cast concrete wall. It was deathly dark inside, and he had paused on the threshold to allow his eyes to adjust to the darkness, before entering.

'Stop!' the cry was almost a scream.

He recalled now, that for a jarring instant, he had thought it was his father calling out. *Stop! Be careful Alex!* He looked around to see a white-helmeted workman, one hand outstretched in an anguished plea, the other holding a yellow-painted portable protective barrier. On his helmet was one word: OTIS.

'Stop! Please mate! The man's eyes were wide, his face draining. The two had stared at each other, the lift man beckoning with his free arm for Alex to come away from the opening. He was trembling.

The realization hit Alex: it was a lift shaft. He stepped towards the man and took hold of his forearm with both hands. 'Sorry I scared you, mate.'

Why had he remembered that experience now? Was it because he was again at a threshold? About to step into a dangerous unknown?

At Perth, these days becoming something of a dormitory suburb of Launceston, Alex turned left, taking the road that skirted Launceston to connect the Midlands Highway with the Bass highway to Tasmania's north-west. With the sun again on his right cheek, Alex was conscious of how the countryside changed as he travelled further. Everything was greener up here. The locals called the state's north-west God's Own Country; their forebears had given it names like Paradise and Nowhere Else.

In heated comfort, he reflected on the changes the highway had undergone since he had ridden pillion behind his father, hugging his dad and peering be-goggled out from behind his leather back to the rushing road ahead.

It was noon when he arrived at Burnie. Alex found a window seat in a waterfront café and ordered fish and chips. The blue waters of Bass Strait sparkled outside; it was surprisingly warm within, sitting in the sun, and he shed his thick jacket.

His watch showed the time to be a little after one when he left the café to walk back to his car. The air was chilly but still, and the sky a startling blue against the green hills behind the small city. After a petrol stop, he would head for those hills and beyond, down the Murchison Highway towards the state's isolated and rugged west coast.

The sun was behind him now, as he travelled south. Hobart to Corinna was a long, roundabout drive, with no direct route available, other than by helicopter. All right for Rick Harding perhaps, but out of the question for Alex Gardner. Turning west off the highway he headed towards the picturesque former tin-mining town of Waratah, each settlement he passed through evoking poignant memories.

His mind was elsewhere as he drove through the spartan mining village of Savage River. The thought that he would miss at least a day at work bothered him a little, as the finalisation of Affinity's competition entry was underway. But he knew that Karl and Annette would cope, and there would still be time when he returned.

The landscape widened as he crossed open button-grass country with distant mountain views all around. Eventually the road started to descend, and the vegetation changed. Soon he was winding his way through thick bush on the familiar white gravel approach to Corinna.

Just as he had on his last visit, before the sun set Alex walked the quiet path by the Pieman. What would tomorrow bring? Was he right about the rocks? Or was this to be yet another fruitless trip?

The deep, dark river glided past, as inexorable as the passage of time, its amber edges stirring in Alex a deep nostalgia, and distilling his resolve.

shifting sands

ALEX BEGAN TO SCAN the beach more intently as he drew close to where the row of rocks should lie. The receding tide should, by his reckoning, be leaving all three rocks exposed.

He had set out from Corinna before dawn, left his car near the end of the bush trail a half-hour later, then, in the bleak dawn light, walked to the big tree. The bike was still there, unmoving in its green cocoon. From there, it was not long before he had succeeded in finding the creek which he knew from the satellite image would lead him to the fateful beach.

In grey light, he bush-bashed his way alongside, and often within, the narrow creek, careless of the frigid water invading his boots and the whipping protests of hostile branches. It was hard going and took longer than he had expected, but eventually he emerged at the coast, where in long shadows cast by the rising sun behind him, the creek made an irregular tannin-stained delta of runnels through the sand, fanning away towards the ocean. This was the beach.

Alex paused to catch his breath and take in the surroundings. Then, not wanting to delay, he gathered himself and set out, walking south on the sand.

He had been walking for twenty minutes. What was wrong? He had expected to arrive at the rocks by now. He eased out of his backpack and set it down on the sand. Opening a flap, he took out the folded satellite images.

Was there any feature he could recognise? Yes, perhaps that patch of rocks a few hundred metres along the beach was this patch in the photo? If it was, then the line would be just beyond it. He picked up his pack and walked on.

And there it was. Surely that was the line of rocks he had seen on the screen in West Hobart. How many times, he wondered, had the rocks been buried, then exposed, by the ever-shifting sands?

Alex stopped, fearful that he would see something that explained away the line. Something that said *this is a natural phenomenon, nothing to do with your father.* But, to his profound relief and mounting excitement, he saw no such explanation.

He walked down the damp sand to the lowest rock and looked up the line towards the dunes. Somewhere in that direction, there might be an answer waiting. He struggled to contain his emotions, remembering previous disappointments. He looked back down at the rocks. The one at his feet sat in a little moat of clear sea-water, the others seemed embedded in the shifting sands. He was struck by the size of them. Surely even his father couldn't have lifted them? *How would you move them Alex?* he asked himself. Or was it his father asking?

Alex looked around. The scattering of rocks he had passed was fifty or so metres behind him. That's it. He would have rolled them from there, perhaps using a branch as a lever to help the process. And look at how they're placed, lengthwise in the direction of the line that they form.

Alex photographed the array of rocks; from the top, from the lower end, from the side. Just then, a little spurt in a sweeping arc of receding water signalled the presence of an obstruction. Alex noticed it only because the little fountain lay in a direct line with the three rocks. Between waves, Alex ventured out to inspect the object. It was the tip of a fourth rock, almost buried in the sand.

At the foot of the dunes Alex put down his pack and sat on the cool, dry sand. He could feel the force of the line running though him. It was mid-morning; his progress had been good, but a rest would be welcome.

He took a drink from his water bottle and unwrapped a muesli bar. Looking at his compass, he determined the direction of the line. He would be heading three degrees north of east. If he kept to that bearing, he should encounter some sign of his father's shelter. But how far? Neither his satellite images nor his new equipment could answer that question. And, with the movement of the dunes and the inexorable incursion of vegetation, would any visible evidence remain after all these years? The awful truth was that he could walk right past some vital sign.

Hoisting his pack onto his shoulders, Alex trudged up the dune, taking with him a piece of driftwood. At the crest, he turned, looked back along the line of rocks, then drove the bleached wooden spar into the sand. This would be his reference point. It would be no use walking on the correct bearing, he figured, if he was moving along the wrong line.

As he loped down the back of the second row of dunes, the chill breeze disappeared and the winter sun was surprisingly warm. The terrain was fairly flat, covered with grasses and low bushes. Alex knew that his father would not have built a hut here, but nevertheless he carefully scrutinised the ground, sweeping his gaze left and right as he moved forward.

He approached the perimeter of the grassland. To his left was a dense stand of tea-tree, to his right the ground was undulating and scrubby. Ahead, the ground rose abruptly, then climbed gently to a wooded hill. He looked back to the signal stick on the dune, far behind him now, and consulted his compass. He had gone off the line just a little; he moved a few paces to the side to make the adjustment.

Close to the bank, Alex's foot struck a rock in the thick grass.

He stood still.

A crew of black cockatoos lurched overhead. Their uneven flight as they flew low above the trees in their little squadrons, crying out their fractured calls, seemed to speak of humble imperfection, of lives endured with dignity and resilience. A gaggle of eight or so flew low over him now; he called to them as a boy might, exhilarated by their presence. As if in response, they came closer and wheeled in their haphazard manner. The sun caught their undersides, their yellow tails flashed a gift of rare beauty to Alex, before they disappeared over the treetops. A strange melancholy came suddenly to him then, as if these creatures knew something that he did not, something at once sad and inevitable.

Alex explored the grass with his boot. More rocks. They seemed to form a circle. *That's no accident of nature, Alex, that's a fireplace.* A fireplace on the line. And where there's a fireplace, there's a campsite, a shelter.

He remained still, feeling the place, allowing its form and detail to reach into his consciousness.

And he became aware that part of the overgrown bank was not *of it*, but an extension to it.

He reached out and pulled at the mass of greenery, where his every instinct now shouted the presence of the handiwork of his father. The tangle came away with surprising ease, and there it was: an opening.

A threshold.

why

ALEX CLEARED THE OPENING a little more. The low afternoon sun entered, bouncing an orange glow from the red stone bank, the rear wall of the hut.

He laid down his pack and tried to calm his seething emotions. Could this place, so long deserted, reveal what had become of his father?

Taking a drink from a water bottle, he calmed himself and, waving aside a tangle of webs, glinting gossamer in the sunlight, stepped into the cave-like hut. The woven wood framework with its bark roofing was poignantly familiar to Alex. Clay and turf over the bark had rendered the hut virtually indistinguishable from the natural embankment.

But the presence of a threadbare, green tarpaulin laid over the bark and beneath the turf surprised him. Found on the beach, Alex had no doubt. It brought to mind the slum dwellings he had seen in Mumbai, where no material was too ignoble to be employed; plastic and cardboard were ubiquitous. *Integrity* of building construction was not, for the slum-dwellers, a concept that made any sense. And here, despite Daniel's almost obsessive desire to build with a profound integrity, he had made a pragmatic choice.

Alex smiled. Was this the obvious but unexpected response to his own fumbling attempts to arrive at an immutable design philosophy? Had he been too inflexible in his own approach, too concerned with an esoteric purity to allow pragmatism to play a part?

The cobwebbed interior of the shelter, blanketed by a thick layer of sand and leaf litter, was simple and compact. To one side, the sagging framework of a low bed platform, on the other a bench topped with drift-wood planks—the kitchen, no doubt—with a simple three-legged wooden stool tucked beneath. Between them, along the rear rock-face wall, a clever shelf structure holding an assortment of dust-covered utensils, tools and cooking implements, cans and boxes, and found objects with potential for some use not yet apparent. A butler's pantry of sorts. It was clear that Daniel must have been here several times, time enough to put the place in such order.

In the back wall of the hut, behind the open shelving, Alex noticed a flat rock set neatly into the bank—a rock that, he could see from its grain and its smoothed edges, was not part of the bank. He worked his fingers around it and found that he could ease it out.

There, behind its stone door, was a spacious, dry niche, cut out of the natural bank. And in the compartment, the life and the stuff of Daniel Gardner.

Alex took a fistful of stiff grass and swept the accumulation of dust, leaves and droppings off the rough bench, then laid his folded ground sheet over it. His hands shaking, he took three articles from within their little mausoleum in the wall and, with reverence, laid them out.

First, a compass. A simple brass compass, darkly dulled with time, attached to a thin leather thong. Second, a wrist-watch. A stainless-steel Seiko calendar watch. Daniel's wrist-watch, confirmed by the inscription on the back: *Daniel Gardner 4th Nov 1967.*

As he felt the weight of the watch in the palm of his hand, felt its reality after the empty years, stared at his father's name, here in this abandoned hut in the wild country Daniel so loved, Alex could no longer hold back the surge within; his body heaved and the tears came.

When the quiet sounds of the bush returned, he turned to the third object. Wrapped in plastic, together with a slim box of pencils and charcoal sticks, was a battered leather portfolio. He remembered it so well.

Fighting the urge to delve into the precious folder, Alex resolved that he would do that only when he was back with his mother, with Daniel's wife.

He examined the remainder of the hut's interior, then went outside and explored its environs. He found a creek nearby, as he guessed he might, but nothing further of interest. Searching further afield, he found no sign of what might have become of his father.

The sun was getting low; it would set before five, and his own watch told him it was now nearly four o'clock. No point heading back, he would spend the night here. The prospect didn't displease him.

He cleared the overgrown fireplace and set a fire. Making some rudimentary repairs to the bed, he laid a few armfuls of ferns and grasses over it, followed by his ground-sheet, then his sleeping-bag. The night would be tolerable.

Sitting in a small cocoon of firelight beneath a wide, cold sky, Alex collected his thoughts. Tomorrow, he would take his father's belongings to his mother in Launceston, and together they would look at the drawings that Alex knew the portfolio would contain. Perhaps, together, they could at last farewell Daniel.

Glancing at his watch before retiring, his father's Seiko came to mind. A calendar watch, in addition to the time it showed the day and date. He picked it up and brought it into the firelight. It had stopped, run down he supposed, at ten twenty-four on Monday the twenty-fifth. The twenty-fifth of which month, he wondered? And how long would the wind-up Seiko have taken to run down?

And the bigger question: with all his precious things safely stored away, what had become of Daniel Gardner?

Why had he not returned to his hut? And to his family?

flash back

NOVEMBER 1991. Seated on a fallen tree outside what was to be his final refuge, not far from the edge of the Tarkine, Daniel Gardner had been drawing—doodling, Mary would have said, had she been there to witness it.

His mind had been taking its own course, until he saw on the page a charcoal face. A face drawn from somewhere inside him, a smudged face at first meaningless, then making a connection deep in his memory. A narrow face, big-eyed, with large ears, oddly appealing.

Lofty McGuiness. That was it, it looked like Lofty. It *was* Lofty. From over there.

Even as Daniel began to ask himself why he had drawn Lofty McGuiness, the answer came; his insides were shaken by the crashing down of long-standing walls, the entombed memory bursting through. Bursting through only now, on this wild coast battered by the Southern Ocean, more than two decades after that fateful night over there. Bursting through with a violence that left him reeling.

It was Lofty, who had not been accounted for when the company had withdrawn from the battle-field. It was Lofty who was still lost, missing in action, weeks later when the unit completed its tour of duty.

Small and hatless, probably dazed, face blackened, it had to have been Lofty. Lofty, whose face had been revealed in a terrible gun-flash. It was surely Lofty, whose face and future he had extinguished, while he himself lived on.

Oh Jesus Christ.

charcoal

MARY RECEIVED THE NEWS of Alex's find with all the appearance of quiet acceptance. But when she took the Seiko from Alex, her eyes glistened.

'His parents gave him this for his twenty-first.'

Alex hugged her. 'I've let Vin know that I'll be staying here tonight. Is that ok, Mum?'

'It's more than ok, Alex. I hoped you would.'

'It was 1991,' Alex's mother was matter-of-fact, as if reading a police report, as she held her husband's watch and spoke to Alex. 'You were eleven. I reported your father missing on the thirtieth of November. I had expected him back home on the twenty-third.'

'What day of the week was that? The twenty-third?'

'It was a weekend. A Saturday.'

'So the following Monday would have been the 25th.'

'Yes.'

'When his watch stopped.'

Mary looked at the watch, large in her hand. 'Yes.'

Mother and son sat on the comfortable lounge in the sitting-room. A small piece of skirting was still missing from the wall beside him, Alex noticed. And did he ever finish painting that door?

Alex recounted his trip slowly, occasionally showing his mother an image on the small screen of his camera. He watched her as she seemed mesmerised by the shots he had taken of the interior of the bush shelter.

Daniel's battered portfolio lay un-opened on the low coffee table before them. The familiar room seemed to be waiting.

'You know Alex, this was something very private to your father.' Mary stared at the object with a mixture of sadness and trepidation. 'It always seemed to me that his drawings were a deeply personal diary; more than that, a kind of release for him. He showed me some, of course; but I never saw all his drawings, never all of *him*.'

Alex moved their tea-cups well clear, looked at his mother, then released the stiffened leather strap and carefully opened the cover of the portfolio.

Inside was a thick sheaf of drawings made up of several bound sketch books, together with numerous loose pages, all of the same size. Some of the loose pages appeared to be butcher's paper, which Alex guessed might be there to protect charcoal drawings.

He opened the topmost sketchbook.

He was surprised and relieved at the condition of the first page. Clearly his father had looked after his drawings, and the outer plastic wrapping had been effective. But that observation was fleeting; the impact of the image immediately overwhelmed any interest the mere wrapping might have had.

Turning the pages slowly, lingering on every detail, every clue, they were stunned by the power of the drawings. Alex, not without talent himself, was taken aback by the skill, the mastery, of his father's work. These were more than highly proficient drawings, they possessed an emotional intensity that raised them to another plane. No bland landscapes, no pretty plants, no tranquil sunsets. Every element, whether incarnate or inanimate, revealed a potent life-force of its own. Several of the works reminded Alex, uneasily, of the more frenzied paintings of Van Gogh, but most were unlike anything he had seen.

Here and there were scribbled words—words whose only connection seemed to be their bleakness, as if Daniel had been spiraling down into some dark place.

unending clouded

Alex could see again, hear again, his father's charcoal striking the page. Had each stroke been an erasure of some regret, some sin? Each slash a savage cut, an expurgation? Or an angry assault on his demons?

unrelenting

It was an hour and a second pot of tea later when Alex and Mary, nearing the last of the drawings and emotionally spent, came across several folded pages. Alex removed them and carefully smoothed out their stiff creases.

The first was a mad scramble of notes and cryptic doodles, the sight of which jolted them both. The confused, erratic hand, far from Daniel's usual meticulous writing, spoke of pain, of anguish. Perhaps of a broken man? Had Daniel been injured? Or was this an eruption of pain of another kind?

Mary's hands were shaking as she held the page. She put on her reading glasses and peered at the writing. Alex moved to look with her and put an arm around his mother's shoulder.

A smudged sketch of a peering face was surrounded by cryptic scribbles and more seemingly disconnected words and phrases:

the flash   gun-flash   the face
Lofty Lofty   God help me   it was Lofty   Lofty
Lofty McGuiness   it was me Lofty   forgive me Lofty

And then, words which rose off the paper to impale them. Words whose implication was devastatingly clear.

forgive me Mary   forgive me Alex

* * *

They sat in silence.

'I think I always knew that your father might have taken his own life,' Mary said, when words could at last come. 'But it's still a shock ...' She dabbed at her eyes with a handkerchief. 'There were times when he seemed so happy ...'

Alex nodded and held his mother closer.

A clock was ticking faintly in the kitchen.

'Do you know who Lofty McGuiness was, mum?'

'No darling, I have no idea.'

It was a strange and un-familiar feeling. *Was it a kind of closure?* Notwithstanding the Lofty McGuiness riddle. There was sadness, certainly, sadness for Daniel and his pain, sadness for his lost life, for what might have been. But as Alex and Mary had a simple meal in the cosy dining alcove off the kitchen, the feeling began to settle wearily into one of acceptance, of finality. Perhaps it *was* closure.

In the adjacent living room, Daniel's portfolio lay open where they had left it, at the loose page—the note, part cryptic, part painfully clear. After dinner they would look at the final few drawings, finish the task.

* * *

Another drawing. The wild, loose sketch was immediately recognisable to Alex; the atmospheric charcoal drawing portrayed the line of rocks, viewed from the top of the sand dunes. In the foreground, the dune grasses, big in perspective, thrashed and cut in mad confusion. Beyond, the line of rocks disappeared into the clouded sea, towards the day's last light on the horizon – a clear, unblemished band of light below a dark, roiling sky.

Then Alex saw it. Farther out in the water, along the line defined by the rocks, small but unmistakeable, drawn with more deliberation than the crushing chaos around, were the head and shoulders of a man. A man in the water. A man following the line, *his line*.

Following the dying day out to the world's edge, and beyond.

the plea

FORGIVE ME, ALEX. As he drove south through the frosty midlands the next morning, Alex tried to concentrate on practical things, for fear that those words, smouldering in the portfolio beside him, would overwhelm him.

He would report to the police and provide them with photographs of his father's last shelter; the case could at last be closed. He would get back to the business of preparing Affinity's competition entry. And he would finish off the work in his mother's sitting-room.

But it was not that easy. His father's last plea reverberated in his spinning mind.

Forgive him for what? had been his immediate response. Then: *For abandoning us, that's what. Didn't you love us enough to stay? All those years of growing up with no father, no husband.*

The surge of anger that rose up in Alex quickly gave way to shame. Shame for his anger. He could not begin to imagine the anguish that his father must have been suffering to act as he did.

Oh, dad.

sabotage

IT WAS CLEAR from the competition brief that the government was expecting a design which would be replicated on the different sites, one benefit being the recognisability of the facilities to tourists moving around the state. To Alex's mind, this was a bit like MacDonalds, those masters of recognisability, of branding. Of the mundane.

Affinity (Alex really) was intent on breaking this rule. The team readily embraced Alex's notion that each VisiTas building should be intimately associated with its particular environment, should *belong* there.

The second stage entry, a detailed design proposal, was due to be submitted next month, August, and the Affinity team was meeting on a cold, rainy Friday to bring its ideas together. Along with scattered sketches, hot coffee and muffins littered the large table. The rain-spattered window above them revealed only a rolling grey wash; the mountain was nowhere to be seen.

'Sure, there will be a common approach to the functional requirements and to things like graphics, and every building could have one recognisable *marker*,' Alex studiously avoided using the term 'sign' as he put his thoughts to the group, 'but each building would be of *its location*.'

'Alex, that would mean we would have to prepare a separate design for each location, wouldn't it?' asked Caitlin.

'In the event that we win the competition,' said Karl, always the realist.

'The designs wouldn't be entirely different,' Alex explained. 'Each would be responding to the same functional brief, so most of the internal workings should be common to all sites.'

'Unless there's something about the particular location which indicates otherwise, of course.' put in Annette, brushing crumbs from her lap.

'Exactly,' said Alex.

Alex had decided that the Affinity entry should be based on the Corinna location, as he had come to know the essence of that place better than the other sites. The concept for Corinna was intended as an example, a model, of how the design of each individual building would be approached, in the other locations.

He flicked through some images on the room's big screen. 'These are some examples of how a building can grow from its site, be part of it rather than some alien object from a place where different things matter.'

The group was quiet as he went on, showing sketches and images from his earlier projects, and of other buildings from other parts of the world. Inspirational buildings in natural settings.

'The spirit of the bush must be allowed to live in the building,' he said, as he brought up several vivid charcoal drawings, 'but this building must not only be a structure rooted in its surroundings, it must accommodate interpretive material which would genuinely interest and inform visitors. This area is not only a place of wild beauty, it's also rich in stories. The first people. The gold-mining. The piners. The history of the settlement itself. Forestry, and the ongoing conflict of the Tarkine.' *And the people who escape to the bush.*

In the still moment after Alex finished his presentation, Caitlin asked, 'Alex, whose were those amazing charcoal drawings? Did you do those?'

'My father,' said Alex.

'Wow. Will you use them?'

'We should,' said Annette, 'they say so much.'

'So powerful,' said Samuel, quietly.

The nodding heads and murmur of agreement around the table resolved that question. Some of his father's drawings would be included.

I wish you could have met my team, dad. I wish you could have stayed around.

As the final entry took shape in the following weeks, the green tarpaulin flapped into his mind, reminding him to curb his single-mindedness. He was learning that life was not always clear-cut; it was a frayed-edged, uncertain assemblage of hope and happenstance.

* * *

'I just ran into Bob Morris at the Institute offices.'

Alex and Karl had been collared by Annette who hurried them into the meeting room and closed the door. Even before they sat, she was talking.

'He's heard on the grape-vine that someone, presumably one of the other entrants, has approached the Minister, objecting to the inclusion of Affinity on the competition short-list. Bob thought it was on the basis of a lack of proven experience and inadequacy of resources.'

Alex's heart sank. The Affinity team had been uplifted by their selection; this news would be deflating. Who might have made such an objection? He straightened up. He would not let this go unchallenged.

'Gerald?' Gerald Marsden was the public servant overseeing the conduct of the *VisiTas* competition. Alex had spoken to him by phone previously, but had not met him. 'Alex Gardner here. Have you got a minute?'

'If it's a question relating to the competition, it should be submitted in writing...'

'I'm aware of that, Gerald. But this is a bit different. Is there any truth in a rumour I've heard that Affinity's credentials have been brought into question? That we shouldn't have been included on the short list?'

The moment of silence on the line sounded like an answer to Alex. 'Can I ask who made the complaint?'

'Alex, I'm not at liberty to talk to you about this...'

'Why on earth not?'

'Let me say this,' Gerald's voice dropped, 'your design credentials are not in question, but if there's anything more you can do to reassure the minister that you have the resources to carry the project through, then, between you and me, I suggest you do it.'

The man was clearly trying to help him; Alex decided not to push any harder.

'There is one thing I can tell you,' said Gerald, 'because it will be made public today. The minister, in his wisdom, has decided to add an additional name to the shortlist. There are now not five but six finalists, and the date for submission has been extended by two weeks.'

'Who is the new name on the short-list?' Alex asked. 'The same party who objected to our inclusion, presumably?' *Not ABC, please. Not William.*

'The new name is Harding Associates.'

Alex breathed a heavy sigh. 'And it was they who objected to Affinity. Right?'

Silence.

Clearly that question was not about to be answered. If not Rick Harding, who else? Who were your allies and who were you enemies? Was there no real ally, no real friend, in the cut-throat world of business? Even the sedate, apparently chummy world of professionals?

* * *

'There's not much we can do about the addition of another finalist, at least not right now.' Alex was again meeting with Karl and Annette. 'We may have to leave that to the probity auditor. As I understand it's very unusual, to say the least,' he said. 'We can, however, address the question of resources.'

'Any ideas how?' this from Karl.

'Yes, I propose that we identify a firm we could partner with—work in association with—in the event we win the competition.'

'Alex, who do you think objected to Affinity's inclusion?' Karl asked.

'What about ABC?' said Annette.

'Seriously? You think they might have ratted on us?'

'No, no, I meant what about partnering with them?' Annette said, then sat back and frowned at the ceiling. 'Although I suppose it's possible they might have intervened, ratted on us, as you say. It's a plum job, and they would hate losing out to an unproven young firm. Assuming they went in for it.'

'Sorry guys, but I trust William,' said Alex. *I do trust him, don't I? Surely he wouldn't do that?* 'I think we should approach ABC to back us up.'

'Good morning William, do you have a few minutes?'

'Morning Alex. First, let me congratulate you and Affinity on getting onto the *VisiTas* short-list. That's quite a feather in your cap, especially considering the quality of the other contenders. Us included.'

He sounded sincere, Alex thought. 'Thank you William. We're realistic about our chances, though.' He swiveled his chair so that he could see the mountain.

'William, we've learned that the minister is unconvinced of Affinity's capacity, in terms of resources, to carry out the project if we were to be selected. I want to put that to rest right now.'

'Go on, Alex'. William's voice on the line was neutral, betraying nothing.

'Yes, I'll be happy to give you a letter from ABC. It will state our preparedness to give you any support you may need. That should nip in the bud any doubts that the minister may have.'

'Thank you William, That's very good of you.' *Was it very good of him? Or had William played it this way? To put his firm in a position to salvage a piece of the action?*

'But Alex, we'll need to put some heads of agreement in place, or at least a memorandum of understanding, so that we don't have any arguments later. In the happy event that you are successful.'

'I agree, William. May I suggest that we leave that to Karl and Peter to work out the details?'

'So if anyone's going to disagree, it'll be them, not us?'

'That's about it,' Alex laughed, a little uneasily.

William was as good as his word. The next morning Alex found a letter attached to an email in his in-box:

Affinity Architects
Att Mr Alex Gardner

Dear Alex
Re: VisiTas project

I congratulate you on your inclusion on the short-list for the Tasmanian Government's VisiTas project.

I confirm our commitment to you to provide any support you may require, in the happy event that you are selected as architect for this important project. From my knowledge of you and your work I have no doubt that, if successful, you will do an outstanding job.

The Government agencies have full particulars of the ABC practice and know its capabilities. I'm sure they will also be aware of the exceptional results achieved on the Otway and Wild South projects, where our professional relationship was cemented.

We wish you well in the next stage of the selection process.

Yours Sincerely

Wlliam Carey MBA FRAIA FAICD
Managing Director
ABC Architects

Cc Minister for Growth and Development

submission

THIS MORNING THE MOUNTAIN had drawn a grey veil of misty rain down over its face, retreating within itself, saying nothing of what the day might offer—the day for submission of the competition entries.

Alex was overseeing the compilation of Affinity's entry, laying out the material to be lodged on the long, 'upcycled' table—a former laboratory bench—in Affinity's meeting room. In accordance with the competition requirements, Affinity would be lodging five A1 size, vertical display panels, the uniform size and orientation being to facilitate the mounting of an exhibition of all entries. The professionally laid out and printed panels displayed design sketches, architectural drawings, computer modelling, photographs and explanatory text. And prints of three arresting charcoal drawings—un-titled, but each marked in miniscule letters with the same attribution: *D. Gardner.*

The principal image of the design, the *hero shot*, showed an elegant structure which might have been part of the very forest in which it was portrayed. A dramatic vertical marker, a sort of high-tech totem pole in uncompromising stainless steel with sculpted timber inserts, signalled the presence and purpose of the building.

The competition conditions, in order to contain both the cost of preparing entries and the exuberance of the entrants, forbade physical models, but Alex had decided to risk testing this limitation. Samuel had made to Alex's specifications, a paper fold-out, which could easily be opened from its flat configuration to extend from the panel face. When opened, it became a delicate three-dimensional web representing the building's deceptively simple structural system.

Alex checked that he had on the table five copies of a DVD containing digital files of all of the material, as required to facilitate the judging process.

Caitlin helped him to wrap the panels together, then held the door for him as he made to leave the office. All Affinity eyes were on him as he looked back. Karl darted across the drawing office to give him a pat on the back and a *well-done*; the others were smiling, nodding their concurrence, and giving him the thumbs-up.

In the street, construction noises from somewhere nearby reverberated in his memory, echoing the remembered sounds of a hammer and a nail-gun, of a father and his son working together.

He hugged the precious parcel to his body, knowing that his father, Daniel, was as much a part of this design as he was.

seeking bogans

WHILE THE JURY GODS DELIBERATED, Alex's life returned to its usual routines. To guard against the disappointment that was the most likely outcome, he tried to put the competition out of his mind.

'Two down: *the purpose of camping outdoors, perhaps:* something, n, something, something, n, something.' He put down his pen, careful not to allow it to mark the doona, and took another sip of tea from his prized post-modern mug.

His distracted brain was getting nowhere; he waited for Vin to arrive at the answer, as she always did, this lovely woman sitting snuggled beside him in their morning-sun-dappled bedroom..

'*Intent!*' she suddenly blurted with a little spray of toast crumbs. 'Oh, that's a lovely clue.'

Alex smiled as he carefully wrote in the answer.

'Only one more to go,' he said, glancing surreptitiously at his watch. Eight-thirty had been his target, it was that time already. He had been hoping to get in an early-morning ride, to free up his mind. 'The hard one. Let's have another go at it, before we look at the straight clue.'

But looking at the 'straight' clues was not an option for Vin, just as reading the instructions when assembling a flat-pack, or asking someone for directions would be unthinkable for Alex.

'Three across: *Illicit night light is unmoved,* two words, nine and five letters.' He showed the nearly-completed puzzle to Vin.

'Well, *night light* could be *moon-light,*' she offered.

'Hang on, yes of course,' Alex said, mentally kicking himself. 'Moon-shine. That's illicit. And look, it fits as the first word. Maybe un-moved relates to the second word.'

His mind was closing in on the answer when Vin exploded with: '*Still!* It's a *moonshine still!*'

Alex looked ruefully down at his watch. Three minutes in the bathroom, two minutes to get dressed; this morning's ride would have to start later than he had hoped. They really would have to look for a bike for Vin.

Filling in the missing letters, Alex said, 'I think maybe I'll leave my ride until later.'

Vin brushed some crumbs away and sat back against her pillows, before turning to the newspaper's real estate section. Since they had decided to look for a house together, they had been learning property-speak, talking to lenders, weighing up suburbs and locations, and scrutinising places on offer.

'Hey Alex,' She looked up from the property pages, as Alex was trying to coax a slice of smoking toast out of an un-cooperative toaster.

'Yeah?'

'Be careful. Have you turned it off?'

Alex smiled to himself. It was what his mother would say.

'What's Moonah like? There's a place here that looks interesting.' She was pointing to one of the array of homes advertised. 'It's in our price range."

'Beyond the flannelette curtain?'

'Pardon?'

'Just a local joke. There's a line, a rivulet actually, over which some of Hobart's more, shall we say *discriminating* citizens would never choose to live. Upright, cultured people on the southern side, flannel-shirted bogans to the north.'

'Excellent!' Vin beamed at him 'Let's go and have a look at the place. It's open for inspection later this morning.'

The place was located in Moonah, in a quiet street that ran parallel to the New Town Rivulet, AKA the Flannelette Curtain. Some back yards actually overlooked, through a stand of immature gums, that little stream, which brought rainwater and snow-melt from the mountain, only a few kilometres away to the west.

As it turned out the house was on the northern side of the street, away from the rivulet. It was a modest brick and stucco building with a gabled iron roof and an attractive deep veranda at the front. Somewhere between the Federation and California Bungalow styles, Alex thought.

It seemed sturdy, the floor plan was simple, three bedrooms (two and a half really), one family bathroom, a small but up-dated kitchen, a generous living area, separate dining room, separate laundry off the back porch, and a separate garage.

Alex noted with pleasure the level, sunny backyard from which the mountain could be seen, and his trained eye saw the potential for opening-up and re-orientating the house.

'Three-fifty K should do it,' the coiffed agent said to him, 'be worth twice as much in Battery Point.'

'Mmmm. Thanks, we'll give it some thought.' Then to Vin, out of the agent's earshot: 'What do you think?'

'I really like it Alex. But not a bogan in sight.'

'Let's go for a walk around the area while we're here. Maybe we can find some.'

They laughed, joined hands and set off towards the river.

a grave encounter

A LANE LED THEM to a gravel path running between the rivulet and expansive green playing fields. Taking the path to Tower Road, then meandering further, the couple came to a latticed steel pedestrian overpass across the busy dual carriageway of the Brooker Highway.

As they made the crossing, the mountain moved behind them, the Queen's Domain rose on their right, while ahead, the hillside suburb of Lutana, which sloped down to New Town Bay, awaited their arrival.

On the far side of the small bay, they could see a hill dotted with coniferous trees and scattered with salt-and-pepper stones. Gravestones. This was Hobart's principal cemetery, named for the idyllic bay on its far side, Cornelian Bay.

Their thoughts went in different directions. Vincenza immediately thought of Christopher Koch's description of the ubiquitous plumes of vapour that rose, then as now, from the zinc works on the edge of Lutana, in his home-town novel, *The Boys in the Island*. Alex, while enjoying the small drama of the aerial crossing, was contemplating the fact that roads, built to connect places, could also brutally divide them.

They walked through quiet, haphazard streets past modest, mid-century, weatherboard houses, bridged the outflow of the New Town Rivulet—a grey heron standing contemplatively in its shallows and its banks crowded with inert gulls and ducks—and paused to enjoy the calm sunshine of New Town Bay, where a lone rower was gliding home from the wide, shining river beyond.

As they walked below a row of gums, the sudden screech and swirl of white cockatoos interrupted the quiet and brought to Alex thoughts and images of other times, other places. What was their raucus message?

The couple trekked in single file along a wire fence around a green rugby field and crossed to a stone-flanked gateway to the graveyard.

Walking up the gentle rise to the cemetery's highest point, they found themselves at the back of a vast crowd, all looking to the east in silent contemplation. A crowd of tall gravestones, as tall as themselves, most sandstone, some painted, some with square heads, others rounded or shaped, some topped with crosses, others with angels. The hushed crowd rolled across the gently undulating terrain, away from them, while behind them, the mountain also looked east, across them all, the dead and the living.

Alex and Vin were reduced to silence. Moved by the same unspoken feelings, both reached for the other's hand.

They walked quietly, hand in hand, through the crowd, on struggling grass, past old, misshapen cypresses, vigilant plovers, and wind-scattered flowers—plastic and real.

As they came upon graves of more recent decades, Alex began to notice the occasional military plaque—bronze plaques bearing the rising sun insignia of the Australian Army.

2078 PRIVATE
B.J.SMYTHE
12 BATTALION
19TH AUGUST 1961 AGE 66
BELOVED HUSBAND OF AILSA MARY
TREASURED MEMORIES

His thoughts turned to his father. At least these people had marked graves; their families must know what became of them, how they died. Must have marked their loved ones' passing.

TX3783 PRIVATE
G.K.FINLAY
2/40 INFANTRY BATTALION
17TH JULY 1975 AGE 77
RESTING PEACEFULLY
LEST WE FORGET

5088 PRIVATE
BRIAN 'LOFTY' McGUINESS
INFANTRY
17TH APRIL 2004 AGE 59
BELOVED HUSBAND OF MARGARET JUNE
LOST, FOUND, LOST AGAIN
AT PEACE NOW

Wait a minute. Alex turned back. *Lofty McGuiness. That's surely my father's Lofty. Same name, isn't it?*

He approached the grave. This Lofty McGuiness apparently lived to the age of fifty-nine. Not killed in Vietnam when he was twenty. So it couldn't be the same person, could it. But the name was too much of a coincidence, wasn't it? Then there's that inscription: *Lost, found, and lost again.* What did that mean?

'What is it, Alex?' Vin's voice seemed to come from far away.

* * *

'I think that grave could belong to a man who served with my father in Vietnam.'

Alex and Vin were sitting outside the little kiosk attached to the Boathouse restaurant, on the foreshore at Cornelian Bay, below the cemetery.

The sheltered bay, a steep, wooded bank on one side, a higgledy row of story-book boatsheds on the other, was mirror-smooth. A score of still yachts shone white in the early afternoon sun, a family of brown ducks busied themselves in the shallows and a lone pelican, a rare visitor, glided sedately above a perfect reflection of itself. On flat grass and in a rollicking playground, mums, dads, kids and dogs did their thing.

'Vin, when I found my father's hut, I also learned what had happened to him.' Alex said as he stirred his mocha. 'But I couldn't yet bring myself to talk about it.'

'Al, you don't have to.'

'It's all right. From what I found it seemed that he had caused the death of a fellow soldier in Vietnam. I can only imagine that he believed him to be one of the enemy. I think he may have repressed the memory of that until much later, when something brought it back to him.'

Vin moved closer and put an arm around Alex's shoulders.

'The man he killed, or believed he had killed, was called Lofty McGuiness.'

'The same name as on the grave?'

'Yes, the same name. The inscription on the plaque makes him the same generation as my father. And he was obviously a soldier at some time.'

Vin waited in silence. The sun gleamed on the bay.

'But This Lofty McGuiness died only ten years ago, not in Vietnam in the sixties.'

Maggie

MARGARET MCGUINESS'S home was a well-kept, iron-roofed, weather-board cottage in a quiet cul-de-sac off Tolosa Street in Glenorchy. From here, the mountain took a different form, more in profile than full-face.

Vin had ascertained from Defence records that the grave was indeed that of the same Brian McGuiness who had served with Alex's father in Vietnam. She searched the electoral rolls and found a Margaret June McGuiness with a Glenorchy address. A phone call established that, yes, Lofty had been her husband, and yes of course you and your fiancee may visit me. Saturday morning would be fine.

The gate was white-painted wrought-iron, set in a low, stuccoed concrete block wall. The path to the house was bordered by narrow garden beds, abundant now with spring bulbs and colourful perennials. Rose bushes dressed the plain, neat lawn.

As they approached the door, Alex squeezed Vin's hand, glad that she had insisted on coming with him.

Alex pressed the doorbell and, somewhere inside, chimes sounded. Through the obscure glass of the front door he and Vin could see a blurred figure approaching the door.

'Call me Maggie.' Margaret McGuiness, short, grey-haired and apron-clad, ushered Vin and Alex into a comfortable front room fragrant with fresh flowers. She sat them on an obese vinyl-covered lounge which faced a large flat-screen television, and bustled into the adjacent kitchen to make tea.

'So what brings you to see me, dearie?' This through the clink of cups and saucers.

'I lost my father a long time ago,' began Alex—he wouldn't lie to Maggie, but there seemed to be no need to complicate matters with the whole truth—'and I'm just trying to fill in some of the gaps in my knowledge of him.' Through an opening into the kitchen he could see Maggie nodding. 'From some papers I came across, I learned that he served in Vietnam with your husband. My father was Daniel Gardner."

Maggie pushed a laden tea-trolley into the room, sat herself next to it and waited for the tea to steep.

'I don't remember him ever mentioning your father, Alex. But then he very rarely spoke of anything to do with the Vietnam years. And all that was before I met him. We married quite late in life.' There was sadness in her smile. 'What little I know about all that has come from others, mainly his parents. They're gone now though.'

She gave the china teapot a little swirl and began to pour.

'I worked in the Glenorchy library, and Brian used to come in often on Saturday mornings. He loved reading, and would take out a new book every week. Fiction or non-fiction, he would read them all.'

The colour of the tea was as deep and rich as the eddying edge of the Pieman.

'But perhaps he didn't always read them.' She looked at her guests conspiratorially. 'He confessed to me later that I was the main reason he came to the library so often.' Maggie smiled at the memory, and Alex and Vin smiled with her.

'My Brian was a lovely man,' Maggie said wistfully as she brushed down her apron. 'Quiet, but lovely. It's been ten years now, but I still sometimes think I hear his van coming into the driveway.'

Vin reached over and touched the older woman's hand.

After a long pause, Maggie said, 'Brian was an electrician—a sparkie. Worked for himself eventually. He loved the work, and loved being independent. And always said he was proud to be a '*norchy boy.*'

'Maggie, I hope you don't mind me asking, but I wondered, we both wondered, about the meaning of the inscription on Brian's gravestone,' Alex was watching her for any sign of discomfort. Seeing none, he went on, '*Lost, found, lost again; at peace now.*'

'His father made enquiries soon after Brian came back,' Maggie said. 'He was concerned about how Brian had changed. Apparently he used to be very out-going, could talk under water according to his mates, but when he returned he was quiet as a mouse. Didn't seem depressed, his father said, but was just vague and unresponsive.'

Maggie lifted the tea-pot. 'Can I pour you another cup?'

'Please,' smiled Vin.

'What about you, Alex?'

'I'm fine, thanks Maggie.'

'Brian's father found out from the defence people that Brian had been reported missing in action, lost, just before his unit was to return to Australia. Apparently he was still missing, presumed killed, when his company came home. I dare say some of his mates from other parts of the country never heard the news when he was found.'

'Did his father find out what had happened to him, Maggie?' Alex asked gently, leaning forward on the couch.

'More or less, yes. Brian stumbled upon a friendly unit, South Vietnamese I think, several weeks after he was reported missing. Literally stumbled, I reckon. He was concussed and exhausted. At that point he could apparently remember nothing.'

'So he had survived all that time alone in a war zone?' whispered Vin.

'Yes, dear, it would seem so.'

As Vin drove them back to West Hobart, Alex was silently trying to make sense of what they had learned from the widow of Lofty McGuiness.

Daniel's scribbles. *God help me, it was Lofty. Forgive me Lofty.* He and his mother had both taken this anguished plea to have screamed forth from a recollection of something awful. Something so un-utterably awful as to drive Daniel to flee from its horror, to walk out into the cold, endless silence.

But whatever Daniel Gardner had done, or thought he had done, he had not harmed Lofty McGuiness.

Perhaps the incident with Lofty, whatever it was, had been for Alex's father a culmination of some sort, a tipping point. Perhaps the damage had already been done.

For his father had been damaged; Alex knew that now.

enemy

NGUYEN VAN THINH of the People's Army was venturing for a third time into the blackness of the battlefield. He had carried two comrades—alive or dead he wasn't sure—back to the aid station.

His breath was ragged. It might be heard, now that the drumming rain had stopped.

The unseen mud was cloying, holding him to the rot-smelling earth, holding him to this terrible place. His wife, his family, his village, were distant dreams.

His boot nudged a sodden mass. Comrade or enemy? He reached down, felt for the familiar fabric, the stitching, the webbing, the pleated pocket. He took hold of a flap—a lapel? a sleeve?—and lifted. The thing lifted too easily. He laid it back down.

A moment of moonlight. He froze. Waited for the return of the blackness.

Was that movement? So close. Had he ventured too far? He was seized by a sudden fear—more like an awful awareness, a fateful knowledge.

The white-hot light, a volcanic vortex the diameter of his wedding band, exploded to fill his vision, to take his world.

From high above the green rice-fields, Nguyen Van Thinh saw three figures straighten and look skyward. Three faces. His family.

editorial

'ALEX!'

Vin came crashing into the bedroom waving their Saturday morning newspaper.

'Look! Look!'

Seeing her excitement warmed his heart. She was so child-like at times. And it couldn't be bad news. She plonked onto the bed beside him and sat close, throwing an arm around his shoulder.

When he took the paper and looked at the front page, it stopped his world. Behind a superimposed headline WE LET THEM DOWN was a drawing that Alex recognised immediately as one of his father's—one of the three that had been included in the Affinity competition entry.

It was a beautifully rendered charcoal drawing of a violent sea crashing onto a formation of weathered rocks, the rocks evocative of bruised, yet resilient, living beings. The pounding adversities of life, perhaps, battering the human spirit.

At the bottom of the picture was a small block of print:

This drawing and others in this issue have been described by our own art critic as 'remarkable'—in her view equivalent in quality to the drawings of renowned artists Kentridge and Blackman.

They were drawn by a man who was used and let down by his country, a man whose startling talent never had a chance to reach its full, rich potential.

Editorial, page 9

'Karl,' breathed Alex.

Vin looked at him.

'The reporter must have spoken to Karl.' Alex found he was having difficulty speaking. The swelling of sorrow and pride that he felt at that moment completely submerged any annoyance he may have felt towards his friend Karl.

After a moment, Vin said, 'turn to the editorial.'
Alex turned to page 9, and together they silently read.

EDITORIAL

The journalists of this newspaper are not easily moved by a story, especially when the story is old news. This is one of those rare exceptions.

This week, when our reporter visited the public display of the entries in the state government's VisiTas visitor centre design competition, she was struck by several drawings accompanying the entry from finalist Affinity Architects. The drawings were attributed to a D. Gardner.

Our reporter has since learned that the author of these compelling drawings was Daniel Gardner, a veteran of the Vietnam war who, it is understood, years ago took his own life after vanishing into wild bush near Corinna, where his drawings were recently unearthed by his son.

The brilliance of Daniel Gardner's drawings is a poignant counterpoint to the brutality of that bloody and ultimately futile war, an unpopular war to which young men were forcibly conscripted, and, in many cases, reviled on their return to their homeland. This was at a time when post-war counselling was absent.

In common with veterans of other conflicts, many Vietnam veterans suffered, and some are still suffering, from what we now call post-traumatic stress disorder, or PTSD, and a shocking number of veterans have taken their own lives.

One can only guess at what the future might have held for Daniel Gardner, and for others, had they been given the support their country owed them.

Too often we have let them down.

'Oh Alex.' The newspaper fell to the bed as Vin threw her arms around him and held him tight.

What vindictive divinity was playing such a chaotic, discordant tune on his emotions? What roller-coaster chord would it strike next?

He made the two-hour dash to Launceston with copies of the Hobart newspaper to see his mother. He wanted to be with her when she read the editorial.

In the pensive solitude of the car, Alex felt the ache of the past few weeks begin to ease, the void begin to fill.

His father had found a way to speak. Daniel's drawings, so long silent, were speaking now, not only to Alex and Mary, but to others too.

The hollowness was no more, replaced by a pride which swelled in Alex, filling his heart and blinding his eyes.

hoping

AS HE LEFT THE FLAT, Alex looked back up at the mountain. The ancient dolerite organ-pipes glowed pink in the early sun, above a thin flourish of mist; the slumbering giant's outline was sharply defined against a yawning, cerulean sky. The day seemed full of promise.

His mother had been overwhelmed when she saw the Saturday newspaper. She had insisted on returning to the capital with him so that she could attend the competition announcement and see how he had worked some of his father's drawings into his firm's entry. She and Vin would see Alex at the venue later.

Down in the city, at the Affinity offices, Alex joined the others for a coffee. Anticipation was in the air. Dare they hope?

Leaving a disappointed Andrea to look after the office, the team set out, an animated gaggle, to walk through the bustling city centre to the dockside building where the competition announcement was to take place.

On one side of the large function space, full-height windows brought the visual feast of the docks into the room. The mountain peered in through rigging and gently swaying masts. Along the opposite wall, on free-standing panels, the competition entries were displayed.

Knots of people pointed and muttered; Alex recognized some of them. There was Bob Morris with several of his colleagues; William Carey had come—he had a vested interest now, didn't he? Was that Lawrence Mellors? Alex nudged Karl as he glimpsed Rick Harding in earnest conversation with someone taking notes.

Around the room, nods and smiles. Nervous laughter. News media: local reporters, photographers, cameramen, sound technicians.

As the Affinity group dispersed around the room, Alex's eyes flitted across the entries. They looked impressive. Colour and shine and computer wizardry. How could he have imagined that Affinity could compete with these established firms?

Where was the Affinity entry? There it was, the panels partially obscured by a small crowd around it. Of course, after the press article they would be curious to see his father's drawings.

Someone was pulling out the fold-out model, grinning. He could hear what sounded like appreciative comments.

Don't start hoping again.

The abrupt crunch of a microphone being tapped brought the room to order, brought the scattered Affinity team back together. Through the subsiding chatter, someone—was it Gerald Marsden?—introduced the minister.

After a predictable, self-congratulatory preamble, the paunchy politician said, 'before I ask Professor Mainwaring to address us, lease join with me in thanking all three members of the judging panel,' he looked to a trio standing to one side, 'it is clear that their task can't have been an easy one.' His theatrical hand-clap generated a ripple of polite applause around the room.

'Now, it is with pleasure that I invite the chair of the panel, Professor Mainwaring, to announce the winner of the VisiTas design competition— the firm who will be engaged to design the network of new visitor centres which will show-case our state's amazing tourism experiences.'

As the eminent architect and academic moved to the microphone, Alex glanced across to where his mother and Vin were standing. Their arms were linked. Vin caught his eye and made a face at him, a funny, nervous *here's hoping*. Whatever the outcome today, he felt like a winner.

'All of the finalists should be congratulated,' the silver-haired, stylishly-dressed professor was saying. She gestured to the displayed entries. 'Any one of the submitted designs would have been a worthy selection. But...' she paused and looked across her spectacles at the small crowd, garnering their attention like the seasoned lecturer she was, '...one entry stood out from the others.'

Alex had stopped breathing. *Be a gracious loser, Alex. The journey has been a good one. We have done well to get this far. Smile and applaud the winner.*

'That entry, the winning design, was submitted by ... Affinity Architects!'

a symphony

THE SQUEAL OF DELIGHT from Vin turned heads, as she embraced Mary. Gasps and happy laughter from the Affinity team. Hugs and back-slaps from Karl and Annette, returned by a dazed Alex. A fist-pump from Samuel, a kiss from Caitlin. Warm applause from the gathering.

The smiling professor waited for the room to quieten.

'What we saw in the entry from the Affinity team was a sensitivity to place that is very rare. Their design concepts demonstrated how each of the new centres would belong intrinsically to its unique location; each could be nowhere else.' She paused, took off her spectacles and, smiling, looked directly at the assembly. 'But despite the uniqueness of each, there is a beautiful consistency of thought which brings the various buildings together, as an orchestra, to play the great Tasmanian symphony.'

Alex looked to where his mother stood, still locked arms with Vin, haloed by the daylight behind her. Her shining eyes caught his.

His gaze swept across the room to where Daniel's drawings throbbed with energy, with life. Where he felt the presence of his father. Saw him. Wild sandy hair, leather, kahki, clutching his portfolio—the secrets of his broken soul.

Alex knew Mary had followed his eyes, was looking there too, looking back through the years, seeing a damaged young man. A man she had loved. Still loved.

In that moment, in that impersonal place, there was no-one else, nothing else; other faces and voices were reduced to a vague background. Just three people locked in a binding triangle—an enduring delta whose sands, once runnelled with despair, now flowed with pride.

A camera flashed.

about the author

Following his retirement from a long and successful career as an architect, Jamieson Allom has found time to re-kindle both his boyhood passion for art and his long-standing enjoyment of the written word.

He lives in Hobart, the capital city of Australia's island state, Tasmania, where he now writes and makes art.

In 2013 Jamieson compiled 'Over the Hill', a little book of his poetry and artwork, published by Forty South Publishing.

MISSING is his first novel.

The author's image on this page is a lino-cut print by the author.